LAST RIDE TO CARTHAGE

LAST RIDE TO CARTHAGE

Prelude to the Series
OLD CHARLIE AND THE PROPHET

DANIEL BAY GIBBONS

Sixteen Stones Press

HOLLADAY, UTAH

Book layout, typography and cover design ©2015 by Julie G. Gibbons. Photo credits, "The Black Horse Runs," under license from iStock; and "Carthage Jail," steel engraving by Frederick Piercy, published in *Route From Liverpool to Great Salt Lake City*, (London: Latter-day Saints' Book Depot, 1855), page 72, now in public domain. Sixteen Stones Press logo design by Marina Teležar.

Sixteen Stones Press
Publisher website: www.sixteenstonespress.com

Last Ride to Carthage
(Prelude to the series, *Old Charlie and the Prophet*)
by Daniel Bay Gibbons

Series website: www.oldcharlie.com

Hardback ISBN 978-1-942640-04-2
Paperback ISBN 978-0-9906387-5-9
eBook ISBN 978-1-942640-03-5

For Julie,
who walked with me through the streets of Nauvoo

To walk with you again in Old Nauvoo—
To step in cadence with the cricket's song,
A quiet chant along Mulholland Street,
Past the mossy stones, the o'er-beetling boughs
Of sycamore and walnut and maple,
Past the dark dwellings of the oppressors,
Destroyers of walls, merchants of old brick,
Red brick of the City's living fabric.
To walk beneath the shining battlements
Of the newly resurrected Temple,
Standing, shining once more on sacred height,
And dropping down now, wending our way down
In the rosy dawn to the quiet grove,
We follow, at last, the endless cortege.
Walking, two last mourners to swell the van,
Behind riderless horses, white and black,
Following the creaking wheels carrying
Joseph and Hyrum home, finally home.
We stand now in the narrow, swelling light,
The chestnuts falling on the blowing grass,
Beneath the trembling boughs, branches waving,
Shouting Hallelujahs to the morning.

DANIEL BAY GIBBONS
SEPTEMBER 24, 2004

CHARACTERS

THE IMMEDIATE FAMILY AND HOUSEHOLD OF JOSEPH SMITH, JR.

Brother Joe, the Mormon Prophet, Joseph Smith, Jr., age 38

Lady Emma, the Prophet's wife, Emma Hale Smith, age 39

Julia, the Prophet's adopted daughter, Julia Murdock Smith, age 13

Little Joseph, the Prophet's oldest son, Joseph Smith, III, age 11

Freddie, the Prophet's second son, Frederick G. Williams Smith, age 7

Alex, the Prophet's youngest son, Alexander Hale Smith, age 6

Lorin, the Prophet's faithful horseman and groom, Lorin Walker, age 21

THE FAMILY OF HYRUM SMITH

Hyrum, the Prophet's brother, Hyrum Smith, age 44

Lady Mary, Hyrum's wife, Mary Fielding Smith, age 42

Lovina, Hyrum's oldest daughter, Lovina Smith, age 16

John, Hyrum's oldest son, John Smith, age 11

Younger children of Hyrum Smith

Historical Animals and Their Owners

Historical Animal	Historical Character/Owner
Old Charlie, a coal-black stallion, the Prophet's favorite riding horse—has been with the family since the early 1830's—ridden by the Prophet to Carthage on June 24, 1844	**Brother Joe,** the Prophet Joseph Smith, Jr., who was murdered while a prisoner in the Carthage Jail on June 27, 1844
Tom Carlin, a large sorrel horse, good natured and somewhat clumsy	**Brother Joe**
Joe Duncan, a highly spirited dark sorrel pacer, used as a riding horse by the Prophet's family	**Brother Joe**
Major, an old white mastiff watchdog weighing 200 to 250 pounds—has been with the family since the early 1830's	**Brother Joe**
Sam, a snow-white stallion—ridden by Hyrum Smith to Carthage on June 24, 1844	**Hyrum,** the Prophet's brother, Hyrum Smith, who died with his brother in the Carthage Jail

FICTIONAL HORSES AND THEIR HISTORICAL RIDERS

Fictional Horse	Historical Character/Rider
Lady Gray, a gentle gray mare	**John Taylor,** the Mormon apostle who stayed with the Prophet in the Carthage Jail and was gravely injured in the attack
Saucepan, a sturdy brown and white paint	**The Big Doctor,** the Mormon apostle and physician, Dr. Willard Richards, who stayed with the Prophet in the Carthage Jail
Jack, a scrappy little stallion	**Porter,** the Prophet's friend and bodyguard, Orrin Porter Rockwell
Pickwick, a chocolate palomino	**Markham,** the Prophet's bodyguard, Stephen Markham
Tramp, a bay gelding	**Blue Dan,** the Prophet's bodyguard, Welsh convert and steamboat captain Dan Jones
Gypsy Queen, a seal brown mare	**Squire Woods,** Joseph Smith's criminal defense attorney, who road with the Prophet from Nauvoo to Carthage
Lather, a fast sorrel thoroughbred	**Brother Samuel** the brother of Joseph and Hyrum, Samuel H. Smith, who rode into Carthage shortly after the martyrdom

Fictional Horse	Historical Character/Rider
Paulina, a bay mare	**Old Man Lott,** Joseph Smith's farm manager, Cornelius P. Lott, and Captain of the Prophet's mounted bodyguard of sixty men in the Nauvoo Legion
Charity, a dark chocolate mare	**Mr. Robert,** the apostate Robert Foster, one of the editors and publishers of the *Nauvoo Expositor*
True Blue, a blue-black stallion	**The Brigadier,** Brigadier General Charles C. Rich of the Nauvoo Legion
Rambler, a light clay stallion	**General Dunham,** Nauvoo Legion Lt. General Jonathan Dunham
Napoleon, a dark sorrel trotter	**The Gov'nor,** Illinois Governor Thomas Ford
Caesar, a gold champagne stallion	**Captain Dunn,** Captain James A. Dunn of the Volunteer Horse Company of the Union Dragoons, who intercepted the Prophet on the road to Carthage
Rust, a light sorrel gelding pacer	**Phelps,** Church leader W.W. Phelps, who preached the Prophet's funeral sermon

Other Historical Characters

Lady Lucy, the mother of Joseph and Hyrum, Lucy Mack Smith

Lady Katherine, the sister Joseph and Hyrum, Katherine Smith Salisbury

John Fullmer, friend of the Prophet, who visited him in Carthage Jail

Cyrus Wheelock, friend of the Prophet, who visited him in Carthage Jail

Long Whiskers, Carthage Constable David Bettisworth, and his posse

White Hat, Carthage Constable Joel S. Miles, and his posse

Artois Hamilton, owner and innkeeper of the Hamilton House in Carthage

Marv, oldest son of innkeeper Artois Hamilton, Marvin Hamilton, age 16

Will, second son of innkeeper Artois Hamilton, William Ransom Hamilton, a private in the Carthage Greys, age 15

Dallas, youngest son of Artois Hamilton, Dallas Hamilton, age 11

Other members of the Hamilton family

Citizens of Nauvoo

Citizens of Carthage

Officers and Soldiers of the Nauvoo Legion

Officers and Soldiers of the Carthage Grays and other anti-Mormon Militia Units

TABLE OF CONTENTS

THE FACE OF THE HORSE

Sleepless animal. In the dark of the night
He stands over the world like a pillar of stone.

There is beauty and intelligence in the horse's face.
He hears the talk of leaves and rocks.
He is aware! He hears the cry of animals,
And the song of the nightingale in the grove.

And knowing all, to whom may he speak
Of his miraculous visions?
The night is hushed. In the darkened sky
The fixed constellations rise,
And the horse stands like a sentinel.
The wind lifts the hair of his tail,
His eyes glow, like two vast worlds,
And his dark mane rustles like a royal robe.

If a man could truly gaze into
The horse's enchanting face,
He would tear out his own useless tongue
And give it to the horse. Of a truth
This magical creature is worthy of it.
And then we should hear words.
Words like red apples, thick
As honey or sweet as milk.
Words, which pierce like a flame,
And kindle in the soul,
Like a hearth-fire in a cabin
Which illuminates the humble room.
Words, which never die
And which are remembered in song.

But now the stable is empty.
The trees spread their leaves in the light,
Narrow rays strike the rolling hills
Warming the rolling summer fields.
And the horse, fixed between the shafts,
Pulls the wagon with its heavy freight
And gazes out of its wise, radiant eyes
Upon the mysterious, motionless world.

By Nikolai Alekseevich Zabolotski
Translated by Daniel Bay Gibbons

Translator's Note: This poem was written in 1937 by the obscure Russian poet, Nikolai Zabolotski. Shortly after publishing this poem, Zabolotski fell victim to the violent purges of Russian intellectuals by Josef Stalin. In 1938 the poet was incarcerated in a prison camp in north-central Siberia (where the translator lived from 2011 to 2014). There he spent most of his remaining years.

THURSDAY, JUNE 6, 1844

Old Charlie rides out on the Carthage Road with Brother Joe

NAUVOO, ILLINOIS – THURSDAY, JUNE 6, 1844

It is nighttime, and Nauvoo, the city of the Latter-day Saints, lies at rest within a great horseshoe bend of the Mississippi River. High on a hill stands the unfinished temple, its stone walls white in the moonlight. Below the temple, the city is laid out in a grid of roads, square with the four points of the compass. The streets are lined with neat rows of shops, houses, stables, outbuildings, fences, gardens, and fruit orchards.

At this late hour the streets are empty. All is quiet, except for the nickering of horses, the sound of frogs and crickets, the distant barking of dogs, and the haunting echo of riverboats sounding their warning whistles in the night. Here and there candlelight winks through the window curtains, but the city of twenty thousand people has settled down for a deep and peaceful sleep.

At the intersection of Main and Water Streets, just above the river, the moonlight filters through the branches of the big trees—maple, sycamore and beech—casting gently moving shadows onto the roadway and buildings. Behind a white picket fence fronting Main Street stands a large, two-story frame house with many windows. A wooden signboard, hanging from two chains, reads, "Nauvoo Mansion." This is one of the finest hotels in western Illinois, with twenty-two rooms. It is also the home of Joseph and Emma Smith and their four children.

Across Water Street from the hotel is a large, two-story stable built of red brick. The stable is surrounded by a lush, fenced-in pasture that runs from the street all the way down to the lapping waters of the Mississippi River.

A stableman carrying two buckets makes his way across the street in the shadows from the stable to the Mansion. A large, white dog, weighing at least two hundred pounds, is lying on the side porch of the hotel. He is Joseph Smith's faithful watchdog, Major. He has been with the family for at least a decade in Ohio, Missouri, and Illinois. The dog stands up as the stableman enters the Mansion and shuts the door for the night. Major walks very slowly as he crosses the street and enters the open stable door.

The moonlight slants through the open shutters of the stable, casting light on the dirt floor. The horses of the hotel guests rest quietly in their box enclosures. Near the door in three special boxes are the horses belonging to Joseph Smith—a strawberry-colored horse called Tom Carling, a dark sorrel called Joe Duncan, and a magnificent, seventeen-year-old stallion, coal-black with a small white star on his forehead, called Charlie.

The white dog walks slowly to a pallet of straw beside Old Charlie's box and lies down.

Is that you Major? Come in. You look kinda stiff in the legs tonight. It's your age, ain't it, old friend? Come lie down a spell and rest your creaky bones. I ain't seen you in days. You've been sleepin' up by the Mansion House, I 'spect, 'stead of here in the stable with Tom and Joe Duncan and me. Well, I'm glad for the company tonight. Can you listen for a spell?

This mornin' Brother Joe and me had a fine, fast ride out ten mile or so on the Carthage Road and back. Tonight my legs are warm and weary. It was right hot outside, fine spring weather with the breeze blowin' and the birds all a-singin' and the flowers a-bloomin'.

I knowed first off this mornin' that we was to go out ridin', 'cause Brother Joe's stableman, Lorin Walker, come out and whistled, the way he does when he wants me to come. I was standin' in my special spot in the pasture, jest lookin' out over the Big River when I heared him and was soon right next to him. Then he brung me in the stable and got me all saddled up. He laid the blanket on my back and hefted the saddle over and cinched it up all snug. Lorin don't say much, but he's got a sure hand with a saddle and bridle. Most times no one rides me 'cept Brother Joe and Lorin. Between times I can also tolerate Lady Emma and even Little Joseph, but no one else.

I s'pose I'm too old to learn to get along with new riders. I pert' near been a one-man horse since I was brung up to Kirtland as a colt. I can't tolerate riders who don't know what they're a-doin'. Brother Joe and Lorin—they know what they're a-doin' in the saddle.

You know that Lorin sleeps up to the Mansion, but spends most hours of the day here in the stables, doin' this and that, fixin' up the saddles and other gear, polishin' Brother Joe's Legion gear, and bringin' in water or feed and whatnot. Lorin's always doin' one chore or another, always workin' away without a lot of talkin'. Fact is, I seldom hear Lorin a-talkin', and when he does talk, it's right low and quiet. Lorin is more about workin' than talkin', 'cept he'll talk to me real low when he feeds me or gives me a rubdown or saddles me up. Same with the other horses—he's always whisperin' to 'em real low. But around people, it's always jest "Yes sir" and "No sir" with Lorin. And 'specially around the ladies Lorin seems right tongue-tied, scarcely speakin' a word.

Lorin takes care of all the hotel horses, which come and go, come and go, but mostly he takes special care of Brother Joe's own horses—me and Tom and Joe Duncan.

I guess you seen that Tom's a good-hearted horse, but kinda big and clumsy. He and I been hitched up together plenty over the years. 'Course Tom warn't with us back in Zion, nor in Kirtland, but still he's ridden with me plenty of miles in the harness. He's a good horse to have by my side pullin' a buggy or a workin' wagon—he jest follers my lead. He turns when I signal, stops when I signal, and never kicks out or makes no fuss.

Now Joe Duncan, on the other side, ain't no horse for the wagon or carriage. Not one bit. He's a ridin' horse like me. He's what Brother Joe calls a "proper saddle horse," pure and fine. But he can be right balky and jumpy. Joe Duncan and I are pert' near the only horses Brother Joe will saddle up and ride when he's leadin' the Legion. Time or two we rode out together on parade with Lady Emma ridin' me sidesaddle and Brother Joe ridin' Joe Duncan. Joe Duncan holds hisself up right proudly in the Legion work, with the band a-playin', and Brother Joe all fixed up in his blue general's gear, and all the hundreds of fellers lined up with their muskets. Joe Duncan steps right proudly in a parade. But mostly, Brother Joe prefers to ride me most days. Legion ridin' or no, I'm the one for him, and that suits me jest fine.

Well, this mornin' Lorin got me all squared away with saddle and all, and then before you know it, I heared Brother Joe a-laughin', and pretty soon he come walkin' into the stable with his little ones. There was Julia ridin' up on her Pa's shoulder, all bright in her yellow dress and her pigtails a-flyin' behind her, and then Little Joseph in his rough and tumble pants and shirt, walkin' right behind Brother Joe, tryin' to act jest like his Pa, I s'pose.

Brother Joe kinda stroked my neck and talked to me a bit, like he always does, and said, "Good boy, Charlie! Good boy!" Little Julia patted my nose.

Little Joseph, short as he is, climbed up on a stump and was tryin' to help with all of the straps and clasps. Then I knowed what was comin' next. Brother Joe said, "Charlie can't go without his treat." The little ones laughed, and Brother Joe reached in his pocket for somethin' and held it right out for me. 'Course he brung me out a piece of sugar from the table, like usual. I licked his hand clean. Lorin set the bit in my mouth, fixed up the bridle, and then cinched everythin' up proper. Brother Joe set Julia down on the ground, then he checked all the straps and swung his long leg up and over the saddle. After Brother Joe got hisself all situated and waved to the young'uns, we was off.

As old as I get, I never get tired of settin' out on a nice ride with Brother Joe. Rain or shine, it's what I hanker for more than anythin' else in the world. I learned early on what we was to do together, me and Brother Joe. With Brother Joe in Kirtland and then Zion, it was everlastin' ridin' around preachin' and talkin' with folks. Same thing in Nauvoo, 'cept now he's ridin' out with the Legion on top of everythin' else. Most every day of his life Brother Joe rides up and down, stoppin' here and there to chat with folks, or goin' into some house or another. He goes for miles and miles, and I 'spect he loves ridin' as much as I do.

Sometimes I think back through all the years and years of ridin' with Brother Joe. Back in Kirtland, I was pert' near the only horse he ever rode. Same thing in Zion. It's close on a thousand mile between them places, but Brother Joe and I rode together back and forth plenty of times over that long road. I'll tell you, Major, sometimes it was real hard work in bad weather, with snow or whatnot, but I never let up. I wanted to ride out with Brother Joe more than I wanted anythin' else, and I always thought that if I looked like I was slowin' down, maybe he'd start to findin' hisself another saddle horse.

First thing after we set out this mornin', Brother Joe and me rode past the little log place where Lady Lucy lives. She's Brother Joe's old mother, you know. Lady Lucy was out in the garden, as usual, jest a-leanin' on her cane and toddlin' around, a-lookin' at all the flowers, I guess, and Brother Joe brung me right up to the fence rail so he could talk with her a bit. The old lady reached out to pat my neck and talked to me in her singsong kinda voice. "Singsong, singsong," she went as she jest rubbed my nose. And then she talked to Brother Joe, "Singsong, singsong," while I dropped my head down and found the sweet grass under the bottom fence rail. Hardly a fly come 'round. Jest had to twitch my skin—that was enough to fix 'em.

The door to Lady Lucy's place opened and out come Lady Katherine. She's Brother Joe's sister, of course, and I knowed her for more summers than I can count, goin' all the way back to Kirtland. Lady Katherine walked over and kinda hooked her arm around Lady Lucy and joined in the talkin' with Brother Joe. It is always right pleasant to be around Brother Joe when he is with his kinfolk. I can jest feel that it perks him right up. Well, after they done talked a spell, Brother Joe leaned way over the fence rail to give Lady Lucy a peck on the cheek and another one to Lady

Katherine, and then he clicked at me, and we was off ridin' again.

We headed on up Main Street. All the shopkeepers was standin' in their doorways, and all the other folks was out a-ridin' or a-strollin'. Most everyone had a word or two for Brother Joe. It was all, "Howdy, Brother Joseph," "Beautiful mornin'," "Weather's fine," "God bless you," and whatnot. Brother Joe stopped off once or twice and leaned down from the saddle, like he gen'rally does, to talk with folks along the way. He's that friendly. Up the street further we passed a crowd of the young fellers, all runnin' in the street, kickin' a ball around and hollerin'. When they see'd us, they all stopped their ball kickin' and turned around and shouted at Brother Joe. Sometimes he stops and joins in the fun, but today he jest hollered a hello at 'em, and we rode on by.

We passed the little clump of trees where Brother Joe does his preachin' some days, with the whole durned town standin' around to listen to him, though there warn't no preachin' today. Then we trotted on up the big hill to the white walls they's a-buildin' up top. He stopped there a spell and dismounted. I see'd him kinda rub his hands up and down, back and forth agin' the stone. He let me graze in the shadow of the walls while he talked some with the men workin' on the stone, who all gathered 'round. They all had white dust spread over their hands and clothes, which makes me sneeze some, so I kept my distance. While I grazed I could hear the low rumble of Brother Joe's voice. He's got the kinda voice you can hear from far off, and when he talks, most times folks stop to listen all serious like. So I heared Brother Joe rumble on for a bit, but then all of a sudden the dusty Stone Men standin' around was all laughin'. That's the way with Brother Joe. He's right serious most times, but then he loves to joke and jibe and make folks laugh. After a bit more laughin' and talkin', Brother Joe waved to the Stone Men and mounted back up, and we was off again.

We rode east up the street he calls Mulholland, past more shops and people and the liv'ry stable where Brother Joe's friend Porter keeps his horses and carriages, and then out into the open country. I went into my buck-trot with the breeze blowin' through my mane, and I could tell that Brother Joe was ready for a nice ride. We rode out a mile to the crossroads where the Carthage Road kinda angles off to the right and down a steep hill toward Carthage, 'bout twenty mile away. Brother Joe's big farm lies jest the other side of Carthage Road, and we slowed down as we rode, I guess so Brother Joe could keep a lookout for what was growin' in the sun. He waved at his farmer, a tall, strong feller named Old Man Lott, who was out tillin' in Brother Joe's field with his sturdy little bay mare hitched to the plow.

Brother Joe rode me right out into the field, and we stopped so Brother Joe could talk a spell with Old Man Lott, who runs Brother Joe's farm and lives out there with his wife and family. His bay mare—Paulina's her name—looked right tired in the harness, and she stood dozin', lockin' one of her hind legs, and restin' on that hip while liftin' the other. I nickered at her, and she flicked her ears, too tired I guess to bother with me. So Paulina and me looked at each other some while Brother Joe and Old Man Lott talked back and forth about fields and crops and fences and gates. Old Man Lott has got a very fine, high-pitched voice, almost soundin' like the voice of a lady, 'cept that Old Man Lott is as strong and tough as any man I ever seen. I seen him rassle young fellers and throw 'em right to the ground.

After a bit of talk between Brother Joe and Old Man Lott, we lit out again in the direction of Carthage and passed the place Brother Joe calls the Cemetery. I can never figure out what goes on there, Major. Time to time Brother Joe rides up there, all dressed up for a meetin', and I can see how the Brethren have gone and dug a big hole in the ground. Always one big hole, with the dirt a-piled 'longside it. Then folks all stand around in a circle around the big hole and sing songs and then hear some sorta preachin'. And then the men slowly drop a long wooden box down into the hole while everyone sings a song, and then the Brethren pick up their shovels and fill the hole right up with dirt. Mighty strange doin's.

After we passed the Cemetery, Brother Joe and me lit on down the Carthage Road. First we jest rode along, Brother Joe not sayin' a word, like usual, and me trottin' along without a thought in my head. Sometimes Brother Joe talks to me when we ride, but today he rode along real quiet. It sounds crazy, Major, I know, seein' how he has to do with so many people all the time, but Brother Joe's really a kinda lonely man. I mean, there's somethin' deep inside him that wants to be alone sometimes, and ridin' me is practically the only time he is alone. Seein' the way he talks and preaches and makes men stand up and listen, or laugh like the Stone Men workin' on the white walls, you'd think Brother Joe was always 'clined to be around folks. But deep down he's a solitary feller. I don't know who would know that if it ain't me, since I spent more time with him over the years than any other creature alive.

We rode nice and easy 'bout ten mile out on the Carthage Road on dry dirt and plenty of shade, my hooves cloppin' steadily like they always do when I know that Brother Joe is mounted. The sun was shinin' through the leaves and the creek windin' in and out through the farms and cow fields. Meadowlarks was singin', and there warn't no wagons or other horses in sight, so we kept on and rode down the road Carthage-ways for eight, ten mile. There was some little hills, and that's what I like, movin' real steady up hill or down hill. Brother Joe don't need to give me much in the way of signals. Canterin' along, I don't think about him any more than I think about the iron nails and shoes on my hooves. Brother Joe is jest there, and when the road is open he gives me my head for a canter or a gallop without holdin' me in, 'cause I'm a big horse, and he knows I can't abide bein' pulled back. I'm a big horse, and Brother Joe is a big man.

'Bout ten mile out of Nauvoo, we slowed and wandered off the road behind some little trees to a burbly creek. I showed Brother Joe that I was thirsty, so he jest let me take a breather, and after I drank, we meandered for a while in the shade while I ate some of the sweet grass. Brother Joe sat alone with his thoughts without speakin', though he did reach down now and then to pat my neck.

Then in 'bout five, ten minutes I sensed that a horse was comin' fast up the Carthage Road toward Nauvoo. Sure enough, 'round the bend come a big white stallion, canterin' smartly with a nice even three-beat clip-a-clop, clip-a-clop. Presently we see'd the stallion through the branches of the little trees. It was Sam, the white stallion that belongs to Brother Joe's big brother, Hyrum. In some respects, Major, Sam and me is exact opposites of a horse, and not jest in color. I'm coal black, and Sam is snow white, but in temper'ment we is as different as night and day. Where I'm what Brother Joe calls high spirited, Sam is quiet. Where I'm proud, he's humble. Where I'm steady, he's jumpy. Sam is a big, strong horse, jest not as fast as me, but he's a smart one. Durned smart. He can scent out the comin' of other horses a mile off, and he jest seems to know what's comin'. I could tell that Sam already knowed I was hidden behind the trees, 'cause he nickered loudly and then gave out a gentle snort as he cantered up, like he was enjoyin' hisself.

Hyrum and Brother Joe are 'bout as close as men can be and ride up to each other's houses most days, and they are always full of slaps on the back and long talks and jinks and jibes and jokes. Somehow I knowed that Brother Joe wanted to s'prise his brother, maybe play a little trick on him. He crouched low in my saddle and moved me over to the edge of the little trees near the road, hopin' to s'prise Brother Hyrum, I 'spect. But Sam already knowed full well where we was behind the trees and lifted up his head and neighed right out to me, kinda like a challenge. I 'spect he smelt me even without seein' me, jest like I smelt him. Hyrum looked all around, s'prised to see what was what. Jest then Brother Joe shouted a little, "Gah!" and spurred me on, and we lit out onto the road jest ahead of Sam and started a proper race back toward Nauvoo.

You know, Major, I always love to have what Brother Joe calls a "dash." And Sam and I had a proper dash this mornin' with Brother Joe and Hyrum in the saddles. Brother

Joe warn't about to let his brother pass us by, and I was of the same mind. I jest lowered my head and doubled down into a gallop, and Sam did the same. We kicked up a mighty cloud of dust, but none of it settled on me or Brother Joe. Time or two I see'd Sam's nose movin' steady up on my left, his snow-white mane a-streamin' in the wind, with Brother Hyrum crouched right over, smilin' over at his brother. But let me tell you, Major, I warn't about to let Sam pass me by today or any other time.

Sometimes a hard gallop also brings the memories, Major. Memories of danger, which make me run all the harder. Runnin' is like a storm wind that blows away all the years and brings back the danger that I seen gather 'round Brother Joe many a time. Sometimes I see the Tar Men, like I see'd long ago in Ohio, with their faces smeared black, strikin' Brother Joe, whippin' him, hurtin' him. But a long gallop with Brother Joe under the blue sky sets everythin' to rights, 'cause I know I can carry him away safely. The world trembles with the thunderin' of my hooves in the dust. I can carry Brother Joe far from the Tar Men, far from any danger. It's hard to explain to a dog, Major, but the long gallops over the hills conquer fear and danger. No one can harm Brother Joe or me when we is runnin' free, faster than any creature.

So we rode hard, Sam and me, side by side, mile after mile, and then I see'd how we was comin' up fast 'longside of the Cemetery and up the long hill leadin' up to the crossroads with Mulholland Street. I always love to go gallopin' hard up the long hills, and that's what I did this mornin' as we rode up the hill into Nauvoo. Sam was givin' it his all, but I see'd how his head fell back further and further, until it was jest me and Brother Joe racin' up the long hill past the green grass. The leather of the saddle creaked, and the metal on the bridle clicked in time with my legs. I struck the smooth road with the flat of my hooves, and life kinda rose up through my legs and withers and spread through every muscle of my long body. Hyrum and Sam fell back like they was standin' still, and it made me feel real good to beat 'em. The Carthage road and the hill, and all the world was jest fallin' further and further behind me and Brother Joe.

We waited to the top of the hill on Mulholland Street, 'cause Hyrum's farm was jest off the road a piece, and we knowed they would be turnin' off to head home. Presently Sam and Hyrum made the top of the hill, and Hyrum reined Sam in. Sam was gruntin' with effort, and I was a mite winded, too, I confess, Major. They gave us the long rein, and we walked along for a piece. They talked back at each other while Sam and I breathed and blew long "hrrrmph" sounds out our noses, feelin' good, walkin' home after a nice ride with Hyrum and Brother Joe.

FRIDAY, JUNE 7, 1844

OLD CHARLIE RIDES TO THE STEAMBOAT LANDING WITH
BROTHER JOE AND PORTER – CHARLIE SEES A STRANGE
TO-DO OVER SHEETS OF PAPER

NAUVOO, ILLINOIS – FRIDAY, JUNE 7, 1844

Morning: Members of the Foster, Higbee, and Law families, all dissenters from the Church, have set up the Nauvoo Expositor *and print one thousand copies of the only issue ever published. It contains libelous material about Joseph Smith and other men and women of Nauvoo. The paper accuses Joseph of "gross moral imperfections" and advocates the violent overthrow of the government of Nauvoo and of the Church. "Let us arise," the* Expositor *states, "in the majesty of our strength and sweep the influence of tyrants and miscreants from the face of the land, as with the breath of heaven."[1]*

Afternoon: Copies of the Expositor *are circulated throughout Nauvoo. The citizens, infuriated by the lies and slanders, threaten to destroy the press. Joseph and others on the City Council deem it better to proceed in a legal manner rather than illegally, thereby saving the citizens from violent retribution.[2]*

After reading the Nauvoo Expositor, *Joseph says, "I would rather die tomorrow and have the thing smashed."*

---

[1] The *Nauvoo Expositor* (Nauvoo, June 7, 1844), "Prospectus" and "Preamble."

[2] B.H. Roberts, ed., *History of the Church of Jesus Christ of Latter-day Saints* (Salt Lake City: Deseret Press, 1951), hereafter "HC," 7:61

Evening: Robert Foster, one of the dissenting editors of the Expositor, *visits Joseph at the Mansion House.* [3]

Hey, Major, old dog. Did you hear all the racket the young fellers was makin' in the streets tonight? They was a-marchin' up and down, blowin' trumpets, and bangin' away on any old durn thing they could find—old cans, pots, drums—anythin' will do as long as they make a racket. Then, they was lightin' a bonfire or two in the street and burnin' big sheets of paper. I see'd it when I passed by ridin' with Brother Joe down Main Street. And not jest the young fellers was there, but proper folks too, and some of the Brethren, jest walkin' up and a-droppin' big sheets of paper into the flames. The sparks was flyin' upwards, but I didn't flinch none as Brother Joe stood me off to the side of the road, jest watchin'. I knowed all about the sheets of paper this afternoon, 'cause Brother Joe and me see'd 'em while we was out a-ridin'.

It was a fine day, and Brother Joe started out in fine spirits, which always puts me in fine spirits, too. I was all saddled up and jest stampin' my hooves outside the Mansion while I waited with Lorin for Brother Joe to come out. Day to day I never know where Brother Joe and me will ride, but as long as I'm with him, I'm ready for it all.

I s'pose Brother Joe and me are 'bout as close together as a man and a horse can get. When we is ridin' alone, he sometimes talks to me. It's all "Charlie this" and "Charlie that." And sometimes I can almost feel like I'm talkin' back to him. Brother Joe always makes me feel like without me he

---

[3] HC 6:438, 442

wouldn't be able to do a durned thing. And wherever we go, he always sees to me hisself when Lorin's not around. Whenever we ride to some meetin' or to the house of one of the Brethren, he'll swing down from the saddle and make sure I'm situated in the shade or have a drink of water or a nosebag, or he sets me out to graze in some sweet spot of blowin' grass. If we is ever to stay someplace overnight, he gets the saddle and bridle off me straightaway and gives me a nice rubdown if we've ridden twenty, thirty mile. He treats me like I'm the most precious thing he has in the world. And I guess I come to b'lieve it, Major. I guess I try to live up to it, if that makes sense.

Well, this afternoon we first headed right up through town to the hill to see the Stone Men workin' on the white walls. It was mighty fine weather when we lit out, and folks crowded the shops on Main Street. From out yonder I heared the big whistle sounds of boats on the Big River. We passed the clump of trees below the big hill and then come up to the white walls. Brother Joe and me rode slowly 'round the block while he jest gazed up at the walls, shoutin' halloos at the dusty Stone Men sittin' up on the long pieces of wood they had rigged up all along the walls.

After circlin' a time or two around the block, Brother Joe and me rode over to the little hotel right across the street from the white walls to visit his friend, the man they call Porter Rockwell. Well, anyways that's his proper name, but I always call him "Porter."

Y'see, Major, I sometimes got my own names for the people Brother Joe sees the most of, people like Porter—it comes easier. They's mostly divided amongst the Brethren and the Soldiers. The Brethren is the ones that do the preachin' in the little clump of trees, and the Soldiers is them that work with Brother Joe in the Legion. Amongst the Brethren there is Doctor Richards—a mighty fat feller. I call him "the Big Doctor." His horse is Saucepan, and I often feel sorry for him, havin' to carry the Big Doctor around and all. Then there's Stephen Markham, who is some kinda main preacher. Him I call Markham, and he rides a little chocolate-colored palomino called Pickwick. Then there's Dan Jones, the feller what comes and goes on his big steamboat, and who I call Blue Dan on account of his blue cap he wears. Blue Dan's got a right interestin' voice, full of strange sounds, sorta' like music comin' out of his mouth when he speaks. He rides a bay gelding called Tramp.

Them's some of the Brethren. Amongst the Soldiers the main feller is General Dunham. He's the main officer in charge of the whole durned Legion, 'cept Brother Joe and Hyrum, who is the commandin' generals. General Dunham rides a big clay-colored stallion named Rambler.

Well, like I said, Porter lives in the hotel on Mulholland. He's a right short feller, at least compared to Brother Joe, but a good man to have in a pinch. He's got kinda a high voice, not deep and rumbly like Brother Joe's, or musical like Blue Dan's. But Porter's a right sharp feller. He's a good one with a gun and as strong as any man or horse I ever knowed. Porter runs what Brother Joe calls the liv'ry stable. There's eight or ten sturdy little horses and some carriages what Porter borrows out to folks here and there. He's also what Brother Joe calls a "bodyguard." Brother Joe's got several of those, but none better than Porter.

The liv'ry stable doors was swung wide open when we rode up, and Porter walked slowly out onto Mulholland

Street, covered from head to foot in dust and a-chewin' on a apple.

"Hey, Porter," says Brother Joe. "I'm glad to find you home. I'd hoped to ride with you out to the steamboat landing."

"Sure enough," said Porter. "Give me five minutes." He jest chucked his apple core out into the street and went into the liv'ry. A minute later he brung out his dirty, little scrap of a horse, called Jack, and tied him to the rail. Jack grunted a bit and shook his mane and then stood with his tail hangin' down. When Porter come out again with the saddle, Jack perked right up and started wavin' his tail in excitement. I suspect he realized then that he was goin' out ridin' and not gettin' hitched up to one of Porter's big wagons or carriages to haul folks or gear here and about. You know, Major, any horse'd ruther ride out with the saddle than get hitched between the shafts of any wagon or carriage. It ain't what horses want. They want to run and move free and not be strapped down to anythin'. Mules and oxen are different. They take to the pullin' of things, but not saddle horses like Sam and Joe Duncan and me. Well, I guess little Jack see'd hisself as a saddle horse, too.

Brother Joe and me jest stood and waited while Porter saddled up Jack. Meanwhile, Porter and Brother Joe talked back and forth. I learned long ago that Brother Joe don't wait patiently for many men, but he always does for Porter, as Brother Joe and him go way back, havin' been raised together as boys in a place called New York.

Porter swung up into the saddle on Jack, and we lit out down the hill and then northwest to the place called Kimball's, on the Big River. As we rode up through the streets and houses and then through the open pastures, we see'd plainly from afar that two of the little river boats was there at Kimball's, with big, white smoke risin' up out of long, black pots sittin' on their roofs. Brother Joe and Porter tied me and Jack up by a little cabin close by, where we could see the water, and they walked up to the door and knocked. The feller named Kimball, who owns the place, come out, and they all shook hands. Then we see'd 'em walk to the dock right next to the water where two little boats was all tied up. They leaned their arms on the rail and jest talked.

The big, smoky boats ride up and down the Big River reg'lar like. There's hardly a day goes by without boats a-comin' or goin'. Most of 'em are small ones, like the two little boats that was tied up at Kimball's that day. But every five, six days the big boats come in jest filled with folks who come into Nauvoo to stay a spell. Most times they tie up at Kimball's, where we was this afternoon, and some other times at the little landin' down here close by Brother Joe's place. Most times when a big boat pulls in, Brother Joe rides up to welcome folks who want to stay at Brother Joe's Mansion House, and Porter hauls their boxes and cases and whatnot in one of his rigs. But there warn't no big boats today. Jest the two little ones.

Jack and me jest waited there by the cabin, not doin' much, and then the whistle on one of the little boats went off, with a noise loud enough to wake every dog and horse in Nauvoo. I didn't flinch, but Jack stood up on his hind legs and screamed right out.

Jest then I heared hoofbeats and knowed that some horse was gallopin' in at a right nice clip. Brother Joe and Porter looked up. And who should come 'round the corner by Kimball's, but Hyrum ridin' Sam. Hyrum jumped right down, not even tyin' Sam up, and headed right over to Brother Joe with a big sheet of paper in his hand. Brother Joe took the sheet in his hands and looked at it real intent like. Porter and Kimball and Hyrum looked over his shoulder.

I don't exactly understand why men look so long at sheets of paper, Major. It puzzles how they can stand or set so quietly jest lookin' and lookin' and lookin'. I don't know what they is a-seein'. Well, as Brother Joe stared at the paper, Porter started to talk here and there, and boy was he gettin' riled up. "Damn them!" he said. And then, "Infernal demons!" and "They'll burn in hell!" and whatnot. He was gettin' mighty red around the face. He was durned mad. I could sense it, like he was ready to go a-fightin'.

Brother Joe didn't say nothin', but when he folded up that big sheet of paper and walked over to mount back up, I could tell that he was riled up, too. His legs was uncommon tense after he swung up into the saddle. Brother Joe was mad. At what, I didn't rightly know. The two others, Porter and Hyrum, mounted right up too, and then we all rode at a fast canter back through Nauvoo and up the big hill. We rode right on past the white walls on Mulholland Street a little piece to some shops. In front of a little two-story place, we see'd a passel of men all a-standin' on the side of the road around a big stack of papers. There was three men with some kinda dirt or black all over their hands, and they was carryin' more and more stacks of the paper sheets down some long stairs on the outside of the shop and puttin' 'em on the stack of papers on the ground.

Brother Joe and Hyrum stayed put in the saddle, but Porter was off of Jack like a flash, and he run up into the crowd. I see'd how he pulled a pistol from his pocket and carried it in his hands.

There was lots of shoutin' and runnin' around. I see'd how fellers was a-runnin' this way and that with bunches of them paper sheets in their hands.

Then I see'd four or five young fellers run up, a couple of the ones Brother Joe and me see'd yesterday playin' kickball in the street. These young fellers started a-shoutin' and was grabbin' the papers out of the hands of one of the fellers with the black and dirty hands, called Robert Foster. I knowed Mr. Robert well, for once he was one of the Brethren and real close with Brother Joe. Many times he would come ridin' with us on his chocolate-colored mare, Charity. Charity was a sweet mare. Well, one of the young fellers was yellin' right into Mr. Robert's face. "Damn you, Foster!" he said. "We'll burn this filth right here in the street," and then he started tryin' to carry off the pile of papers from Mr. Robert's hands. Mr. Robert tried to pull the papers away. Then Porter stepped up with his pistol in his hands.

It looked like it was fixin' to become a big fight, with Mr. Robert and Porter right in the middle of it, but Brother Joe jumped down out of the saddle and run over. I heared him shoutin'. He was yellin' for folks to jest calm down. He pushed Porter and the young fellers away. "Let it be!" he kept shoutin' at 'em. "Let it be. Let the law take care of this."

So Brother Joe calmed things down, but by now there must have been two, three hundred men in the street and some women too. And everyone was a-carryin' these paper sheets and a-lookin' at 'em intent like as they walked away. And most of 'em looked as mad as Porter, 'cept none of 'em had drawn out any pistols about it like Porter done.

We rode home pretty soon after that, jest Brother Joe and me. Brother Joe was mighty quiet on the ride, kinda sunk down deep in his own thoughts, 'specially when we passed them young fellers a-lightin' fires. They had lit up a couple of big bonfires right in the middle of Main Street, and I see'd how lots of folks was wanderin' over with them pieces of paper in their hands and jest droppin' 'em in the flames. It was right strange.

After we got back to the stable, Brother Joe went right over to the Mansion House. Lorin took off my saddle and bridle and put me in my box in the stable. You know how Tom and Joe Duncan and me each got our own special little stable doors what open out onto the big pasture 'longside of the stable? Well, I jest wandered outside and went over to my reg'lar spot. There I stood, jest a-watchin' the Mansion across the street. It was mighty quiet, but I could feel some kinda tension, like a storm was blowin' in.

As the sun was settin' and the shadows got long across the fence lines, a whole lot of horses started comin' in— horse after horse—mostly belongin' to the Brethren and some of the Soldiers. Lorin brung the horses into the pasture by the stable, one by one, and let 'em jest wait with their saddles still on. There was General Dunham's big stallion, Rambler, and Markham's palomino, Pickwick, and lots of others besides. They was all there, the horses grazin' in the pasture and their riders standin' in the street, talkin' in little groups, a-leanin' on the fence. And then Brother Joe come out of the Mansion to say howdy to everyone. Brother Joe was walkin' here and there, jest a-talkin' to 'em. As far as I could make out, all of 'em was sayin' we was in a mighty bad way. Hyrum was the last to come, ridin' up on Sam. I guess they was all waitin' on him, for after he rode up, Brother Joe and all the men went into the Mansion. I suspect they was all inside talkin' with Brother Joe about them pieces of paper while we horses waited outside.

It got dark outside, and the windows in the Mansion started to light up. All the horses in the pasture and in the stable stood real quiet, with only the sound of a grunt or a nicker now and then. After a while the moon come up, and the whippoorwills started callin' out in the trees by the Big River. I was startin' to wonder if Brother Joe would talk with the men all night. Sometimes he does that. The visitin' horses stood quiet with their saddles on, jest a-waitin' for their riders.

Then all of a sudden, I see'd how one more horse rode up in the moonlight. It was Charity, the chocolate-colored mare what belongs to Mr. Robert Foster, the feller who was in the tussle with all the sheets of paper this afternoon up on Mulholland. Mr. Robert rode her up hard, right to the gate— I see'd how he jerked her head this way and that with the reins—and then he climbed down and put Charity into the waitin' pasture with the other horses. She stood in the open gate, I guess not knowin' what to do, 'cause it was dark and kinda ghostly in the moonlight. She started walkin' back out onto Water Street, but then Mr. Foster jerked her head back around and slapped her hard right on her behind to get her movin' into the pasture and shouted out her name. She come in with the other horses, and Mr. Robert closed the gate. I watched as he stood in the street a blink or two, fixin' his collar, and then walked fast over to the Mansion.

Charity stood alone over agin' the fence, away from the other horses. I nickered at her, and she walked over to my reg'lar spot. Her tail was right between her legs, and her ears was laid flat, so I knowed she was afraid. I sniffed her nose, and she sniffed back. Then she jest stood agin' the fence quiet, not movin' a bit, but jest a-waitin'.

Then, after a short while, Mr. Foster come walkin' back across the street. He yelled at Charity—she run right over to him—and then he hauled her back out of the pasture. He climbed back up and rode her hard down Water Street. I could see how he was kickin' her sides right hard.

It got me thinkin' about the difference between Brother Joe and most other riders I ever seen. You know, Major, how Brother Joe respects every livin' creature. I 'specially understand that when he's ridin'. It's right surprisin' how few horsemen ever bother to speak a kind word to a horse or give him praise. They jest stick to hard words and sharp heels when a horse has done somethin' wrong, like Mr. Robert done with Charity. They never understand how a horse likes praise and responds to it. They push their horses as hard as they can. Their horses might as well be handcarts on the road, how they get pushed. But that's not proper ridin'. Brother Joe is a proper rider. He's always ready with a word of praise. It kinda makes you want to stand up and do whatever he asks you to do.

And I would do practically anythin' for Brother Joe.

SATURDAY, JUNE 8, 1844

LITTLE JOSEPH RIDES OUT ON OLD CHARLIE – CHARLIE
SEES THE COMINGS AND GOINGS AT THE RED BRICK
STORE – BROTHER JOE TALKS ABOUT THE WHOLE TOWN
BURNING DOWN

NAUVOO, ILLINOIS – SATURDAY, JUNE 8, 1844

The skies are clear throughout the day, with thunder and rain all evening and through the night.[4]

10:00 a.m. to 1:00 p.m. The City Council meets in the morning at the Red Brick Store to discuss the publication of the Expositor. Joseph speaks in favor of suppressing libels: saying that he knew it would be dangerous and bring the wrath of the surrounding communities upon them, but that it was their responsibility as men of "enlarged minds" to protect the "injured and oppressed," and to declare the press a nuisance and destroy it.[5]

Hyrum speaks concerning the character of the editors of the press: saying that Robert Foster and the Law brothers had persecuted the poor while in Missouri, and that William Law had offered Joseph Jackson $500 to kill Joseph.

Joseph proposes that they pass an ordinance against libels. Witnesses swear that they heard the conversation of the night before between Foster and Joseph at the Mansion. In the presence of witnesses, he expressed regret for publishing the Expositor and proposed to return

---

[4] Scott H. Faulring, *An American Prophet's Record: The Diaries and Journals of Joseph Smith* (Salt Lake City: Signature Books, 1989), hereafter "APR," 488-89; HC 6:434-39

[5] HC 7:62-63

to the Church. Joseph told him to come back with three or four friends to meet and talk. Foster agreed, but never returned. He sent Joseph a letter saying, "I have consulted my friends in relation to your proposals of settlement, and they, as well as myself, are of the opinion that your conduct, and that of your unworthy, unprincipled clan, is so base, that it would be morally wrong, and detract from the dignity of gentlemen, to hold any conference with you."[6]

A committee is appointed to draft a resolution ordering the destruction of the Nauvoo Expositor.

Joseph predicts that the city of Nauvoo will lie in ashes within five years, unless they go to Oregon, California, or some other place.[7]

Major? Is that you? Things have been mighty quiet around here. From one day to the next I never exactly know what to 'spect from Brother Joe.

I knowed durin' this whole week that there was somethin' in the wind. We horses can almost smell any uneasiness or tenseness, you know Major. I could kinda feel the stress buildin' up, and I know the other horses felt the same. Like when a big thunderstorm blows through, and y'see all the little birds flyin' on the wing here and there. The animals sense things like that before they happen.

I didn't ride with Brother Joe none today. This mornin' he come over to the stable, and I perked right up 'spectin' that we was to have a fine ride out in the sun, but he jest patted my neck and talked to Tom and Joe Duncan and me some and then walked away down Water Street.

---

[6] HC 6:434-37

[7] Scott H. Faulring, *An American Prophet's Record: The Diaries and Journals of Joseph Smith* (Salt Lake City: Signature Books, 1989), hereafter "APR," 488-89; HC 6:434-39

A little later on, Little Joseph come out into the stable with Lorin, and I knowed that I was to go out ridin', jest not with Brother Joe. Little Joseph is a fearless rider just like his Pa. He's a small feller, hardly able to sit in a saddle, but he jest loves to ride. When we lived in Quincy two, three summers ago, Brother Joe brung home Tom for Little Joseph to ride. I 'spect Brother Joe thought Tom would make a fine ridin' horse for him, but Tom's too big and clumsy for proper ridin', 'specially for a little feller like Little Joseph. Little Joseph jest seems to prefer to ride me, like his Pa, so now and again he comes out to ride.

'Course a little feller like Little Joseph would ordinarily have a hard time gettin' my saddle and bridle all situated, so Lorin come out into the stable to help. Lorin seems to love to fix Little Joseph all up for ridin'. I jest stood still while Lorin saddled me up, then he handed the reins to Little Joseph, and he led me out of the stable by the pasture fence.

I 'spect I already told you, Major, that I never allow nobody to ride me, 'cept Brother Joe, Lorin, Little Joseph, or Lady Emma. And Little Joseph and me got ourselves a sorta game we play whenever he comes out to go a-ridin' with me.

It all started this way. Long 'bout a summer or two ago, Little Joseph come out one day and found me all saddled up outside the house. I was jest standin' in the street, waitin' for Brother Joe. Little Joseph must have had a notion to ride me, for he untied me from the waitin' rail by the front door and then tried to climb up into the saddle. Now Little Joe could scarcely lift his foot up into my stirrup, so in order to mount up he done untied me and led me over to a fence rail across the street. I 'spect he thought he could jest climb up the rails high enough to scramble onto my back. Now I was waitin' on Brother Joe and warn't too sure about ridin' off with Little Joseph. That put a piece of mischief in my mind. So as Little Joseph started to climb up the fence, I sidled over toward the little feller, pinnin' him tight agin' the fence. I never hurt him none, but I jest thought it best not to be ridden off when I was waitin' on Brother Joe. He kept tryin' to climb up the fence, but I didn't let him, 'cause I knowed he jest wanted to mount up. When he stopped tryin' to mount up, I eased up on him, but every time he tried to climb up, I pinned him agin' the fence. This went on, over and over. It was jest a sorta little game I played with him.

But you know that now and then Little Joseph has got mischief in his own mind, too. He finally pushed me away from the fence and run into the Mansion House. I figured he was tired of tryin' to ride me, but presently he come back outside and tried again to climb the fence and get on my back. Once more, I sidled over and pinned the little feller agin' the fence. But this time, I suddenly felt a prickin' feelin' in my side. The little rascal had gotten a sharp pin in his hand and was jest a-prickin' my side. It didn't hurt me none, but was annoyin'. Well, I waggled my ears back and forth and shook my head and then finally stood away from the fence and let Little Joseph clamber up onto my back.

So today Little Joseph and I played our game when he tried to mount. I pinned him agin' the fence, and he set to prickin' my side, and I let him up. Then we set out through the streets of Nauvoo. Lorin had raised up the stirrups as high as they could go, and Little Joseph sat in the saddle like a proper little horseman. We rode up and down and all through the streets. Little Joseph didn't seem to have no destination, but jest felt the joy of ridin'. All the people in Nauvoo know Little Joseph, and there was plenty that waved at him or yelled out their halloos. We rode up to Brother Joe's farm, then on north a mile to Hyrum's farm. I was lookin' for Sam to be out in Hyrum's pasture, but didn't see him as we rode up. There was two other horses in Hyrum's big pasture—the big farm horse, Nimrod, and the little brown pony, Peter Simple. As we come cloppin' up to Hyrum's farmhouse, out come runnin' Hyrum's boy, John. He's 'bout the same age as Little Joseph, but a mite bigger. John climbed up the fence and sat, and the two boys talked back and forth about things boys discuss, I guess. Few minutes later, John run off to fetch a little saddle, and he fixed up Peter Simple for a ride. Peter Simple is John's ridin' pony, 'bout twelve hands high. Brother Joe says that I'm fifteen hands from the ground up to my withers.

And then we set off. I s'pose we looked a sight, Little Joseph ridin' me and John ridin' Peter, one big horse and a small pony ridin' side by side. But the boys was havin' a time of it. We rode back down Mulholland Street into upper Nauvoo, then back past the Stone Men workin' on the white walls on the top of the hill, and finally back down to Brother Joe's Red Brick Store.

Little Joseph and John tied me and Peter Simple up with all the other horses waitin' outside the Red Brick Store and went inside. There was all the same horses what was in the Mansion House pasture last night—the Big Doctor's Saucepan and General Dunham's Rambler—plus a bunch more. Sam was there, I see'd, and I figured Hyrum had ridden him down hisself.

After we arrived, the man called John Taylor rode up. I like his mare; she's a real, nice young filly—good goer too—named Lady Gray. He tied her up next to me. John Taylor strolled over and stroked my nose some and said, "How are we doin' today, Charlie?" I'm partial to John Taylor, as he always has somethin' kind to say to me or a pat on the head. I know Brother Joe is partial to him as well, as he is always askin' John Taylor to sing a song. He's forever singin' his songs to Brother Joe or singin' out loud in the big meetin's up to the clump of trees underneath the big hill.

John Taylor went on inside the store, and then I jest stood and waited. There was lots of people comin' and goin' at the store. Some was there to buy somethin', I suspect, as they come out with parcels or bags and carried stuff or loaded it into wagons. But most of 'em like Hyrum and General Dunham and Markham, whose horses was tied up out front, was there upstairs to talk with Brother Joe. I knowed Brother Joe was there, for out of the upstairs windows I could hear his voice now and again. It was warm outside and all the windows was open. Well, I figured Little Joseph had gone inside to set for a time and listen to the men, for I see'd him and John a-sittin' by one of the open windows upstairs, watchin' somethin' all intense like. I waited out in the street with the other horses.

From time to time I heared angry voices or shouts comin' down out of the open windows, but mostly, there was jest the monotonous sound of one or two voices talkin' all solemn like. Near's I could tell they was talkin' about the sheets of paper I see'd bein' looked at and bein' burned in Main Street yesterday.

The meetin' in the store broke up 'bout an hour after Little Joseph and I got there. Pretty soon we see'd the men comin' out of the store. Hyrum was walkin' with his boy, John, and Brother Joe was carryin' Little Joseph on his shoulder. I wondered if Little Joseph had climbed up a fence rail to mount up on his Pa, like he done with me. The horses perked up when the men come down, all talkin' in kinda low and solemn voices. Brother Joe was speakin' quietly with Hyrum and the Big Doctor, while Little Joseph climbed down and come over to reach up and stroke my neck. Near's I could tell they was still talkin' about the sheets of paper. And then, I heared Brother Joe's voice loud and clear. He said that inside five years Nauvoo would be burned right to the ground. He said that the whole place would be on fire, 'less we all up and go off to a place called Californee or the Rocky Mountains or some other place out West.

I'm puzzled about that, Major. First off, I'm not too keen about the whole town gettin' burned down. And I don't rightly know where Californee is, nor the Rocky Mountains.

But I do know this. If Brother Joe wants to ride there, I'll carry him.

SUNDAY, JUNE 9, 1844

Old Charlie and Tom pull Brother Joe's buggy to the steamboat landing and back to the Mansion House

NAUVOO, ILLINOIS – SUNDAY, JUNE 9, 1844

Joseph Smith is ill and stays most of the day at home in the Nauvoo Mansion House. His brother, Hyrum Smith, preaches the Sunday sermon in the grove.

2:00 p.m. The Osprey, a large steamboat, arrives in Nauvoo at the upper steamboat landing. Joseph helps bring several passengers with their luggage to the Mansion House.

6:00 p.m. There is a meeting at the Mansion House.

Lay down, Major, and get some rest. I'll jest tell you about today while you rest your eyes, old soldier.

I see'd Brother Joe walk back to the Mansion from the Red Brick Store yesterday. He was a-coughin'—sounded like a dog barkin', it was that deep in his chest. I figure this mornin' he was jest a-restin' in the Mansion, for I didn't see him. I see'd a lot of other folks walkin' in their best clothes or ridin' in carriages, so I knowed that there must have been some preachin' goin' on up to the trees below the hill, but 'parently Brother Joe warn't doin' no preachin' today, with his cough and all. Most times when the preachin' is goin' on, the whole hillside is filled with people. Brother Joe has a mighty voice, and a whole crowd of people can hear him speak. Other preachers have a hard time gettin' heared proper in a big gatherin' outside, but not Brother Joe. He's a big man with a big voice. The only bigger voice I know is Hyrum, who is even bigger than Brother Joe.

I warn't 'spectin' to go out ridin' today, as Brother Joe is coughin' and all, so I was s'prised in the afternoon when Lorin come into the stable and hitched me and Tom up to Brother Joe's fancy black buggy, the same one he likes to take Lady Emma out in on a fine day. First he hauled us out of the pasture and brung us out into the yard by the street. Tom and I stood untied by the water trough waitin' for the next part, which we both knowed was comin'. Lorin brung out the two big soft collars, which he unhooked and slipped up over our heads and around our necks. Then he laid the big back straps up and over our shoulders. Next he put the funny-feelin' straps over our rumps, which he calls "britchens," which kinda spread the weight of the buggy over our whole bodies, makin' it easier to pull. Then he hooked us up to the pole straps and placed the bridles on us, with the long drivin' reins. Then Lorin brung me and Tom out away from the trough to stand together for the next part. He laid down the long loopin' heart rings between us to keep the drivin' reins all straight, so they wouldn't twist up. Then, finally, he hooked the long pole up to the buggy.

Tom is always a good horse to work the harness with me. He don't always know what to do or how to step and pull, but he follers me, and I have more than enough sense for the two of us. As we stood waitin', I thought of the steady black stallion Jim, who pulled in the harness with me from Kirtland days through Missouri until we arrived in Illinois. He was the steadiest and trustworthiest of all the teammates I ever had, but he died along the road after we got Lady Emma's wagon across the Big River on the ice.

When we was all harnessed up, Lorin drove the wagon out in front of the Mansion, and Brother Joe and Little Joseph come out. Brother Joe took the reins, and we set out up Main Street. As we was drivin', I heared the big whistle of a steamboat on the Big River. I was 'spectin' to turn up past the trees and onto the big hill, but 'stead we went on north and west to Kimball's to the steamboat landin'. We pulled up jest as the big boat was a-slidin' in by the dock. There was a bunch of people there, includin' Porter. He had Jack with him, all hitched up to one of his haulin' rigs with another scrappy little horse called Switcher. Brother Joe pulled his buggy next to Porter's, and Jack nickered a hello. We watched the men on the boat dock. Soon a crowd of people was pilin' off the boat. Brother Joe stood by a-talkin' to the people as they passed. Men was carryin' trunks and boxes. Soon Brother Joe come back up to the buggy. He had three men and two ladies with him—hotel guests by the way they looked. Porter was a-carryin' all their gear—trunks and suitcases and whatnot—and piled it in the back of his rig. We then set out, follerin' the other horses and wagons back into the city.

Back to the Mansion, Lorin unhitched us from the wagon, and I spent the rest of the day in the pasture by the stable. We horses prefer to be out in the open. Rain or shine I'd ruther be out where I can see around me, than cooped up in the stable. You can see that my box in the stable has got its own door openin' out onto the pasture, and most times Lorin lets me come and go as I please. I got me a favorite spot to the far end of the pasture, where I stand right reg'lar.

From there I can see the whole layout—the stable, the pasture, and the road with the Mansion House across the way. The whole get-up. I can also see the Big River and the boats, big and small, a-movin' up or down.

You know, Major, Brother Joe's got hisself two boats what he rides out on the Big River. He's got one little boat and one big boat. The big boat is a steamship with a big wheel in the back and a black round tub up top that spews black smoke out into the air. It's a big boat and can carry a passel of folks out on the river. Brother Joe's friend, Blue Dan, is the captain. Many a time I seen him out on the water, standin' on the railin' up top, leanin' out over the water with his blue cap on. Brother Joe calls Blue Dan's steamship the *Maid of Iowa*.

And then Brother Joe's got hisself a right small boat, only big enough for three, four bodies to set in. It ain't got no wheel or smoke stack, but Brother Joe gets it movin' by strokin' these two long poles back and forth in the water. Many times I seen Brother Joe take Little Joseph out on the water, and they jest stroke them poles back and forth, then settle in one spot for the longest time, workin' somethin' in the water. Brother Joe calls it fishin'. Brother Joe keeps his little skiff in the stable, where it stands leanin' agin' one wall. I can smell the river water on it when he and Lorin or Hyrum help him carry it in. In fine weather, Brother Joe is fond of bringin' it out many a day, and I can see 'em walkin' down to the water's edge and settin' it in the water from my special spot in the pasture.

Main thing, though, is I can stand in my reg'lar spot and see Brother Joe's Mansion house and watch if Lorin is a-comin' over to fetch me and saddle me up, or see Brother Joe or Little Joseph comin' out for a ride or for a talk or to give me some sweet sugar from Lady Emma's kitchen.

'Bout feedin' time, Lorin started to let all the visitin' horses into the pasture. He was jest openin' and closin' the gate as the riders come in and let their horses wander in the pasture. There was Saucepan and Pickwick again and Sam, of course. And then up rode Blue Dan ridin' his bay-colored gelding called Tramp.

I s'pose the riders was all across at the Mansion talkin' with Brother Joe. I never could figure, Major, how Brother Joe and the others could do so much talkin' all the time. Seems like there's a-time for talkin' and then there's a time for doin'! Horses are all about doin', if you take my meanin'. We was born to be up and doin'. Long as I knowed him, Brother Joe has been a mighty good talker, preachin' all the time and a-visitin' the people. But then sometimes he's all about doin'. Well, these days it seems like a time for talkin'.

But I'm ready when Brother Joe is ready to up and do things again.

MONDAY, JUNE 10, 1844

NAUVOO, ILLINOIS – MONDAY, JUNE 10, 1844

It is cold and cloudy. The east wind blows.

10:00 a.m. to 5:30 p.m. The Nauvoo City Council meets all day in the upper room of the Red Brick Store.[8]

Joseph reads from the Illinois Constitution, which speaks of the responsibility falling upon the press for what it prints. Others read from Blackstone *on nuisance law. The council votes to declare the* Nauvoo Expositor *press a public nuisance, believing the best way to rid the city of the nuisance is to "smash the press and pi the type." Councilor Warrington says he believes it would be too harsh to smash the press, and that it would be best to fine the editors for each libel. Orson Spencer says the editors will never pay the fine, that they have perjured themselves before thousands, that they will bring an armed mob upon the city, and that it would be better to die at once than to have Nauvoo burned by an invading army. Councilor Phelps compares their actions to the Boston Tea Party. The City Council declares the* Expositor *seditious and a public nuisance. Orders are given to the City Marshall, John P. Greene, to destroy the press.*

The City Council also orders Jonathan Dunham, acting Major General of the Nauvoo Legion, "to assist the Marshal with the Legion, if called upon to do so."[9]

---

[8] APR 489

[9] APR 489

8:00 p.m. Marshall Greene returns and reports that the press has been destroyed. The posse that accompanied the Marshall gathers in front of the Mansion House to hear a few words from Joseph. He tells them that they will not be hurt for destroying the press, that they were simply carrying out the orders from the City Council, and that he would "never submit to have another libelous publication established in the city."[10]

It's been a-blowin' all day, Major. The wind feels good blowin' through my mane and puts me in mind of ridin' fast over the prairie or through the trees. Sometimes when I'm not out ridin' I like to stand in the wind.

This mornin' I was standin' in the wind in my reg'lar spot in the pasture. It was real clear, and the wind felt fresh comin' in off of the Big River. I was jest watchin' two fellers in a little fishin' boat down past the bank when I heared the back door to the Mansion House slam, and then I see'd Brother Joe run out of the Mansion. I was a-hopin' he'd come over to saddle me up for a fine ride out on the Carthage Road and back, but 'stead he run across the road and out of sight down Water Street. I 'spect he's been up to his Red Brick Store all the day talkin' with the others. I waited for Little Joseph to come, but he never did. Lorin come in and freshened up the water and the feed and brushed down my coat some, but I was home all day long.

Then after the sun went down, things started to happen for sure around here. I told you how sometimes men are all about talkin' and never doin'. Well, tonight Brother Joe started doin' 'stead of jest talkin'.

'Long 'bout dark I was standin' in my box in the stable, when I heared a big commotion way up yonder on the big

---

[10] HC 6:439-48; APR 489

hill, like the sound of men shoutin'. I wandered out into the pasture, and then I smelt smoke carried on the wind, like somethin' was burnin' up on the hill or out by the farms. I stood with my ears all perked up and a-sniffin' the wind, when I heared the sound of hooves on the road, and so I run up and down the pasture fence to see what was what. Then I see'd 'bout twenty, thirty horses comin' from the east along Water Street. They was turnin' onto Water Street from Durphy Street, and they come runnin' right on past the stable. I could make out seein' Porter ridin' Jack, and Markham ridin' Pickwick, and Blue Dan on Tramp. Then they stopped, and the horses was jest a-wheelin' and circlin' around in the street next to the Mansion House.

I also see'd General Dunham from the Legion in his uniform ridin' his big clay-colored stallion, Rambler, and four or five other Legion cavalry riders besides in their uniforms.

All the riders seemed mighty agitated, and the horses kinda picked up on that. I could hear the horses all blowin' and snortin', so I knowed they was all excited. I see'd how two of the men was carryin' torch fires in their hands, held up real high, and the men was all talkin' at once, and a few was laughin' and shoutin' out to each other. The horses wheeled around in the street, turnin' this way and that.

The lights was all ablaze in the Mansion, and pretty soon I see how Brother Joe had walked out into the street to talk to the men. They all calmed the horses down as much as they could, and all I heared was the low sound of Brother Joe's voice. There's somethin' about his voice that soothes a body. I seen it with man and beast, Major. Jest the sound of his voice calms a body down, and he was a-calmin' down the men and horses in the street. There warn't no laughter or shoutin' after he talked, jest a calm.

Well, after he had talked a spell, Lorin run over and fetched me back into the stable and saddled me up quick and led me over to the front of the Mansion. The horses and riders was all still there, jest a-standin' in the road, and Brother Joe mounted right up and turned me up Main Street. I went, and all the other horses follered. We cantered up past all the shops. The streets was filled with people, who was all wavin' and shoutin' to Brother Joe as we passed. We headed straight up the big hill, past the white walls and Porter's livr'y. Up ahead I see'd in the road a big smolderin' fire right plumb in the middle of Mulholland Street with a crowd of people standin' or walkin' around and jest lookin' on. The yellow light from the flames shone in their faces. Brother Joe circled me around the fire, which looked like a pile of broken wood and metal. There was also plenty of pieces of paper blowin' around the street, some of 'em on fire.

There was bunches of folks standin' all around, some near and some far, and by the side of the road I see'd Mr. Robert Foster jest watchin'. He looked mighty unhappy, but I remembered how he had mistreated his chocolate mare, Charity, and didn't feel sorry for him none when I thought about that. Then some fellers started in on him, shoutin' at him, and so he walked down the road and into his house and slammed the door.

The smell of smoke was real strong in my nostrils, and all the other horses got hold of that smell and started to snort and blow. The men was all a-shoutin' and a-talkin', and a lot of 'em seemed right happy, but I couldn't make out why.

What makes a man happy, Major? I can't figure that out any more than you can. Some men seem happy when things is gettin' burned and the smoke is blowin'. But Brother Joe didn't seem happy none. He was right quiet settin' there in the saddle with all the hubbub goin' on around him.

You know Major, when I see'd that big fire in the middle of Mulholland Street, I remembered that Brother Joe had said that the whole town would be a-burnin' in five years, unless the people all moved west to Californee or the Rocky Mountains or some other place.

Well, I s'pose the burnin' has already a-started.

TUESDAY, JUNE 11, 1844

BROTHER JOE RIDES OLD CHARLIE TO THE UPPER
STEAMBOAT LANDING – THEY SEE TWO SNAKES
FIGHTING IN THE ROAD – MEN SHOUT AT BROTHER JOE
AND ONE OF THEM DRAWS A PISTOL

NAUVOO, ILLINOIS – TUESDAY, JUNE 11, 1844

The weather is overcast and cool.[11]

In the early morning Joseph is in council with the brethren at the Mansion House. He issues a proclamation announcing the reasons for the destruction of the Expositor and calls upon all officers to help him in support of maintaining the peace of the city against mob violence.[12]

Joseph hears that Robert Foster and the other dissenters have predicted the utter destruction of Nauvoo.[13]

The destruction of the Expositor has stirred up Joseph's enemies. Citizen meetings are held in Warsaw and Carthage. Robert Foster and other members of the Foster and Higbee families begin to sell their Nauvoo property and move out. Francis Higbee departs from Nauvoo and predicts, "in ten days there will not be a Mormon left in Nauvoo."

Joseph goes to the upper steamboat landing at the request of the captain of the steamer Osprey. As he and others look at the river and the ship, Charles Foster calls to his fellow passengers to look at Joseph Smith, "the meanest man in the world." A Mr. Rollison on board the ship also

---

[11] HC 6:450-52
[12] HC 6:449
[13] APR 490

shouts abuse at Joseph Smith. A Mr. Eaton on board the ship tries to silence Foster and Rollison. Rollison begins to draw a weapon.[14]

2:00 p.m. Joseph goes to the court session in the Red Brick Store, where many have come to observe the proceedings. Joseph tells the people, "I am ready to fight, if the mob compels me to, for I would not be in bondage." Joseph asks the people present if they will stand by him, and they shout, "Yes!"[15]

This was a day of doin', Major, and no mistake. All night long I smelt the smoke in the air, and this mornin' I knowed that I would be ridin' out with Brother Joe to start doin' things.

In the early mornin' the pasture was right filled up with the visitin' horses. All of 'em was there: General Dunham rode up on Rambler, and then there was Sam, Lady Gray, Saucepan, Jack, Pickwick, and Tramp. One of the first ones in was the big sorrel called Rust, what belongs to the man Phelps. He's a loud man, Phelps, with a voice like a steamboat whistle. I heared him a-speakin' two blocks out as he come ridin' down Water Street. He also has a laugh like a trumpet, but his horse Rust is mighty quiet. He kinda keeps to hisself, and when all the horses was in the pasture together, Rust wandered over to the far corner closest to the riverbank and jest nibbled the grass alone.

I see'd how all the men went into the Mansion House, but they broke up the meetin' after an hour, and they all rode off 'cept for Blue Dan's bay gelding, Tramp. He jest stood with me and Tom and Joe Duncan in the grass, a-waitin'. Pretty soon after that, Lorin and Brother Joe come

---

[14] APR 490

[15] APR 490; HC 450-52

out of the Mansion House with Blue Dan. Brother Joe had his hand restin' on Blue Dan's shoulder. When they walked up I see'd water drops all over Blue Dan's face. Drops was fallin' on his shirt, and he was uncommonly quiet. Funny thing, Major, how sometimes folks has water drops on their faces, like it's been rainin'. I can't figure out where the water comes from. Well, the drops of water was jest pouring down Blue Dan's face. Brother Joe stood agin' the fence, with his big hand a-restin' on Blue Dan's shoulder, and looked him plumb in the eye while he said somethin' to him. Then Blue Dan kinda threw his arms around Brother Joe, then mounted up on Tramp and rode off.

Meantime Lorin fetched me up and saddled me, and I knowed that things was startin'. Straight off, Brother Joe and me headed up into the city. Things was quiet in the streets, but you could feel the difference in the air, kinda tense like. Brother Joe didn't have much to say to me as we rode, but I could feel that he was ready for somethin'.

We passed all the shops, where folks waved at Brother Joe, and then started headin' out on the road to Kimball's steamboat landin'. Then up ahead, in the middle of the road, we see'd some sorta creatures swirlin' around in a heap. Brother Joe pulled me up and walked to the side of the road. Then he had me stop so he could get a good look. I see'd right plain it was two big snakes in the road, all twined together and turnin' this way and that like they was fightin'. I couldn't help myself and roared right out loud, risin' up on my hind legs so I could strike out with my front legs. But Brother Joe could see how the snakes put a fear in my body, and he led me wide around 'em. Then we rode on toward the steamboat landin'.

Brother Joe tied me up on the rail, close to the boat dock where the big steamship was still settin'. There was plenty of people walkin' around, and Brother Joe went up amongst them, noddin' his head here and there at folks. A big fat man standin' on the boat see'd Brother Joe and called his name, then walked down the gangplank to shake his hand. I knowed that it was the captain of the boat, 'cause he wore a blue cap, jest like Blue Dan, who is the captain of Brother Joe's little steamboat. Well, Brother Joe and the captain jest stood leanin' on the rail, a-lookin' at the people gettin' on the big steamboat and talkin' amongst theirselves, when I see'd up on the top part of the boat some men talkin' real loud. All the people looked up to them. And then one of the men—he was wearin' a jacket with long coattails—started to shout down to Brother Joe. He shouted Brother Joe's name and pointed straight at him. Then he looked around at all the other people on the boat and started to shout. I couldn't make out all that he shouted, but I understood him to say that Brother Joe was "the meanest man in the world," and some other things. All the people on the boat and on the land was lookin' at Brother Joe, who stood not sayin' a word on the dock.

Then another feller on the boat started to shout. He was a big tall man wearin' a black hat. Black Hat pointed at Brother Joe, and shouted out that he was a "dirty scoundrel" and lots of other words I couldn't rightly understand, but they sure did agitate up the people. Some shouted right along with Black Hat at Brother Joe, but a few shouted at Black Hat and told him to be quiet. Then I see'd how a man in a green jacket walked right fast along the top of the boat and went up to Black Hat and kinda pushed him backward, tellin' him to "shut up" and that he didn't know what he was a-sayin'. Well, Black Hat reached right into his jacket and pulled out a gun and pointed it right at the heart of Green Jacket. Then there was even more shoutin', and the captain hurried back onto his steamship to calm things down.

I never see'd how things worked out on the steamship 'cause Brother Joe mounted right up, and we rode off at a fast canter. Brother Joe seemed mighty agitated, but he didn't say nothin' on the ride home.

We passed the place on the dirt road where the two snakes had done their fightin', but I didn't see 'em or any trace of 'em.

WEDNESDAY, JUNE 12, 1844

OLD CHARLIE AND JOE DUNCAN ARE SADDLED UP FOR
A RIDE TO THE CEMETERY – CHARLIE WATCHES WHILE
BROTHER JOE IS ARRESTED BY THE CARTHAGE
CONSTABLE

NAUVOO, ILLINOIS – WEDNESDAY, JUNE 12, 1844

1:30 p.m. Joseph and others stand outside the Mansion House, waiting for the body of Dan Jones's oldest son to be brought out and buried. The little boy's name was John Madoc Jones, who died at age 2 years and 2 months.[16] *While waiting in the funeral cortege, Joseph and fifteen others are arrested by Hancock County Constable David Bettisworth from Carthage for destroying the* Expositor.[17]

Bettisworth reads the arrest warrant, which demands that Joseph be brought before Justice Thomas Morrison in Carthage "or some other justice of the peace." Joseph, upon hearing the words, "or some other justice of the peace," tells Bettisworth that he will willingly be arrested right here in Nauvoo and be inspected by a Nauvoo judge. Bettisworth swears that he will not leave without taking him to Carthage. Joseph resists him and asks if he intends to break the law. Upon producing a writ of habeas corpus, *Joseph is released.*[18]

---

[16] *Nauvoo Neighbor*, 3 July 1844

[17] Letter from Dan Jones to Thomas Bullock, 20 January 1855, quoted in "The Martyrdom of Joseph and Hyrum Smith," *BYU Studies*, 24 (Winter, 1984), 95; HC 6:487 and 7:66-67

[18] George D. Smith, ed., *An Intimate Chronicle: The Journals of William Clayton* (Salt Lake City: Signature Books, 1991) (hereafter "JWC") 132-33; Richard Bushman, *Rough Stone Rolling* (New York: Alfred A. Knopf, 2005) 541; HC 6:543-58, 7:66-67

Joseph is placed under house arrest until he can appear in Nauvoo Municipal Court the next day.

The Warsaw Signal *reports the destruction of the* Nauvoo Expositor *to its readers: "Citizens ARISE, ONE AND ALL!!!—Can you stand by, and suffer such INFERNAL DEVILS! To rob men of their property and Rights, without avenging them. We have no time for comment, every man will make his own. Let it be made with POWDER AND BALL!!!"*[19]

Mighty strange doin's today, Major. I don't know what all y'see up to the side porch of the Mansion House where you lay most of the day, but I seen plenty beneath the saddle today.

It started early afternoon when Lorin come out into the stable and saddled me and Joe Duncan up. Joe Duncan was pawin' and snortin' like anythin', as it had been a while since he had gone out ridin'. Sometimes I feel bad, Major, since I seem to get all the ridin' that there is in Brother Joe's family. Seems that every time Brother Joe or Lady Emma or Little Joseph go out a-ridin' they choose me. It makes me feel kinda proud and happy, but I know that it's hard for Joe Duncan, who is a saddle horse from the tip of his ears on down to the bottom of his hooves. Whenever Lorin comes to saddle me up, I notice that Joe Duncan is always jest forever shamblin' 'round and 'round in his box. Well, I tell you that he was one happy horse to be in the saddle today. I see'd how Lorin fixed him up with Lady Emma's sidesaddle, so I figured Brother Joe was fixin' to ride out with Lady Emma. I was as excited as Joe Duncan, rememberin' how Brother Joe and Lady Emma loved to take long rides together down the

---

[19] *Warsaw Signal,* June 12, 1844

country roads and out over the fields. Lady Emma is a fine horsewoman herself and knows how to handle herself right proper in the saddle. Lots of times Brother Joe and Lady Emma will carry their food in the saddlebags and set out on a soft blanket in the green grass for what she calls a "pick-a-nick." We'll ride out six, eight mile and find a quiet spot, and they'll eat and talk while Joe Duncan and me wander and graze to our heart's content on a loose tether. Well, I figured we was goin' to have a pick-a-nick today, but there was somethin' different.

When Lorin brung me and Joe Duncan around to Brother Joe's house, I kinda noticed a clink, clink sound in one of my hooves, which annoyed me some. Well, I soon forgot about that, for out front of the Mansion was a mighty strange gatherin' of horses and wagons. Blue Dan was there, settin' quietly in a little wagon with his blue cap on, pulled down close over his face. He had Tramp all hitched up in the shafts. Settin' by Blue Dan's side in the rig was a lady all dressed in black with a black cloth hangin' down over her face, so I couldn't see who she was. But I figured it must have been somebody close to Blue Dan, like his wife, 'cause he had his arm around her shoulders. I could see that Blue Dan had more drops of water on his face, like he done yesterday when he talked real earnest like with Brother Joe. There was lots of other folks there on horseback or in buggies, 'cludin' the Big Doctor ridin' his old brown-and-white paint, Saucepan, and Hyrum ridin' on Sam. I also see'd John Taylor on Lady Gray, Porter on Jack, and Markham ridin' his Pickwick. When Lorin walked up pullin' Joe Duncan and me along by the reins, Brother Joe was standin' next to Blue Dan's rig a-talkin' in a low voice to him and the lady all in black. Blue Dan didn't look up, but jest sat there with his blue cap pulled down low. Lady Emma was standin' next to the lady in black, jest a-strokin' her arm. Joe Duncan and me waited while they talked.

Well, after Brother Joe said his piece, he helped Lady Emma up into the saddle on Joe Duncan, and then he mounted me. But we didn't ride right off. 'Stead we formed up in a long line of horses and carriages right behind Blue Dan's little wagon. Lady Emma and Brother Joe was the first in line on Joe Duncan and me, right behind Blue Dan's little wagon. And then we and all the others jest stood there, not a-movin'. Everythin' was quiet, 'cept the soft sounds of the horses and the song of birds up in the big trees. Finally, the front door to the Mansion House opened up, and four men carried out a little wooden box. Then Blue Dan took off his cap, and all the other men jest took off their hats. The four men with the box walked real slowly, without talkin' or makin' a sound, and laid it real careful like in the back of Blue Dan's rig. The four men was follered by a couple of ladies who had spring flowers in their hands, and they reached over the bed of the little wagon and laid the flowers up top of the little wooden box. When I see'd the box, I figured Blue Dan was fixin' to travel somewhere, and he was all packed up to go and jest wanted to take them flowers along with him.

Then, Blue Dan clicked at Tramp and shook the reins, and we began walkin' real slow up Main Street, all stretched out in a long line, as still and quiet as a summer's day.

Then things started to happen, Major, let me tell you. First, I heared the sound of lots of horses comin' down the road toward us from far up Main Street, and pretty soon I see'd 'bout twenty, thirty horses ridin' fast toward us. I thought—What the heck's comin' now? Some shenanigans, I'll lay. Well, when the horses got close, I see'd how the riders looked at us real intent like, and then they pulled out their pistols and rifles and held 'em right up, pointin' 'em in our direction. The first horseman was a big stout feller with long, wispy whiskers 'longside of his mouth, and he was carryin' what Brother Joe calls a scattergun in his hands.

The horsemen rode right past Blue Dan's wagon, and then surrounded me and Brother Joe. I reared up on my hind legs and was ready to dash on a signal from Brother Joe, but he didn't make no sign to gallop off. The riders jest moved in among the long line of horses and buggies and Blue Dan's rig and separated Brother Joe and me and Hyrum and Sam from the rest. Soon, it was jest me and Sam, with Brother Joe and Hyrum on our backs, standin' alone in the middle of a circle of horses.

"What's this?" said Brother Joe. "Who are you?"

The man with the long whiskers and the scattergun said his name, which I didn't catch, and he said that he was from Carthage. Then he said to Brother Joe, "You're under arrest." He then called out the names of 'bout ten, fifteen men besides Brother Joe and Hyrum. I recognized Porter and John Taylor and the Fat Doctor and Markham and others bein' mentioned. These men he called up, and they rode up on their horses and come and stood 'longside of Brother Joe and Hyrum.

Well, I didn't know what the heck was goin' on, but I do know that Brother Joe and Hyrum and the other fellers had 'bout twenty guns pointed at their chests. Then Long Whiskers pulled a paper out of his pocket and started to read it right out loud. It didn't make much sense to me, but as close as I could tell it was a paper that said that these horsemen could point guns at Brother Joe and take him and the other fellers back down to Carthage.

It's a funny thing, Major, about all them papers. I seen men settin' for hours on the porch, or leanin' back agin' a tree trunk, jest a-starin' at one little stack of papers they call a book. And then I think about all the fuss in Nauvoo about those sheets of paper we see'd burnin' in the street. And then I often seen folks bringin' out little green pieces of paper and givin' 'em to the storekeepers and gettin' back in return all kinds of things—food and tools and barrels filled with who knows what. And now, Long Whiskers was goin' to take Brother Joe to Carthage, all 'cause of a piece of paper.

I still was hopin' that Brother Joe would spur me on, and I was ready to gallop so far ahead of Long Whiskers and the other men with guns that they would never catch us, but Brother Joe jest sat cool and collected in the saddle. Then I sensed that he was pullin' somethin' out of his breast pocket, and I turned my head to see him unfoldin' another piece of paper, which he read out loud to Long Whiskers. Near's I could tell, it was sayin' that we didn't have to go to Carthage after all, but that Brother Joe could stay in Nauvoo. I couldn't figure that all out, Major.

Well, Long Whiskers rode close up and snatched away Brother Joe's piece of paper, and he looked at it a long spell. Then one of the other fellers with guns rode his horse next to Long Whiskers' horse, and he took the paper, and he looked at it a long spell. Meanwhile all the other fellers kept their guns a-pointin' right at Brother Joe and Hyrum and the rest.

Then Brother Joe spoke up and asked for Long Whiskers' piece of paper. Long Whiskers handed it over to him, and Brother Joe looked at it then handed it over to John Taylor, and he looked at it some. So, meantime, we was jest standin' in the street. All the men on their horses and Blue Dan in his rig and all the rest of folks follerin' Blue Dan was jest a-waitin' while the men was lookin' and lookin' at them pieces of paper. Seemed like they was doin' battle with their papers.

Finally Brother Joe spoke up and said how he'd be willin' to be Long Whiskers' prisoner, only they wouldn't go to Carthage, but instead jest wait in Nauvoo 'til tomorrow and go all together down to the Seventies Hall to look at all them papers again. By this time, a whole passel of Nauvoo Legion fellers had arrived on horseback with their guns and was standin' around in a ring behind the Carthage fellers with their guns. There was lots of shoutin' goin' on, and I see'd that Long Whiskers was lookin' a mite worried. Then he said okay to Brother Joe. "We'll wait until tomorrow." And things calmed down some.

Well, the rest of the day, Major, we had Long Whiskers and his men follerin' us around everywhere we went, like blue flies on the backside of a mule.

First they follered us up to the Cemetery. We rode slowly up Main Street behind Blue Dan's rig, then down Mulholland to the crossroads. When Blue Dan's rig stopped, the four fellers come back and picked up the little wooden box and carried it under the trees over to a hole in the ground. Lady Emma and Brother Joe dismounted and walked over with the rest of the folks. They all stood in a big circle around that hole. Long Whiskers and his fellers stayed on their horses jest a-watchin' and talkin' quietly amongst theirselves. After a spell I could hear the folks yonder singin', and then I heared Brother Joe's voice, all soft and reassurin'. Then they lowered Blue Dan's box down into the hole with ropes, so I guess he warn't travelin' nowhere after all. Then the folks jest got back in their wagons or on their horses, and we all rode back into Nauvoo.

Well, Long Whiskers and his fellers all follered Brother Joe and Lady Emma back here to the Mansion, and there's been two or three of them fellers with guns standin' in the street outside the Mansion House all afternoon and evenin'. I 'spect you see'd 'em as you sat on the side porch.

Are you still listenin', Major? Hear that clink when I walk about in my box? I 'spect I got a shoe comin' loose. Hear that clink, clink? Are you still awake?

THURSDAY, JUNE 13, 1844

Old Charlie visits the Blacksmith and waits during the Meetings outside the Seventies Hall – Brother Joe talks about the Snakes

NAUVOO, ILLINOIS – THURSDAY, JUNE 13, 1844

The weather is clear throughout the day, with rain in the evening.[20]

9:00 a.m. Joseph presides as judge at Municipal Court in the Seventies' Hall, where all the men named in the arrest warrant of the previous day seek and obtain writs of habeas corpus. *All prisoners are discharged and Constable Bettisworth and his men return to Carthage.*[21]

In the evening Joseph rides back to the Seventies' Hall and attends a meeting where George Adams preaches.

At the end of the meeting, Joseph takes the stand and relates his dream of two large snakes. In the dream, Joseph is out riding with "his guardian angel." As they pass the temple, Joseph sees two large snakes intertwined so tightly that neither has any power over the other. Joseph is told the meaning: "Those snakes represent Dr. Foster and Chauncey L. Higbee. They are your enemies and desire to destroy you; but you see they are so fast locked together that they have no power of themselves to hurt you." Then Joseph sees himself on the prairie without his guardian angel. All at once, Joseph is seized by William and Wilson Law. They tie his hands behind him and throw him into a pit from which he cannot escape. He finally gets his hands loose and jumps high enough to get hold of some grass at the edge of the pit. He sees Wilson attacked by wild beasts, who cries for help from Joseph. Joseph replies, "I cannot, for you

---

[20] HC 6:460-62

[21] APR 491

have put me into this deep pit." In another direction he sees William, blue in the face, green poison coming from his mouth, being crushed by a snake. The snake is beginning to eat him, beginning at the arm. He also cries for help. Joseph replies, "I cannot, William; I would willingly, but you have tied me and put me in this pit, and I am powerless to help you or liberate myself." Joseph's guide soon appears and helps Joseph out and they go their way "rejoicing."[22]

Robert Foster and the Law brothers leave Nauvoo.

Joseph receives news that a large mob of armed men has begun to assemble in Carthage.[23]

Well, Major, things is back to normal tonight, thank the stars. It looks like Brother Joe has got hisself rid of Long Whiskers and all the gunmen from Carthage once and for all.

By the way, I was right about that shoe bein' loose, Major. Lorin saddled me up in the mornin' and took me first thing over to the Mansion House to wait on Brother Joe. When Lorin walked me 'round the corner, I see'd right off that there was Long Whiskers and his fellers already mounted up and waitin' by the front door. I also see'd that Brother Joe was standin' in the doorway talkin' with Lady Emma. When Brother Joe heared my hoofbeats comin' 'round the corner of the road, he stopped his talkin' and looked over toward me. I could tell he was watchin' to see how I was walkin'. Then Brother Joe kissed Lady Emma and stepped down and called my name. I walked over to him.

---

[22] Andrew F. Ehat and Lyndon W. Cook, eds., *The Words of Joseph Smith: The Contemporary Accounts of the Nauvoo Discourses of the Prophet Joseph* (Salt Lake City: Bookcraft, 1981), (hereafter "WJS") 378; HC 6:460-62
[23] Bushman, 542

He picked up my hooves, one by one, and looked at 'em all. Then he stroked my neck and scratched my ears. "We're goin' to the blacksmith, Old Charlie."

I'm sure I told you before, Major, how I hate the blacksmith more than anythin'! They call the blacksmith Mr. Webb, and he's a kind enough feller, and so are his brothers what work with him. He's a good feller, as far as that goes. Good at his job, that is, and he's kind to the horses. But it's the flames and smoke I hate and the way Mr. Webb kinda blows up the fire with this contraption that he pulls down, over and over until the fire is a-roarin'. And then I hate all the hammerin'. And 'course it's indoors, and folks is comin' in and out all the time with strange horses and walkin' around behind you where you can't see.

Well, Brother Joe rode me right over to Mr. Webb's blacksmith shop, with Long Whiskers and all them Carthage fellers follerin' right behind. I was clinkin' about in the street while Mr. Webb stood holdin' my bridle while he talked with Brother Joe. Then Brother Joe left me while he and Long Whiskers and the rest of 'em walked right next door to the brand new Seventies Hall. Mr. Webb led me into the blacksmith shop. 'Course I was nervous, but Mr. Webb had me fixed up in a jiffy. He then led me over to the Seventies Hall, where he tied me up next to the other horses.

Can you smell my hooves where they've been singed by the fire? I'm mighty particular about my feet. Most horses are. Horses have got the strongest and the lightest feet of any creature in the world. They can stand up to anythin' and ride for miles and miles. A horse is extra careful to look after his feet. I'm mighty particular about where I put my feet. I don't like streams or marshy ground. And I don't like the blacksmith. Well anyway, it's all finished now.

After gettin' my hooves seen to by Mr. Webb, I stood all mornin' at the hitchin' rail next to the Seventies Hall. There was most of the horses that went out to the Cemetery with Blue Dan and his wagon yesterday—Lady Gray and Jack and Pickwick and all the rest— and then over yonder all the horses of Long Whiskers and the men from Carthage. Mr. Webb tied me up between Lady Gray and Pickwick.

And so there we stood quietly all mornin' in the shade of the trees—Long Whiskers' horses on the one side of the grass, and me with the local horses on the other. As I said, I was tied up between Pickwick and Lady Gray. Pickwick kinda kept to hisself, not acknowledgin' me in the least, but jest a-flickin' the flies away with his tail and shakin' and turnin' his head away whenever I nickered a friendly hello at him. He's a big chocolate-colored palomino ridden by Markham.

I got to thinkin' about Markham while I was standin' there. He's a proper rider and a great friend to Brother Joe. I seen him from time to time in a tussle with fellers what got out of hand in Nauvoo, and he knows how to handle hisself in a pinch. Same with Porter and Blue Dan. Sometimes they call theirselves Brother Joe's bodyguards. I don't exactly know what that means, but I do know that they is all strong men and true friends to Brother Joe.

Seein' Long Whiskers' horse tied up over yonder, I also got to thinkin' about him. Yesterday I heared Long Whiskers read his piece of paper and call out the list of men he was fixin' to point the rifles at, and Porter and Markham was two of 'em. So was John Taylor, who rides Lady Gray. I 'spect

Long Whiskers wanted to take Brother Joe and Hyrum and Markham and Porter and John Taylor and all the rest with him back to Carthage.

Lady Gray nudged me from the other side, so I knowed she wanted to play some, but I jest stood still, 'spectin' Brother Joe to come out. Sure enough, the doors to the Seventies Hall swung open, but it warn't Brother Joe. It was Long Whiskers and a bunch of his fellers what had pointed guns at Brother Joe. They was puttin' on their hats and walkin' out of the Seventies Hall real fast. They didn't say much, but got on their horses and rode right off.

And then I heared Brother Joe's voice and see'd him walkin' out with all his fellers. They was mostly all smilin' and slappin' each other on the back and whatnot, so I knowed Brother Joe was in a good mood, and that he warn't goin' to Carthage. The men all stood next to the hitchin' rail by us horses, talkin' for a spell, laughin' and jokin' with one another. They was havin' a grand old time, while we horses waited. I couldn't make out what they was sayin', but then I heared John Taylor say the name "Robert Foster." Mr. Robert was the one what was carryin' all them pieces of paper that caused all the shenanigans last week and then come and visited Brother Joe in the night down to the Mansion. Well, I heared that Mr. Robert was clearin' out of Nauvoo for good, that John Taylor see'd him loadin' up all his stuff in a wagon this mornin'. I thought about his sweet little dark mare, Charity, and wondered if she was pullin' the wagon.

Then Brother Joe started talkin' in a low voice, and suddenly all the jokin' and talkin' stopped amongst the other fellers, and they crowded around Brother Joe in a circle, kinda tippin' their heads in to listen. Brother Joe told 'em all about the two snakes we see'd in the road on the way to the steamboat landin', and then about how he see'd the snakes again while he was asleep at the Mansion. I didn't understand how that could be, but as far as I could tell Brother Joe was sayin' that Mr. Robert and his friends was kinda like snakes, and mighty dangerous snakes. Markham and Porter and the rest of the fellers jest nodded their heads. Then the group broke up, and we rode on back home.

I was standin' around in the pasture most of the afternoon, and then in the evenin' Lorin hitched me and Tom up to Brother Joe's buggy, and he drove us back over to the Seventies Hall, with Lady Emma and Lady Lucy and Lady Katherine ridin' along. They went inside the hall with a hundred other folks for some meetin'. While Tom and me was jest standin' in the buggy harness outside, jest waitin', it started rainin'. Then there was some thunder. Lorin run outside from the meetin' and put the top up on Brother Joe's buggy so the seats wouldn't get wet, then he went back inside the Seventies Hall. I looked around, and all the other horses was jest bowin' their heads down, lettin' the rain run down their withers and off their backs. It felt right good after a hot day, but I was glad when the meetin' ended and we rode on back home with Brother Joe and the ladies.

And it's still rainin', Major. Can you hear the patterin' sound on the roof of the stable? Are you awake? Major? Oh! Goodnight, then.

FRIDAY, JUNE 14, 1844

OLD CHARLIE AND BROTHER JOE RIDE OUT ON THE
CARTHAGE ROAD WITH THREE OTHER MEN TO LOOK AT
THE COUNTRYSIDE – BROTHER JOE DRAWS IN THE DIRT –
THE FOUR HORSEMEN HAVE A RACE BACK INTO NAUVOO

NAUVOO, ILLINOIS – FRIDAY, JUNE 14, 1844

It is pleasant all day, but some clouds appear in the evening.

Joseph begins planning for the military defense of Nauvoo.

In the evening Joseph writes a letter to Illinois Governor, Thomas Ford, giving the reasons for their actions in destroying the Nauvoo Expositor. He said, "After a long and patient investigation of the Expositor, and the character and design of its proprietors, the Constitution, the Nauvoo Charter and all the best authorities on the subject . . . the City Council decided that it was necessary for the 'peace, benefit, good order, and regulations' of said city, 'and for the protection of property,' and for 'the happiness and prosperity of the citizens of Nauvoo' that said Expositor should be removed. . . . I send you this hasty sketch that your Excellency may be aware of the lying reports that are now being circulated by our enemies . . . and that nothing has been transacted here but what has been in perfect accordance with the strictest principles of law and good order."[24]

---

[24] HC 6:466-67; Dean C. Jesse, ed., *The Personal Writings of Joseph Smith* (Salt Lake City: Deseret Book Company, 1984) (hereafter "PWJS") 586-87

Joseph prophesies in the presence of several men at the Mansion House that if the mob attacks Nauvoo, it will return upon their own heads "with fury and vengeance."[25]

Hello, Major. Lay yourself down and have a listen. I had a fine long ride today out in the countryside with Brother Joe and two of his brothers. We was joined by General Dunham of the Legion. You know that he's one of Brother Joe's main generals. Brother Joe's got hisself lots of generals and colonels and whatnot, but General Dunham's the biggest of 'em all. He's the biggest, 'cept Brother Joe and Hyrum, of course.

I 'spect you know, Major, that Brother Joe's a mighty 'portant man around Nauvoo. Near's I can determine, he's the head man in charge of jest 'bout everythin'. He's in charge of what they call the Church, meanin' he's the main preacher in town and the leader of all the Brethren. The Brethren is men like Brigham Young and John Taylor and the Fat Doctor and such. And then Brother Joe is what they call the Mayor. That means he is in charge of the whole city and all the streets and buildin's and the policemen that walk up and down the street at night with their sticks. But then Brother Joe is also what they call the Lieutenant General, meanin' he's the main feller in charge of all the soldiers in the whole durn Legion. He's got the charge of the whole shebang, with all their horses and cannons and muskets and pistols and the thousands of men in their blue uniforms. That's a lot of responsibility for one feller, but he's up to it. I never seen a man more up to anythin' than Brother Joe, and

---

[25] JWC 133

I'm up to it, too. I help him with everythin' he does. Whether he needs to ride out to preach or see the Brethren, or go to his Mayor meetin's, or ride out in his Lieutenant General uniform with the Legion, I am always with him.

We had three other horses up here today. First General Dunham come ridin' up to the Mansion House on his horse, Rambler. I was standin' in the pasture in my watchin' spot when I see'd him ridin' up. General Dunham was a sight to see, Major, all dressed out in his Legion uniform. He's not a young feller, but still mighty robust and vigorous. He ain't tall out of the ordinary, but he's got broad shoulders, and he has a kinda go and dash about him. The way he was turned out today was right smart, 'cept smart ain't even the word for it. He had on white pantaloons and a blue jacket all covered with them gold buttons and gold braid and two big gold things a-settin' right on his shoulders. He also had gold spurs on his high black boots, and his hat was sorta looped up with a gold-colored piece on it, and there was a long black feather stuck in it, kinda floatin' over the top. He had on long leather gloves and a red silk sash tied around his waist.

Lorin come runnin' across the road when he see'd General Dunham ride up and opened up the pasture gate to let Rambler have a graze. General Dunham climbed down out of the saddle and set his uniform all straight, then walked on over to the Mansion. I kinda wandered over to nicker a hello at Rambler, and he nickered back, nice and civil and nothin' quarrelsome, but he let me know that he warn't in no mood to visit. I'm tellin' you, Major, that Rambler is a real fine horse, from his nose to the end of his tail. He makes me feel kinda like a small-time cob. His coat was all groomed so that it shone all over, real glossy and shiny in the sunlight. He is always real quiet around other horses, with his head held high, kinda like he knows that every other horse recognizes that he is the best. Every time he moves, he is very refined and confident. But I also have the feelin' that he is more than show. I'm a big strong horse, but I got the feelin' like Rambler could give me a proper run in a long gallop over twenty, thirty mile.

Rambler warn't the only visitors we had to the pasture this mornin'. In a short while, Hyrum rode up on Sam. Lorin brung him into the pasture, makin' 'bout eight, ten horses, countin' Joe Duncan and Tom and a couple hotel horses. They was jest all grazin' here and there, and a couple of 'em rollin' around to scratch their backs. Sam walked up and nickered at Rambler, who didn't give him no nevermind. I see'd that this depressed Sam, who come over to my spot in the pasture to stand by me. I was jest watchin' the door to the Mansion yonder, knowin' that Brother Joe might be ridin' out today and waitin' for him to come over.

Then, 'bout an hour later, up come one more rider to the stable. It was the younger brother of Brother Joe and Hyrum, who lives on a big farm down Carthage way. Brother Joe and me have ridden down there a time or two. His name is Brother Samuel, and he rides a big sorrel thoroughbred named Lather, who is the fastest horse in all of Illinois, so I heared Brother Joe say. Lather ain't much to look at, specially compared to General Dunham's Rambler. He's kinda dirty and ruffled up, not all groomed over proper like, but Brother Joe is sure right about Lather's speed. There ain't many horses what can keep up with me on a long ride, but Lather is one of 'em. He's jest kinda full of get-up-and-go and can gallop down a straight road like lightnin'. But he ain't the most dignified horse in a pasture by a long sight. Lorin brung him in, and Lather immediately headed for the water trough, where Sam was drinkin'. Well, Lather kinda tried to nose Sam out of the way, so Sam wrinkled his nose in disgust and stepped away to let him drink. Then Lather run all the way around the pasture fence, along Water Street, around the back of the stable, and all the way down to the Big River. I see'd how he sniffed the water, then jerked his head up and run on back up the hill and straight over to the alfalfa pile Lorin had forked underneath the fence rail. Rambler was there havin' a quiet feed by hisself, and Lather tried to nose in on him, but Rambler warn't havin' none of it and snorted twice at him in challenge. Lather kept tryin' to come in, and finally Rambler kicked out at him, which sent Lather runnin' off to the east side of the pasture. And that's how it went all mornin', Lather runnin' up and down, this way and that, while we all waited in the pasture.

Finally Lorin come out and whistled for me, and I went over into the stable to get all saddled up. I stepped around happy while he cinched the saddle on, knowin' I was 'bout to go out ridin'. Lorin led me back outside by my bridle, and I waited with the other horses, Rambler and Sam and Lather, by the pasture gate. Then I see'd the men a-comin', Brother Joe walkin' in the middle with his brothers, Hyrum and Brother Samuel, on one side and General Dunham on the other. Hyrum had a bunch of long papers rolled up in his hand. I said that Brother Joe and Hyrum is also big generals in the Legion, but they didn't have on their uniforms, only their reg'lar ridin' clothes. But the uniform didn't make no nevermind, and I could tell that General Dunham was lookin' to Brother Joe to tell 'em all what to do. Uniform or no, he knowed that Brother Joe was the Lieutenant General.

Well, Brother Joe and the others mounted up, and we all rode out into Water Street. There was Brother Joe on me, Hyrum on Sam, General Dunham up on Rambler, and Brother Samuel on Lather, four fine horsemen canterin' along together on four fine horses.

Brother Joe rode me east on Water Street. The others follered, and we turned up Durphy Street to Parley Street, then we headed straight east. I could tell that Lather was hankerin' for a nice dash, 'cause he went right into a buck-trot, but Brother Samuel reined him back, 'cause all the men was talkin' as we rode, and I 'spect he wanted to listen in. General Dunham was talkin' about cannons and guns and diggin' trenches 'round about Nauvoo.

We passed the Cemetery, where two days ago we had all ridden up behind Blue Dan's wagon with Long Whiskers and his fellers follerin' behind. We rode past Brother Joe's farm, and then we headed on down the Carthage Road. I wondered if we would ride all the way to Carthage, which is twenty mile or more, but we jest stopped right in the road 'bout a mile or so distant. The men talked a while amongst theirselves, and then we split up, ridin' off the road into the grass and trees in different directions, but we stayed near the road and kinda wandered around in the open countryside.

Brother Joe and me headed through a field, and he had me jump over a low farm fence. Then we splashed down through a little cold stream and rode up the side of a big hill. On the top of the slope we stopped, and Brother Joe jest sat in the saddle, lookin' out over the countryside. We could see the Carthage Road down a ways, right clear even though there was clumps of trees all over the place. The road looked like a little brown line meanderin' back and forth and up and down through the green fields and little hills as far as I could see. The horizon was a bit hazy, and there was big billowy clouds up in the sky. It was all green grass, blue sky, and white clouds. I could feel a breeze blowin' nice and fresh.

Suddenly Brother Joe whistled out real loud and waited a minute and then whistled again. Pretty soon we see'd General Dunham comin' through the trees down yonder on Rambler. He jumped the little fence, too, and come through the stream and on up the hill. They jest stood 'longside of us, and the men talked some in quiet voices. Then General Dunham twisted around in the saddle to open up his saddlebags and pulled out a pair of bottles, which he held up to his eyes. What was they? Don't ask me, 'cause I don't understand it, but he jest sat there forever holdin' up them bottles.

Brother Joe whistled again, real loud, and pretty soon we see'd Sam and Lather comin' together up the hill from the other side with Hyrum and Brother Samuel. Pretty soon all four horses was standin' together on that hill while the men talked.

"Now, General," said Brother Joe, pointin' out over the country toward Carthage. "How far will the cannon carry, do you think? Is this close enough to the road?"

"It's elevated enough," said General Dunham. "It's a good spot." And then he went back to starin' this way and that through them bottles.

"Where can the rifles dig in?" asked Hyrum. And then General Dunham and Brother Joe started pointin' out over the countryside and talkin' about shovels and trenches and whatnot, and they looked around in pert' near every direction, General Dunham with his bottles, and the other men with their hands shadin' their eyes.

The four of us then rode down the hill and around in the fields for a while, Brother Joe and General Dunham sometimes talkin' and pointin'. We rode out into a big field between the hill and the Carthage Road and stopped there for a spell, and then rode up another little hill where General Dunham looked again through them bottles, and finally back to the first big hill where we started. The four men then climbed down out of the saddle and stood on the edge of the slope lookin' out over the road and talkin'. Then Brother Joe stooped down and started scratchin' in the dirt with a long stick and pointin' here and there. Hyrum and General Dunham got their own sticks, and they started pointin' and scratchin' in the dirt theirselves. They was at it a long time, talkin' real low and serious. Meanwhile Sam and Rambler and Lather and me wandered around a bit, feedin' on the grass on that there hill, but not goin' too far. Lather kept wanderin', so Brother Samuel walked over and hobbled him down so he couldn't stray.

Finally, the voices of the men got loud and happy. Brother Joe said that he was right hungry, and 'cause of that I knowed we was finished. Sure enough, they mounted up, and we got back on the road and headed up toward Nauvoo.

I could tell that Lather and Rambler wanted to gallop, and for a few minutes the men reined us all in, but when we got near Brother Joe's farm and headin' up the long hill to the crossroads, suddenly Hyrum clicked at Sam, and they lit out like a flash. Brother Samuel then kicked, and we watched them two brothers gallopin' up the hill on Sam and Lather. Then, suddenly, General Dunham took off on Rambler, and I see'd the three horses ahead. Then finally Brother Joe shouted at me and bent down low over my neck, and we was off after 'em.

It was a proper race, Major, and no mistake. We was all 'bout a mile from the top of the hill. Brother Joe and me was ridin' behind them three other horses and gallopin' hard, and lickety-split we passed Sam, who was runnin' out of steam. Then we passed Rambler, who was runnin' as hard and strong as any horse I ever seen. Then, finally, we passed Lather. Brother Samuel looked over at Brother Joe as we passed and smiled. I knowed we had 'em all beat, but then if you can b'lieve it, jest as we got close to the crossroads and Mulholland Street, Lather suddenly passed us on the left, and jest like that we was beat. Then I knowed Brother Samuel had been a-holdin' Lather back. Maybe he is the fastest horse in Illinois. Up on Mulholland Street, we all four slowed down, the men laughin' and talkin', and the four of us horses tossin' our heads and blowin' friendly "hrrrmphs" out of our nostrils, jest like we was sayin' to each other, "nice little run, boys."

Back to the stable, I was right heated up, and it felt good when Lorin took my saddle off. Guess you don't know, Major, what it's like to have a saddle strapped to your back for hours on end, 'specially in the sun. Feels good to get home after a long ride and have Lorin pull that saddle off and give me a proper rubdown. Then Lorin always makes sure the water trough is filled and I got plenty of feed. That's the life, Major. That's the life.

SATURDAY, JUNE 15, 1844

Brother Joe takes his family to see a painting of a
pale horse – Old Charlie and Brother Joe ride
outside Nauvoo to watch the Legion soldiers
digging in the dirt

NAUVOO, ILLINOIS – SATURDAY, JUNE 15, 1844

Joseph orders the Nauvoo Legion to build defenses and stand guard outside Nauvoo to defend it from attack, if necessary.

Samuel Smith, Joseph's brother, goes off to the Illinois State Capitol in Springfield to carry letters and documents to Governor Thomas Ford that explain why they destroyed the Expositor.

2:30 p.m. Joseph Smith and his family and friends view the oil painting, Benjamin West's "Death on a Pale Horse," which has been on display in Joseph's Red Brick Store for the previous three days.[26]

Afternoon: Joseph rides outside the city with his bodyguard, Orrin Porter Rockwell, to inspect the construction of military defenses.[27]

Evening: Two messengers come riding into Nauvoo to report that Colonel Levi Williams of the Illinois State Militia is demanding that all Mormons surrender their weapons. The messengers ask for advice from Joseph Smith. He tells them, "when they give up their arms, they give up their lives with them."[28]

Been an interestin' day, Major.

You know that we had Lather stayin' all night with us in

---

26 APR 491-2

27 HC 6:471

28 JWC 134

the stable, 'cause Brother Samuel was over at the Mansion House. I didn't sleep proper, what with all of Lather's constant movin' around and fussin'. I know you left the stable in the night, yourself. Did you sleep on the porch? Well, Lather is what you call one high-spirited horse. I told you how he runs. Like a windstorm, he goes. But he seems right fretful when he's behind a fence or in a stable box and not out ridin'. He's kinda like a dog chained to a barrel, if you understand my meanin'. Well, he was kickin' and snortin' this mornin' plenty, until Brother Samuel come out bright and early and saddled him up. Lorin come out with him to make sure Lather had some feed, and I heared Brother Samuel tell Lorin that he was carryin' some pieces of paper for Brother Joe and takin' 'em to Springfield for the Gov'nor. I been a time or two to Springfield with Brother Joe, and it's a right long road, a hundred, hundred-twenty mile. Brother Samuel told Lorin that he wants to make it in two days. After seein' Lather ride, I 'spect they'll make that jest fine. Then they was gone like a flash. I never see'd a horse happier to be saddled up than Lather.

In the afternoon Lorin come out and saddled me all up and then hitched Joe Duncan and Tom to Brother Joe's big open carriage. Joe Duncan warn't happy about bein' in the shafts, let me tell you. He was a-tossin' his head and neighin' right out loud. He's a natural-born ridin' horse and thinks it below him to be pullin' a wagon or carriage or any kinda rig.

I figured we was goin' out on a long ride with Emma and the little ones. Sure enough, they all come out of the Mansion all dressed up fine. Lady Emma had on a dress the color of autumn leaves, and it kinda swirled around her feet when she walked. She was holdin' hands with little Julia.

Brother Joe was herdin' all his little boys outside to get in the carriage. 'Course you know there's Little Joseph, who is already a strong little feller. Then there's the two little fellers, Fred and Alex, who is as full of mischief and jokes as their Pa. Fred run around the back of the carriage and fussed with somethin', while the other youngsters shouted and pulled on the hands of their Ma and Pa. Brother Joe helped Lady Emma up into the carriage, and then the youngsters all piled around her. He then walked around to pat Joe Duncan and calm him down, as he was lookin' mighty agitated and depressed in the harness. Last of all, Lorin got in the driver's seat and took the reins. Lorin click-clicked at Joe Duncan and Sam, and they took off.

Brother Joe waved at his boys and then walked over and swung right up into my saddle, and we follered along behind the carriage.

Fred was kneelin' backwards in the back seat, a-danglin' a long string off the back of the carriage. I see'd that it was tied to a little wooden horse on wheels, which he was a-tryin' to drag behind the buggy. Trouble was, the road was so full of rocks and sticks that it never got to rights, and jest bounced along behind. I heared Brother Joe laugh.

I was s'prised that we didn't ride far, for Lorin pulled the carriage right up to Brother Joe's Red Brick Store, which ain't more than a short gallop from the Mansion House. Brother Joe dismounted and tied me up at the end of the hitchin' rail, next to the light sorrel gelding called Rust, what belongs to one of the Brethren named Phelps. I see'd that Pickwick was there, and Porter's little scrap of a horse called Jack. Then Brother Joe helped Lady Emma out of the carriage and then the youngsters. Lorin stayed in his seat in the carriage lookin' on.

Jest then I see'd Hyrum and his family ride up in his carriage, with Sam between the shafts with one of Hyrum's other horses called Clinker. I see'd his Lady Mary and then his boy John and finally the girls, Lovina and the little ones whose names I don't rightly know, gettin' out of his carriage. Lady Mary walked over and gave Lady Emma a hug and said somethin' about goin' up to Hyrum's farm for supper. 'Course I knowed Lady Emma and Lady Mary from years back, when we was all in Kirtland, and I knowed that them two is as close as close can be, 'specially with all the youngsters around.

Hyrum's daughter Lovina is a right proper lady and nearly growed up. I knowed her since she was a little sprig of a girl in Kirtland. She was wearin' somethin' all in blue and smiled pert' near all the time from the moment they drove up. She kinda brushed out her dress as she walked up to the store. Then I was right s'prised to hear Lorin Walker speak up. "Howdy, Lovina," he said. Lorin don't say much, and 'specially to the ladies, but he did chat on a bit today with Lovina, which s'prised me. She stood next to Brother Joe's carriage and smiled at Lorin, tellin' him how they was goin' inside to see a picture inside the store and what fine weather we was havin' and whatnot. She didn't seem a bit anxious to go on into the store, but jest smiled and chatted away. Lorin put in a word here and there, but mostly he jest smiled back at Lovina. Finally she said she needed to go inside, as Brother Joe and Hyrum and their families had already walked into the store. Lovina held out her hand toward Lorin, and durned if he didn't take it in his hand and jest touch the back of it to his mouth, jest like that! After Lovina left, Lorin jest sat in his carriage seat, jest smilin' and kinda lookin' up into the sky.

A passel of folks was comin' and goin' out of the store. One of 'em I heared talkin' about some pale colored horse they see'd inside the store. I couldn't make heads or tails of that, how a horse could be inside Brother Joe's Red Brick Store. Then I heared the loud, boomin' voice of Phelps. He come walkin' out of the store with two, three other Brethren, and Phelps was a-talkin' all about horses and how there was four of 'em—a black horse, a white horse, a red horse, and then last of all a pale one. Well, that confused me, Major. I ain't never seen one horse in Brother Joe's store, let alone four of 'em. I wondered at first if he warn't talkin' about me and Sam, seein's how we is black and white, and how we went out gallopin' around yesterday with Lather, what is red, and Rambler, what is kinda pale colored.

Well, Phelps went on and on, almost like he was a-preachin' to them fellers, and I didn't understand much, only that there was four horses. But then he pulled out one of them little books filled up with papers that all the Brethren carry around with 'em. He flipped through the papers and then looked down at one page and spoke out some words, sayin' that the name of the feller ridin' the pale colored horse was "Death," so I knowed the pale horse warn't Rambler at all, seein's how his owner is General Dunham.

Well, after that, Phelps rode off, and I stood around for a piece until Brother Joe walked out of the store with Porter, who mounted right up on Jack. Brother Joe said goodbye to

Lorin and mounted up on me, and we headed out, ridin' side by side with Porter and Jack.

We follered the same roads we done yesterday and cantered on down to the exact same hill we stood on yesterday. Brother Joe and Porter talked a bit back and forth as we went. Let me tell you, Major, when we rode up to the hill, things was mighty changed overnight. General Dunham was ridin' around on Rambler down in the field, and there was a whole troop of Legion men in their blue uniforms—fifty, sixty of 'em. They had dragged one of the Legion cannons up to the top of the hill and was pilin' rocks and tree branches 'round about it, and down below the Legion fellers was diggin' long holes in the ground and pilin' the dirt up to the side facin' the Carthage Road.

It put me in mind of the long holes the Brethren had dug back in Far West before all the soldiers come in to attack Brother Joe and the Brethren. In Far West I see'd how Brother Joe and the Brethren stood in the holes in the ground with their guns, jest a-waitin' for the soldiers to come up. Well, I figured Brother Joe and General Dunham was thinkin' the same thing would happen in Nauvoo, and that they 'spected the armies to march right up the Carthage Road. Standin' on the top of that there hill, I looked down the Carthage Road 'spectin' to see the armies comin' any minute, but there warn't none. Only our Legion boys diggin' in the dirt. Brother Joe jest sat quietly in the saddle lookin' around. He didn't say nothin', but I could feel his pulse through the saddle, real calm and even.

Finally General Dunham came a-ridin' up the hill on Rambler and lifted his hand up to his forehead, real smart like—that's how all the Soldiers say hello to Brother Joe.

Then he and Brother Joe talked a spell, while Rambler and I jest stood up by the cannon. After that we walked down to the flat where we rode up and down, watchin' the Legion fellers at their work. We stopped while I had me a mouthful of grass and a drink by the little creek. The Legion men was standin' around in their blue shirts with shovels in their hands. I see'd that their muskets was a-leanin' agin' the fence rail yonder. They all lifted up their shovels and come over when they see'd me and Brother Joe and took a breather, leanin' on their shovels. I see'd that they was all sweatin' somethin' terrible in the sun, and some of 'em had taken their shirts off, but they all had big smiles on their faces while Brother Joe talked to 'em. He and Porter got down and said their piece to the men in blue for a while, while Jack and me nibbled on the June grass down along the creek. All the while this feller or that would walk up and stroke my mane or pat my neck and say, "Hey, Old Charlie," or "Good boy, Charlie."

Funny thing, Major, how all the Legion men seem to know me, even when I don't know them. Some of 'em I recognize the smell of, but mostly I scarcely see'd 'em before in my life. But they know me and always have a kind word or a pat on the nose. They always gather 'round me when I ride up, jest like they gather 'round Brother Joe. Makes me feel kinda important, like Brother Joe and me is the center of everythin' that happens in Nauvoo.

SUNDAY, JUNE 16, 1844

OLD CHARLIE AND JOE DUNCAN PULL BROTHER JOE'S
CARRIAGE TO THE GROVE – BROTHER JOE PREACHES –
OLD CHARLIE HEARS TALK OF THE MISSOURIANS –
BROTHER JOE RIDES OLD CHARLIE THROUGH THE CITY
IN THE AFTERNOON

NAUVOO, ILLINOIS – SUNDAY, JUNE 16, 1844

Word is received that fifteen hundred armed Missourians are crossing the Mississippi River over into Illinois to attack Nauvoo. Joseph counsels thousands of Saints to stay calm, to prepare for the defense of the city.

10:00 a.m. Joseph preaches his final sermon in the Grove below the unfinished Nauvoo Temple. He says, "The doctrine of the plurality of Gods is as prominent in the Bible as any other doctrine. It is all over the face of the Bible. It stands beyond the power of controversy. A wayfaring man, though a fool, need not err therein."[29]

The sermon is interrupted by heavy rain.

Judge Jesse B. Thomas tells Joseph he should seek to be examined and cleared before a non-Mormon judge on the charges of riot, which have been filed against him.[30]

2:00 p.m. Forty men from Madison arrive by steamer to inquire into the Expositor affair. Joseph invites them into the Masonic Hall, and

---

[29] WJS 378-383
[30] HC 6:479

Willard Richards reads the Council minutes, which declared the paper a "nuisance." The men leave satisfied.[31]

4:00 p.m. Joseph speaks from the stand in the grove east of the temple, ordering Major General Jonathan Dunham to have the Legion in readiness to protect the city and suppress all illegal violence in the City.

Joseph issues a proclamation explaining the situation in Nauvoo: "If, then, our charter gives us the power to decide what shall be a nuisance, and cause it to be removed, where is the offense? What law violated? If, then, no law has been violated, why this ridiculous excitement and bandying with lawless ruffians to destroy the happiness of a people whose religious motto is 'Peace and good will toward all men?'" Joseph sends delegates to all the surrounding towns with the proclamation.[32]

Joseph sends another letter to Governor Ford: "The Nauvoo Legion is at your service to quell all insurrections and support the dignity of the common weal. . . . I wish, urgently wish, your Excellency to come down in person with your Staff, and investigate the whole matter, without delay and cause peace to be restored to the Country—and I know not but this will be the only means of stopping an effusion of blood."[33]

You look more stiff and slow than ever, old Major. It's the rainy weather, I 'spect. You can feel it in your bones.

Well, rest a spell, and I'll tell you what Brother Joe and me did today.

I worked the harness with good old Tom Carlin. We pulled Brother Joe's carriage up to the trees below the hillside where they is buildin' them white stone walls. Pert' near the whole city was there, and about two, three hundred

---

[31] APR 492

[32] APR 492; HC 6:484-485

[33] PWJS 589

horses as well. Brother Joe and Lady Emma drove up in the big carriage with Lorin and all the young'uns.

Before we left the Mansion, Tom and me were standin' under the elm trees, in the shafts of the carriage, jest waitin' to set off. It was smellin' like rain was a-comin', but cool and nice for a change. Lorin was standin' by my head holdin' the reins. Then, who do you think come out of the Mansion first? It was little Julia. She come runnin' down the steps and through the gate and bounced right up to Lorin.

"Do you think you'll see Lovina today?" she asked Lorin.

Why she ever asked him that, I can't make out, but Lorin's face turned red, though he didn't answer her nothin'. Then Julia come up to Tom and me in the harness and talked to us a bit, strokin' our noses. She's a talker, that one, and I like that. Her dark hair was all set in rings, and she smelt like lilac flowers.

Then the boys come out, Little Joseph and Fred and Alex. I see'd that Fred carried a piece of wood made to look like a musket, and he stood jest like a Legion soldier by the buggy, with the stick over his shoulder. Finally Brother Joe come out of the house with his arm kinda crooked so that Lady Emma could hold on. When they walked down the front steps to the carriage, Fred put his hand up to his head real smartly, jest like a soldier. Brother Joe helped Lady Emma up inside the carriage, and the little boys climbed in the back. Lorin and Little Joseph climbed up to the front seat, and we was off. We stopped first by Lady Lucy's little place, and Brother Joe and Little Joseph helped her climb slowly up into the carriage.

Durin' the drive up Main Street to the hill, I could hear the youngsters of Brother Joe bein' right lively. All through the trip, Fred was talkin' about soldiers and guns and the Legion. Julia and Alex was laughin' and playin' right 'long. Then Fred started makin' shootin' noises with his mouth. Suddenly Lady Emma spoke up loud and clear, "Put that gun away! I'll have no more of that talk!" Things got real quiet in the carriage for the rest of the trip. Brother Joe didn't say nothin'.

At the woods at the bottom of the hill, we could hear all the people singin' as we drove up. There was hundreds of 'em, like I said, pert' near the whole durned city I 'spect, and it seemed like every face was turned to watch us as we drove in. Lorin pulled us up into the shade by the other carriages, a little ways down from all the folks and stopped us right next to the buggy of Brother Hyrum. Sam was there in the shafts with Clinker. They neighed as we pulled up, then Sam nickered at me as we settled down to pull at the grass at our feet.

I 'spect you never seen preachin', Major. In the middle of the clump of trees there's this old tree stump. The folks jest stand all around or set theirselves up on the hillside and listen. After the singin', first one feller and then another climb up onto that stump and start to preachin'. Sometimes they go on and on for hours, but the folks don't seem to mind none. Actually, they seem right happy and placid. It's uncommon strange to see so many people all together and only one of 'em talkin' at a time and everybody else jest listenin'. 'Course they might now and again say a word together all at once real loud, somethin' like "Ay-Men," 'specially when a feller has finished his piece, and sometimes they will all laugh together at once, without any warnin', which startles the horses nibblin' at the grass under the trees off to the side. Mostly they laugh when Brother Joe stands on the platform to say his piece.

But they warn't laughin' today. They was unusual quiet and seemed most solemn like and silent and respectful, 'specially as Brother Joe climbed up on the wooden stump to talk. He done almost all of the preachin' this mornin', and the folks listened right intent like. He's a big man, and he's got a mighty big voice, and if folks is quiet, I 'spect that every last one of the folks can hear every word he says, even the ones settin' far up the hillside yonder. I knowed they all heared him loud and clear this mornin', and most of 'em had them curious drops of water runnin' down their faces, which I figure shows that a man or lady is listenin' right intent like. Brother Joe's that powerful a preacher.

He went on a mighty long time, and I see'd that the clouds was startin' to get black while he talked. I knowed that a storm was a-comin', but the folks in the trees and up on the hill didn't seem to notice none.

Then, I heared Brother Joe's voice loud and clear, ringin' out like the ringin' of a bell. He was lookin' at his little stack of papers in his book and sayin' somethin' about "God a-standin' in the congregations of the mighty," and jest then a clap of thunder boomed out in the sky, and it started to rain. Well, the meetin' ended real quick, and folks was runnin' for their houses with shawls held up over their heads or mountin' up on their horses or climbin' into their buggies.

Lorin set up the canvas rain bonnet on the carriage, lickety-split. Then there was some odd doin's. First Julia come runnin' up, water drippin' off her dark curls, to speak real urgently with Lorin, who stopped workin' the cover to look over at the people comin' through the trees toward the horses and wagons. Julia seemed real intent on tellin' Lorin somethin', and she kept lookin' over her shoulder. Then, a moment later, I see'd Lovina, the daughter of Brother Hyrum, up yonder amongst all the folks walkin' close by Lady Mary under a big black tarpaulin that Hyrum and John was holdin' up over the ladies. Suddenly Lovina left the tarpaulin and come runnin' up real quick to Lorin Walker, who was actin' real strange, fumblin' with the canvas cover, and when he talked to Lovina his voice sounded strange. The two of 'em talked back and forth a bit, right intent like, until both the families of Brother Joe and Brother Hyrum walked up. The two families climbed into the carriages, out of the rain. Then we waited another spell on Brother Joe, who was standin' in the rain talkin' a long spell with Brother Hyrum and another man I didn't know. I heared Brother Hyrum call the man "Judge Thomas," and then I heared Brother Joe say somethin' about "the Missourians," and how they was a-comin', sure as rain. That made me prick my ears up, rememberin' all the trouble we had with them Missourians all them years ago in Far West.

Then Brother Joe climbed into the carriage, and Lorin started to drive us home. I see'd Lovina in Brother Hyrum's carriage as we rode off. She was jest a lookin' over towards us with a smile on her face.

We pulled up to the Mansion House jest as the rain quit. 'Stead of goin' right in, as usual, Brother Joe come up to talk to me a bit and scratched my ears and nose under the bridle.

The rest of the afternoon was ordinary, 'cept Brother Joe saddled me up hisself and rode me up to the new place he calls the Masonic Lodge. The roads was still muddy from the mornin' rain, but the sun was peakin' out from behind the clouds. There was a passel of forty, fifty strangers and a couple of the Brethren, includin' the Big Doctor, what piled into the buildin' for a little spell. It was gettin' a mite warm in the sun, and the windows was open, so I heared Brother Joe's boomin' voice. Close as I can figure, he was talkin' to them strangers about the pieces of paper that caused all the shenanigans last week and how they burned all the papers and such in the street that night.

Then Brother Joe rode me back up the hill by the white walls, where he talked a spell with a bunch of fellers, a lot of 'em dressed all out in their Legion uniforms. General Dunham was there with Rambler. All I understood was that Brother Joe was orderin' General Dunham to watch over the city. Seein' how the Missourians are a-comin' and all, that sounded right sensible, and when I see'd General Dunham put his hand right on up to his head, like the soldiers do, I knowed that he would do jest like Brother Joe asked him.

MONDAY, JUNE 17, 1844

BROTHER JOE IS ARRESTED WHILE RIDING OLD CHARLIE
THROUGH THE STREETS OF NAUVOO – HUNDREDS OF
HORSES RIDE OUT TO THE FARM OF SQUIRE WELLS

NAUVOO, ILLINOIS – MONDAY, JUNE 17, 1844

Morning: Joseph Smith and several others are arrested again on charges of "riot," this time by Constable Joel S. Miles of Carthage.

2:00 p.m. Joseph and his fellow prisoners are brought before Nauvoo Justice of the Peace Daniel H. Wells at his house, where they are examined and released.[34]

Late evening: Stephen Markham reports to Joseph Smith the forming of mobs in Carthage and Warsaw and the possibility of an attack on Nauvoo.

Joseph sends a letter requesting the immediate return of Brigham Young and other members of the Quorum of the Twelve who are serving missions. He writes: "Mass meetings are held upon mass meetings drawing up resolutions to utterly exterminate the Saints. . . . You know we are not frightened, but think it best to be well prepared and be ready for the onset; and if it is extermination, extermination it is, of course. . . . Large bodies of men, cannon and munitions of war are coming on from Missouri in steamboats."[35]

Well things have sure enough been in an uproar these last few days, Major. I 'spect you seen a passel of

---

[34] HC 6:487-491
[35] HC 6:486-494

folks comin' and goin' over at the Mansion. Let me tell you, things have been happenin' around here in the stable.

I was 'spectin' a calm summer, Major, takin' it easy in the stables and out in the pasture. I was 'spectin' that Brother Joe would be stayin' right close to home for a nice quiet spell during the summer. I was kinda lookin' forward to some good rides through town with the buggy, or with the saddle out over the hills and farms 'round about. It's fine weather for a good ride, and Brother Joe is grand company for a gallop with Lady Emma or Little Joseph down along the Big River or out over the prairie. But we ain't had no quiet rides of late.

More shenanigans went on today while we was out ridin'. Seems like one day after the next Brother Joe's got hisself in one predicament after another. Well, he and me was out ridin' this mornin', as usual. Brother Joe rode up the hill to talk some with all the dusty Stone Men. He walked me all around the white walls, speakin' to one man and then another as they was workin', when suddenly I heared the sound of hooves, and I knowed there was a heap of horses a-comin' up the hill on the Carthage Road. Pretty soon the heads of all the men turned eastward and, sure enough, a big crowd of men on fifty, sixty horses come ridin' into town. Up ahead was a stout feller with a big white hat ridin' a gray gelding. Several of the fellers ridin' 'longside of him started pointin' in the direction of Brother Joe and me, and I heared their voices, all excited. Quick as lightnin', all the horses rode up to the white walls and all around us. White Hat rode real close and looked right in Brother Joe's face and said, "You're under arrest, Joe Smith." Another feller grabbed my bridle, which didn't set right with me, and I started to rear up. But Brother Joe was right calm, and he said, "It's going to be all right, Charlie. Steady, boy."

Well, Brother Joe dismounted, all civil like, and the man with the white hat pulled out a piece of paper and started speakin' from it to Brother Joe. There was two men with guns, pointed right agin' Brother Joe's chest, on this side and that. Brother Joe jest sat hisself down on the ground, leanin' back agin' the white walls. White Hat got down hisself and four or five of his fellers, and the rest rode off into the city with pieces of paper in their hands.

Brother Joe was jest a-chattin' with White Hat and his fellers, right civil and friendly like, and all the Stone Men stood around with their hammers in their hands. I was tied up on a picket line with White Hat's gray gelding and the other horses with him. Then one by one White Hat's men started bringin' up Nauvoo men, with guns a-pointed at 'em, and they joined Brother Joe, a-settin' or a-standin' agin' the white walls. Pretty soon there was twenty Nauvoo men, Brethren and Soldiers and whatnot. They was the same men what had the trouble with Long Whiskers a few days back, including Porter and John Taylor and Markham and Blue Dan and all the rest.

Well, then there started some arguin' back and forth between Brother Joe's men and White Hat. Close as I could understand, White Hat was insistin' on takin' Brother Joe back with him to Carthage, but the Nauvoo men was sayin' that we would have to go first to see Squire Wells, what has a farm between the farms of Brother Joe and Hyrum.

"You ain't bein' examined by no Mormon judge," White Hat was sayin' to Brother Joe.

"Squire Wells ain't no Mormon," Porter said. Then he kind of spit off to the side.

Well, there was much arguin' back and forth, but finally it was agreed that Brother Joe and Hyrum and all the rest of the fellers White Hat wanted to take back to Carthage would ride out to Squire Wells's farm to sort it all out, and that White Hat and his horsemen would go with us to make sure we didn't run off.

So we headed out, canterin' up Mulholland Street to the crossroads and then down the hill on the Carthage Road, with all the guns still a-pointin' our direction. Brother Joe rode me 'longside of John Taylor, and the two of 'em talked in low voices as we rode. John Taylor's horse, Lady Gray, was ridin' right close to me, and I could tell she was agitated by the guns, 'cause she was shiverin' as she cantered along. I looked back down Mulholland Street as we turned on the Carthage Road and see'd that there was more horses in the street than I had ever seen before. Hundreds of 'em. Folks was comin' out of their houses and jest follerin' right along, 'til it seemed the whole town was ridin' behind us.

You should'a seen it, Major! They was all ridin' behind us down the Carthage Road. Hundreds of horses with riders. We cantered into Squire Wells's farm lickety-split. You know, Major, it lies pert' near right between the farms of Brother Joe and Hyrum, jest off the Carthage Road not far from the Cemetery. Well, I see'd how the curtains of Squire Wells's window moved, and he looked out, mighty s'prised I'm sure, to see all them horses a-ridin' right into his farmyard. There was the twenty, twenty-five men of White Hat, all with their guns pointin' at Brother Joe, and the ten, fifteen other men what was s'posed to go to Carthage, and then 'bout two, three hundred other friends of Brother Joe ridin' behind on horseback or in wagons.

Well, Squire Wells come out of his house, a-wipin' his hands on a rag, and White Hat went up and talked to him a bit, handin' him a piece of paper. Squire Wells put down his rag on a bench and looked down at the paper for a spell. Then Brother Joe and Hyrum went into the house with Squire Wells and White Hat and two, three other gunmen. White Hat was a-carryin' his piece of paper in his hand, and John Taylor was a-carryin' one of his own. I suspect they was goin' to look intent like at all the pieces of paper and let Squire Wells decide which paper wins. The rest of us all waited outside, a-starin' at the guns of the other men from Carthage. Time or two I heared loud voices comin' through the open window of Squire Wells, and then suddenly the men all come out of the doorway. Jest by lookin' at White Hat, I knowed he was beat. He was a-stuffin' his paper in his pocket, and he called to all of his men. I guess Brother Joe's papers was stronger than the Carthage papers, again. So all of 'em packed up their guns and mounted and rode off.

When we see'd the dust rise up on the road to Carthage, Porter stood up on a barrel in Squire Wells's yard and let out a mighty whoop and a holler, and then all the men cheered. Some of 'em throwed their hats up in the air. Brother Joe mounted back up in the saddle, but I could feel that he was quiet, deep down, and thinkin' mighty hard.

Funny how I can tell what's goin' on inside of Brother Joe, jest by the way he sits in the saddle. I s'pose he and me are 'bout as close as a man and a horse can be. That's what happens when you ride with a man through so many summers and winters, day after day, nighttime and sunlight, rain and snow, down through so many years. Well, ridin' back into Nauvoo from Squire Wells place, I jest knowed that Brother Joe was deep in his thoughts, and I wondered myself, what will happen next.

TUESDAY, JUNE 18, 1844

Brother Joe puts on his General uniform and rides Old Charlie in a parade with the Nauvoo Legion – Brother Joe climbs up on the platform and speaks to the Legion

NAUVOO, ILLINOIS – TUESDAY, JUNE 18, 1844

Almost overnight, Nauvoo becomes an armed camp.

8:00 a.m. Thousands of members of the Nauvoo Legion assemble in front of the Masonic Hall on Main Street under full military orders. Joseph and his staff ride from the Mansion House to the Masonic Hall and then lead the Legion in a parade up Main Street to the Legion parade grounds northeast of the temple. Thousands of observers follow in the parade.[36]

1:45 p.m. Lieutenant General Joseph Smith declares the city to be under martial law. With no promise of help from Illinois Governor Ford and fearing an immediate attack, Joseph orders the Nauvoo Legion to assist the Nauvoo police force in blocking all roads leading into the city.

The Nauvoo Legion's ranks have swelled from three- to five-thousand men, as many have come into Nauvoo from surrounding regions to defend the city. Legion members are called out to patrol the streets and to inquire into any suspicious-looking characters who are in the town.[37]

---

[36] WJS 383-384; HC 6:499-500

[37] Richard E. Bennett, Susan Easton Black and Donald Q. Cannon, eds., *The Nauvoo Legion in Illinois: A History of the Mormon Militia 1841-1846* (Norman, Oklahoma: The Arthur H. Clark Company, 2010), hereafter "NL", p. 239.

2:00 p.m. Joseph, in full military uniform, stands atop the scaffolding across the street from the Mansion House with his brother Hyrum and other Nauvoo Legion officers. Thousands of uniformed men stand in the street or on horseback.[38]

Joseph addresses the Nauvoo Legion for the last time in uniform. He says: "We are American citizens. We live upon the soil for the liberties of which our fathers periled their lives and spilt their blood upon the battlefield. Those rights so dearly purchased shall not be disgracefully trodden under foot by lawless marauders without at least a noble effort on our part to sustain our liberties. Will you all stand by me to the death, and sustain at the peril of your lives, the laws of our country, and the liberties and privileges, which our fathers have transmitted unto us, sealed with their sacred blood? ("Aye!" shouted thousands.) It is well. If you had not done it, I would have gone out there (pointing to the west) and would have raised up a mightier people." Drawing his sword and presenting it to heaven, he said, "I call God and angels to witness that I have unsheathed my sword with a firm and unalterable determination that this people shall have their legal rights, and be protected from mob violence, or my blood shall be spilt upon the ground like water, and my body consigned to the silent tomb. While I live, I will never tamely submit to this oppression; and it would be sweet, oh, sweet, to rest in the grave rather than submit to this oppression, agitation, annoyance, confusion, and alarm upon alarm, any longer."

3:15 p.m. Joseph rides again in front of the Legion up to the parade grounds.

9:00 p.m. Messengers arrive from Carthage, reporting that the armed mob is willing to act with or without the help or command of Illinois Governor Thomas Ford.[39]

---

[38] HC 6:496-503

[39] APR 494

Is that you, Major? Did y'see the Legion sentries in the street? I been hearin' 'em walkin' up and down in the dark. Somethin's happened in the city, and no mistake. I never see'd so many guns and sentries in my life, 'cept back in Far West when the whole durned army turned out agin' Brother Joe. But at least we knows the sentries is protectin' Brother Joe, and it's right comfortin' to know that they is watchin' out over the Mansion while Brother Joe sleeps.

It's funny, Major, but you can feel somethin' different in the whole city—in the men and the women, I mean. It's in the way they stand, the way they move and hold theirselves. It's in the sound of their voices. Somethin' is different today. The whole durned city is fillin' up with soldiers. More and more is comin' every day, almost every hour.

I 'spect you heared all the soldiers startin' up early this mornin' and musterin' in the streets. They was marchin' all around the city before dawn, and so I knowed that Brother Joe and me was goin' to be doin' proper Legion work today. Sure enough, first thing Lorin brung all the Legion stuff around to the stable. See Major, there is a different saddle and bridle and whatnot that I use when I'm ridin' with Brother Joe in the Legion. Lorin calls it the military gear, and it's black leather polished up right fine, with yellow buckles on the straps and bridle. There's also them little black pouches that Lorin calls my military housings. Brother Joe keeps his cartridges and whatnot in 'em.

Well, after Lorin got me all saddled up, Brother Joe stepped across the street all dressed up dandy in his Lieutenant General outfit—blue coat, buff trousers, high military boots, two horse pistols and holsters on his belt, and a straight steel sword in a scabbard by his side. He also had a red sash wrapped all strange like around his waist, and on his head Brother Joe had a big general's hat decorated with some long bird feathers a-wavin' on top.

Lorin held the bridle while Brother Joe swung up in the saddle, and we rode out into the street. There was 'bout sixty horsemen waitin' for us in front of the Mansion, all fitted up in their Legion uniforms and armed with swords. They was Brother Joe's Legion bodyguard. One horseman rode up to Brother Joe, and I see'd that it was Old Man Lott from Brother Joe's farm, 'cept 'stead of his old farm clothes, he was dressed right proper and fine in his Legion uniform, in his blue coat with gold fringe hangin' off one of his shoulders, and with his sword and guns. I wouldn't have knowed him right off, 'cept I heared his high-pitched voice and recognized his mount, the bay mare named Paulina, what I seen hitched to the plow in Brother Joe's field. But now Paulina was brushed down smooth as silk and had a fine saddle on and held her head right high. I see'd, though, how she rested on one hip, liftin' the other one off the ground like I always see'd her do in the field.

Brother Joe then led me out in front of the other horses belongin' to his bodyguard, and they all fell in line, and we lit out up Main Street at a nice canter. Then I see'd how every man, woman, and child in Nauvoo seemed to be out on the sidewalk or in the side streets watchin'. There was a cheer that went up when I rode by with Brother Joe, let me tell you.

It was a perfect day, all sunny and warm, and I was steppin' lively as we rode up Main Street. Then up ahead, by the Masonic Hall, I see'd all the foot soldiers lined up in their blue uniforms, with their muskets leanin' on their shoulders.

It was a sight to behold, as there was hundreds and hundreds of 'em. Their sergeants and corporals yelled at 'em, and all at once they brung their hands smartly right up to their caps and looked at Brother Joe and me as we passed by. Up ahead I also see'd the other officers, the ones that ride close by Brother Joe in the Legion—Hyrum on Sam and all the rest. Then I heared the big boom of the drum, and the brass band started a-playin'. We passed the band, led by a stout and strong feller they call Dimick, a-liftin' his stick in the air and bringin' it down in time with the music. There was another feller out in front carryin' one of them colored cloths on a long pole, all red and white with a big patch of blue. Brother Joe and me rode right past the drummer, a big black feller they call Isaac Manning, who was carryin' the big bass drum up agin' his breast, a thunderin' and beatin' it as loudly as he could. I'm sure the sound of that drum could be heared all the way out on the Carthage Road, past Brother Joe's farm and the Cemetery. Maybe all the way to Carthage.

Up ahead was General Dunham settin' steady and calm on Rambler, with his arm raised right stiff with his hand up agin' his general's hat. We stopped right in front of him, and General Dunham brung his hand suddenly away from his head. As near as I can tell, this was the signal that he knowed Brother Joe was the big man in charge of the Legion, 'cause all the men cheered, and folks lined up on the street was wavin' their hats and yellin' and cheerin', too. Brother Joe took command of the Legion, and he and me walked at a slow pace on up Main Street, the band playin' loud and clear, and the officers, bodyguard, and the hundreds of soldiers marchin' right behind.

It was a right impressive moment, Major. It's hard to explain, but the sky was blue, and the gardens was all filled with flowers, and the air felt kinda different, if you know what I mean, like there was a big change in the wind. The ladies and the little children was runnin' in and out of their houses, and I watched while a little girl handed out little flowers to some of the soldiers, who stuck 'em right in the lapels of their blue jackets. I also see'd the smiles on the faces of the soldiers, Major, and I 'spect some of 'em felt like this was the best day of their lives, to march along behind me and Brother Joe.

Well, all the soldiers follered Brother Joe and me up the hill, past the white walls on the hill and out onto the wide open parade grounds. We waited while the soldiers lined up all straight and even, and then Brother Joe rode me up and down the line while he looked at the fellers standin' there. One feller rode with us—the one Brother Joe calls Charlie Rich when we is at meetin's with the Brethren, but in the Legion they all call him the Brigadier. He was mounted up on his black stallion called True Blue. I like the Brigadier, 'cause he always has a word and a pat for me. The Brigadier is real short with dark hair, and the way I size him up, he ain't the smartest of Brother Joe's generals, but I can tell the men all think the world of him. Brother Joe had put him in charge of all the musket men on foot—they was called the First Cohort, and there was more of them than anythin' in the Legion. So the Brigadier and True Blue was in charge of the whole outfit.

Brother Joe rode me off to the side, and we stood there with Hyrum on Sam and General Dunham on Rambler while the Brigadier rode off to talk to his fellers. Brother Joe and the others looked on and talked back and forth while the soldiers marched here and there over the parade ground. Then they set off the big cannons, blastin' out toward the marshland in the north. Every time the cannon was set off, I see'd every horse on the parade ground kinda flinch and lay their ears back, and some of 'em reared up on their hind legs. After the cannons was set off, all the cavalry men rode out onto the field on their horses, a-swipin' at poles stuck in the ground and bales of straw with their swords. The cavalry is called the Second Cohort, and I could tell they thought of theirselves as better than the Brigadier's foot soldiers in the First Cohort.

While we stood around—Sam and me and Rambler— there was a lot of talkin' back and forth between Brother Joe and Hyrum and General Dunham. They was talkin' about the Missourians and their cannons and musket men, about their cavalry, and how we was to get ourselves and our boys all ready for 'em in case they ever come a-marchin' up the Carthage Road. They also talked some about Long Whiskers and White Hat and their gunmen. They was the ones what pointed all their guns at Brother Joe and tried to take him down the road to Carthage. I heared Hyrum say that that warn't *never* goin' to happen again, and then they talked some about the Legion and how our soldiers would keep the city safe from the armies, and then they talked some about how they had set up some kinda soldier law in the city, 'stead of jest lettin' folks ride in and out willy-nilly. And near as I could tell, General Dunham was sayin' that now that we had soldier law in the city, we would never worry again about Long Whiskers or White Hat or any other men ridin' right into Nauvoo to grab hold of Brother Joe or anyone else, or to fire off their guns and hurt folks and maybe set fire to the city.

Finally, after a couple of hours of watchin' the Legion doin' what Brother Joe calls their "maneuvers," we headed back down the hill to the Mansion House. All the Legion boys—infantry and cavalry—follered right behind us. When we got close to the Mansion, I see'd that there was more people standin' in the street than I ever see'd there in my life. And not only Legion fellers, but the Brethren and all the ladies from the city.

Brother Joe and Hyrum and General Dunham dismounted and handed our reins off to Lorin Walker to hold. Then they climbed right up a little ladder onto a wood platform on Water Street, right across from the Mansion House. Some of the other officers climbed up with 'em. I looked and see'd Brother Joe a-standin' there in his general's uniform, a-lookin' this way and that at the crowd. Somebody whistled out and yelled, "Quiet!" and all the soldiers lined up in the street to listen to Brother Joe. It took a few minutes for folks to settle down, and then things got right quiet. Folks was standin' in Water Street and way up Main Street, with hundreds of other folk behind 'em. I looked over by the Mansion House and see'd Lady Emma standin' by the side of the house with Little Joseph and Julia and several other ladies, a-watchin'.

Lorin stood by the side of the ladder where Brother Joe had climbed, holdin' my reins and the reins of Sam and Rambler. General Dunham walked to the edge of the platform and yelled, "Attention!" and suddenly all the Legion fellers brought their hands up to their caps and jest stood still. The only sound was the fussin' of the horses.

Then they kind of snapped their arms back down to their sides, with a sound like a flock of birds takin' off.

Brother Joe stepped up to the edge of the platform and started speakin'. He must have talked an hour to the soldiers. All the time, the fellers in the Legion was right attentive. I couldn't make out much of what Brother Joe said, but I do remember that near the end, Brother Joe called out to all the people, and said, "Will you stand by me to the death?" and then all the soldiers and all the folks 'round about shouted out "Aye!" like it was one big voice. Then Brother Joe looked right peaceful, and I see'd him reach down and pull out his sword from its scabbard, and he raised it right up in the air and said somethin' about him promisin' to defend Nauvoo from the mob and that he wouldn't never again put his sword back into the scabbard until we was all safe again. All the ladies and most of the men had them water drops runnin' down their faces, and when Brother Joe had finished sayin' his piece, they all shouted again, but not quite as loud, sayin' "Ay-men!"

Well, after Brother Joe and the others had done their talkin' to all the soldiers and the folks of the city, he climbed down the ladder and mounted up on me again, and we went back up Main Street to the parade ground, where we spent the rest of the day watchin' the men march and shoot their muskets, and listenin' to the officers yellin' at em, doin' this and that and whatever they was ordered to do.

And through it all, I could feel Brother Joe's pulse throbbin' through the saddle. He didn't say much, jest watched and listened, but I knowed that he was the center of things. He was my whole world, I knowed that already, but seein' all the soldiers marchin' this way and that, I suddenly knowed that he was their whole world, too, and that they would do whatever he told 'em to do to defend Nauvoo from the other armies.

So I jest stood there and waited for Brother Joe to tell me what to do, like I always done.

WEDNESDAY, JUNE 19, 1844

BROTHER JOE RIDES OLD CHARLIE FROM THE MANSION
HOUSE IN FULL MILITARY ORDER TO THE PARADE
GROUND – THE NAUVOO LEGION DRILLS ALL DAY

NAUVOO, ILLINOIS -- WEDNESDAY, JUNE 19, 1844

The Warsaw Signal publishes this against the Mormons: "Exterminate, utterly exterminate . . . strike them!"[40]

Orders are given to secure gunpowder and to put state-issued guns in the hands of all members of the Nauvoo Legion. Picket guards are placed on all streets in Nauvoo. The city is on constant alert, day and night.

8:00 a.m. The Legion assembles at the parade grounds and begins drilling, remaining until late in the afternoon. Of these days, one Legion soldier later remembered, "I was in the city . . . during which time every man almost slept on his arms and walked armed by day, ready at a moment's notice to lose their lives, or lay them in jeopardy in defense of our rights."[41]

11:00 a.m. Legion troops from Green Plains, Iowa, arrive in the city and muster outside the Mansion House. Joseph Smith rides before them up to the parade ground. [42]

Joseph learns that there are anti-Mormon gunmen and hostile militia groups gathering and growing stronger by the hour around Carthage, Warsaw, and across the Mississippi River in Missouri. Word

---

[40] *Warsaw Signal,* June 19, 1844

[41] Oliver Boardman Huntington, "Diary of Oliver B. Huntington," typescript, page 45, copy in author's possession

[42] APR 494; HC 6:504

comes that the only thing that will satisfy the enemy is for Joseph to be taken prisoner to Carthage to be tried.[43]

Y ou look mighty tired out, old Major, and I guess I am, too.

I 'spect you heared all the picket guards passin' by again in the night, a-walkin' up and down Water Street. I heared 'em all night long. They was walkin' down by the Big River, too, up and down, jest talkin' quietly amongst theirselves. Then in the early mornin', a steamer stopped down to the lower landin' below the stable, and I heared a whole crowd of men all a-talkin'. I 'spect it's all part of the soldier law that General Dunham was talkin' about yesterday. Soldiers marchin' up and down, and comin' and goin'. Well, as long as it keeps Brother Joe safe, I'm all for it, gettin' waked up at night or no.

Brother Joe was all dressed up in his General uniform again today, hat and sword and all, and there was lots of ridin' around today with him, which suits me jest fine. Fact is, Major, Brother Joe spent pert' near the whole day ridin' in the saddle.

'Course, there's never any tellin' what Brother Joe is goin' to do. You and me both know that, down through the years. I'm used to him jest up and goin' off on his mission trips, or to Springfield, or shuttin' hisself up for days on end for councils or meetin's and whatnot with the Brethren. And these last days there's been a lot of shuttin' hisself up in the Mansion House, talkin' with the Legion soldiers and with the Brethren.

---

[43] HC 6:505-507

Brother Joe and me headed out first thing back up to the parade ground in the mornin' sunshine, jest like yesterday 'cept there warn't crowds of people watchin' us go, jest the Legion fellers. Brother Joe's bodyguard was waitin' on us in front of the Mansion House, Old Man Lott ridin' Paulina and ten, fifteen of his men on their horses. And then there was hundreds of blue Legion soldiers on foot, all standin' in a long line on Main Street waitin' on Brother Joe, most with their muskets all propped up on their shoulders and little packs on their backs, though some of 'em didn't have no muskets. They hurrahed when we come ridin' 'round the corner. Brother Joe sat in the saddle for a bit, talkin' to 'em. I heared somebody say the soldiers was from Green Plains, and they had jest stepped off the steamer to join the rest of the Legion soldiers. There was smiles all around, and Brother Joe walked me up and down the line, stoppin' to chat with this feller or that. Then, we lined up and marched up Main Street. Old Man Lott and ten, fifteen other horsemen rode with Brother Joe and me, stretched out in two lines to either side of us, and all the fellers from Green Plains follered behind on foot, keepin' time as they marched.

The sun was jest hittin' the white walls on top of the hill when we passed, and up there we could already hear the sound of boots comin' from the direction of the parade ground, all steppin' together. I tell you, Major, marchin' sounds mighty peculiar in the distance, and it makes you prick your ears right up. When we rode into the parade ground we see'd that all the other Legion soldiers was already up there, hundreds and hundreds of 'em, all standin' straight and marchin' this way and that. They all let out a mighty "Hurrah" when they see'd Brother Joe and all the Green Plains men, let me tell you. The new men marched over to join the long line, and Brother Joe and me rode to the little hill to watch. I see'd Hyrum and General Dunham already waitin', jest settin' there on Sam and Rambler. John Taylor rode up 'longside of Brother Joe as we took our place, all dressed in his blue coat, with a sword by his side. He handed Brother Joe some papers and stood by while Brother Joe looked at 'em real intent like. John Taylor's mare, Lady Gray, gave me a nice, friendly nicker, and I answered back, and when we got real close I jest nuzzled her friendly like to say I was glad to see her again. Sam tossed his white head and pawed the ground real playful like, but Rambler turned his head away and flicked his ears. He warn't havin' none of the friendliness. He was all business, so I figured I ought to be all business, too, and jest stood to attention next to Sam and Lady Gray, waitin' for what was next.

General Dunham spoke real quick to Brother Joe and then went out onto the parade ground, ridin' this way and that, tellin' the soldiers what to do. They was all spread out in long lines over the parade ground, and it looked to me like there was even more of 'em than yesterday—more than I can count. I been around Brother Joe and General Dunham long enough to know that they calls the reg'lar blue soldiers—the ones without horses—the infantry. Then there are the fellers on horses, and they're called cavalry. And finally, there are a few fellers what move around the big guns on little wheels—called 'tillery.

Most of the reg'lar infantry fellers stood in big, straight lines with their muskets or rifles restin' on their shoulders. You could see here and there the officers standin' 'longside of the reg'lar men. I knowed the officers 'cause they all had on big hats like Brother Joe's, some of 'em with feathers stickin' out up top. In the distance, I see'd that all the cavalry horses was waitin' up to the far end of the parade ground, with their riders tryin' to keep 'em in line. I could hear 'em neighin' and callin', all excited. Pert' near all I see'd up on the parade ground was blue coats in straight lines, 'cept one of the companies was all dressed in red. It was a sight to see—more soldiers in one place than I ever see'd, even in Missouri when pert' near the whole army of Missourians come to circle around Far West with their guns and cannons.

After a short spell, it looked like the whole Legion—infantry, cavalry and 'tillery—was goin' to practice shootin' with their guns. I heared the officers shoutin' commands. I see'd how the infantry fellers stretched out in a long single file, almost as far as I could see. Then they all turned together toward the open marsh where they aimed their muskets and rifles, and on the shout of "Fire!" they let loose! Suddenly there was sparks of fire comin' from their muskets and rifles, and the air was filled with the cracklin' noise of muskets—real loud and startlin'. I could hear the sound of the bullets flyin'—zip! zip!—and a couple of *'Yooow'* noises when one of 'em bounced off a stone. There was a big cloud of gray smoke rollin' out of the end of their muskets over the ground, makin' it kinda hard to see all the blue soldiers for a minute. Then I caught a whiff of the gun smoke, all sharp and tangy like in my nostrils. I could see that some of the horses didn't like it and shook their heads this way and that. Then the infantry fellers stood and reloaded and fired off again two more times. I heared the cracklin' noise of the muskets again, and the smoke kinda rolled over the open field in big waves. When the first bang went off, Lady Gray let out a scream next to me and reared up on her feet, and I see'd across the field how some of the cavalry horses did the same. Sam and Rambler was steady, and I didn't flinch none, seein' how I'm used to the bangs.

I remember the first day I ever heared the bangs. It was when I was a colt and went out huntin' with my first owner in a place called Kentucky. I was skeered out of my wits, let me tell you—dancin' about all over the place and rearin' up, practically throwin' my rider. But I got used to it, and later on when I was brung to Kirtland and joined up with Brother Joe, it seems like I lived with the sound of guns reg'lar like ever since. I don't like it, but I know that if I'm with Brother Joe there's bound to be bangs now and then. With Brother Joe, I know that if there ain't bangs right now, then there is going to be bangs sooner or later.

Well, after the reg'lar Legion soldiers got done with their bangin', they moved off to the side, and here come the cavalry, and they lined up to set off a bang or two theirselves with their guns. Most of the cavalry fellers shot little guns, what Brother Joe calls horse pistols, held in their hands 'stead of the long muskets like the reg'lar fellers use. I could see that some of the cavalry horses didn't like the bangin' goin' on right above their heads at all, but most of 'em stood steady enough. Then, after they finished their bangin', the cavalry fellers all pulled their swords out and pointed 'em straight up toward the sky and let out a whoop and a holler. I see'd how the sun kinda glinted off the steel of their swords.

Then, the cavalry horses all moved back in position, and the 'tillery fellers moved up, draggin' three little cannons behind 'em. They was 'bout the size of a little tree stump, but made all of metal and heavy. I could see the fellers strainin' to pull those things to the side of the field and turn 'em around to aim 'em north toward the open country and the Big River yonder. Well, there was dead silence amongst all the other soldiers lined up watchin', and we see'd a little spark of fire atop each cannon, and then a big "Boom!" altogether, which sent out three long stretches of fire over the ground and three big clouds of smoke follerin' right along. The cannons kinda jumped back on their wheels. I didn't flinch none when I heared the sound, 'cause I'm used to it, but most of the cavalry horses was a-squealin' and two of 'em run off a piece with their riders strugglin' to haul 'em back into line.

You know, Major, I been ridin' with Brother Joe in the Legion for four summers, now, and I'm used to the noise and the shoutin' and the bangs. Why, sometimes on Legion parade I ride right 'longside of black Isaac Manning, what carries the big bass drum, a-bangin' away with his big sticks as he marches, his white teeth flashin' in a mighty smile as he goes, and I don't flinch none, not even toss my head away. And a time or two I been standin' to attention in a line with Brother Joe while the cannon is set off—Boom!—close 'longside of me, and the smoke rolls all about me, and its smell is kinda burnin' in the air and in my nostrils, but I jest hold my head high and kinda blow a trumpet blast out of my nostrils to clear 'em out. I ain't skeered by the sound of the cannon or the bangin' of the drum, as long as Brother Joe is safe in the saddle and tellin' me what to do and where to go.

THURSDAY, JUNE 20, 1844

BROTHER JOE RIDES OLD CHARLIE OUT OF THE CITY TO
INSPECT THE MILITARY DEFENSES – THE NAUVOO
LEGION PARADES ALONG THE MISSISSIPPI RIVER

NAUVOO, ILLINOIS – THURSDAY, JUNE 20, 1844

Early morning: Lieutenant General Joseph Smith, Major General Dunham, and other Legion officers ride outside of Nauvoo to continue preparations for a military defense of the city. Joseph pledges his farms in order to gain the necessary provisions to meet the coming attacks of the mob.[44]

10:00 a.m. A cannon is reported to have arrived at Warsaw.

11:00 a.m. Joseph Smith reviews the Nauvoo Legion facing the Mansion House, after which the full Legion parades along the banks of the Mississippi River.

Joseph Smith sends a letter appealing to John Tyler, President of the United States, informing him of mobs gathering from Missouri and Illinois with the intent to "exterminate" the Saints, and requesting him to take action against it to "save the innocent and oppressed from such horrid persecution."[45]

Many men are deposed saying that outside of Nauvoo, in the surrounding settlements, men are forcing people to take up arms to fight against Joseph, or to go into Nauvoo and join the people there, or to give up their arms. Those who are not Mormons also come to report these things. Many people outside of Nauvoo are forced to leave their homes.[46]

---

[44] HC 6:514-515
[45] HC 6:507-508
[46] HC 6:508-514

Willard Richards sends a letter to James Arlington Bennett requesting assistance: "We are already being surrounded by an armed mob; and, if we can believe a hundredth part of their statements we have no alternative but to fight or die."[47]

10:00 p.m. Joseph Smith gives orders to commence the manufacture of more artillery. He reads a letter from the Mormon apostate Robert D. Foster that the mob intends to besiege Nauvoo and cut off all communications and supplies.[48]

Joseph Smith advises his brother Hyrum to leave for Cincinnati with his family on the next steamboat. Hyrum replies, "Joseph, I can't leave you."

"I wish," Joseph tells his friends, "I could get Hyrum out of the way, so that he may live to avenge my blood, and I will stay with you and see it out."[49]

Last night was a short night, Major. Seems like I had jest settled in after a long day of riding, when I see'd Lorin a-standin' there in the stable with his lantern, a-whisperin', "Charlie, Charlie," in the dark. Tom and Joe Duncan stirred in their boxes, and the hotel horses was all fussin' around in the straw while Lorin fixed me all up in the Legion saddle and bridle and straps and led me outside into the early mornin' light.

I see'd right off three horses all saddled up and tied to the post and ready for ridin'. It was Hyrum's big white Sam, and with him was Jack and Tramp, what belong to two of Brother Joe's reg'lar bodyguards, Porter and Blue Dan. Lorin tied me up likewise and kinda sat on the stump lookin'

---

[47] HC 6:517-518

[48] HC 6:520

[49] HC 6:519-520

toward the Mansion House and pulled out a green apple and started chompin' on it. Sam 'clined his head toward me and gave a little welcomin' nicker. And we jest all waited— four horses and Lorin Walker chompin' on his apple. I kinda nuzzled Lorin's shoulder, and sure enough he reached in his pocket and pulled out another apple and gave it to me. Then we all jest waited. That's what it seems like I spend half my life doin', Major, jest waitin' for Brother Joe. There warn't so much as a wisp of cloud in the sky, jest a little red and purple on the horizon, and it looked to be a real scorchin' day. The skeeters warn't out yet though.

Pretty soon Brother Joe come out of the house with his brother Hyrum. Both of 'em was all dressed out in their blue General jackets with white trousers, ridin' boots, gold buttons, and their big hats carried in their hands. Lorin stood up when he see'd 'em walkin' across the street and started to unhitch me from the post. Brother Joe and Hyrum put their big hats on, and I could see the bird feathers up top a-blowin' in the mornin' breeze. Pretty soon Porter and Blue Dan follered right along, all dressed in their blue Legion uniforms. Lorin handed my reins to Brother Joe, and he and the other three riders swung right up into their saddles. We stood there a minute while the men got situated. Lorin handed Brother Joe his gloves and his black belt with the horse pistols. Hyrum and Brother Joe was talkin' back and forth, and Brother Joe hesitated jest a minute in the stable yard, lookin' at his Mansion House, and then the four of us rode out into the street where there was another little bunch of Brother Joe's bodyguard detail all in blue on their horses, includin' Old Man Lott ridin' on his bay mare, Paulina.

We galloped out along the Big River on Water Street, then all the way out along Parley Street to the Carthage Road crossroads. The men was talkin' loud, and the horses all seemed in fine spirits. We turned down the Carthage Road and moved steady out into the open country, where we see'd the little lines of soldiers here and there. They all snapped their hands right up to their foreheads as Brother Joe and Hyrum passed, and a few spoke out a friendly hello, and Brother Joe answered back. Out 'bout three, four mile, Brother Joe stopped on the Carthage Road and joined up with another group of Legion men on horseback. One of 'em was General Dunham. Rambler looked mighty steady and confident, jest lookin' around as he stood in the sun. Brother Joe sat in the saddle talkin' a bit to General Dunham. Blue Dan's Tramp nickered to Rambler, but he never nickered back, jest actin' kinda superior.

Then we all left the Carthage Road and rode down into the creek bottom where we splashed through the stream and then worked our way across the open country, where there warn't no reg'lar roads. Here and there we see'd Legion soldiers in their blue coats. It was new country for me, and I was puzzled where Brother Joe was takin' us, but I knowed he had a direction. We was jumpin' over low fences and cuttin' through the trees and bushes and all. Sam and me didn't have no trouble with the fences, as Brother Joe and Hyrum love to jump when they is out ridin'. Once or twice it seemed like Tramp was kinda fumblin' in his tracks, trippin' on a rock or branch here or there. When we come over a little wooden bridge, I see'd Tramp kinda falter at the hollow-like sound of his own hooves on the planks. Jack was steady, though he warn't as sure about jumpin' the fences, and 'course Rambler was as strong and sure as any horse I ever see'd. We come to a deep ravine, right steep, with water runnin' in the bottom, and we splashed right down into it. The horses hesitated in the water until Brother Joe kicked me to pick it up, and we kinda surged up the other side, with Tramp comin' up last.

On the other side of the ravine the bushes was pretty thick, and there was big ditches here and there with Legion soldiers diggin' theirselves cozy little seats in the dirt, and there was campsites close by with tents and a place for fire and all. The men all seemed happy to see Brother Joe and me, and he must have leaned low in the saddle and shook a hundred hands along the way. Brother Joe was forever praisin' the soldiers and tellin' 'em their soldier work was the best he ever seen. He told 'em here or there to dig a deeper ditch or to set up logs jest so, but he'd always remember to put in a joke or a good word or a pat on a shoulder as we left. Everywhere we went it was, "Howdy, General," or "Hey, Brother Joseph." Now and then one of the soldiers would ask, "How's your horse today, General?" and pat my flanks or stroke my nose, and Brother Joe would say, "Old Charlie's jest fine. Couldn't ask for a better horse," which made me step up all the finer.

We got to some farms and a mill by a big stand of trees, then headed back in the other direction from which we come. We crossed the creek in a different spot and kinda meandered our way back. When we got back close on to the Carthage Road, we come up to the hill where Brother Joe had scratched lines in the dirt with a stick a couple of days back. There was some of our blue Legion fellers swarmin' all over it. They was workin' on a little wall of rocks in front of the Legion cannon up top.

Brother Joe and Hyrum rode on up to the top of a little hill with General Dunham. Blue Dan and Porter stayed behind to keep watch from the bottom of the hill. Brother Joe and Hyrum and General Dunham all dismounted and let us horses wander to the far side of the hill where there was green summer grass. We had a feed while Brother Joe talked with the others.

I tried to act real friendly to General Dunham's horse, Rambler, but he warn't havin' none of that. When I tried to move in too close to him, he tried to kick out at me, so after that I jest let him be and fed close to Sam. I looked over a time or two and see'd General Dunham jest a-lookin' into those two bottles of his. Brother Joe had some papers in his hand he was lookin' at real intent like.

After a while Brother Joe whistled for me, and he and General Dunham and Hyrum mounted back up, and we rode back down the hill. Hyrum called Blue Dan and Porter, and we lit out north for the Carthage Road. By this time, there was a proper line of soldiers marchin' back into the city right behind us.

At the crossroads, we headed right into Brother Joe's farmyard, where we stopped for a long time while Joseph and the men went inside. 'Bout then, two other men rode up in a long wagon with a white canvas coverin', full of supplies, I s'posed. They warn't dressed in uniform and went into Joseph's farmhouse carryin' some papers. Sam and me and Jack and Tramp stayed out in the yard, tied up to the long rail with 'bout a dozen other horses. Then after a bit, the men all come out and shook hands all around with the fellers in the big supply wagon.

We rode back into Nauvoo proper on the Carthage Road and then on Mulholland Street. The city was right filled with soldiers, and as we 'proached home, the sides of the street was lined with men in blue, who set up a proper "Hurrah," with whistlin' and clappin' for Brother Joe as we pulled up to the Mansion House.

Well, Brother Joe stopped in the street and shouted a big hello at all the men, and they cheered. Brother Joe then led right out in another parade, this one along the Water Street, past the Red Brick Store and on down on the flat close to the Big River. The whole durned Legion follered along behind, with all the brass band blarin' and the big bass drum boomin'. Down by the Big River, we stopped and watched the Legion fellers march around a bit, and they even set off the cannon a time or two, aimed out over the river water.

Finally, 'bout the heat of the day, Brother Joe and me returned home to the Mansion House, and Lorin took off the saddle and gave me good feed and water and a rubdown after a long day. Brother Joe's old Uncle John from Ramus, one of the little towns out in the countryside, come ridin' up all excited to talk with Brother Joe. When he rode into the stable and gave his horse off to Lorin, he said somethin' about how guns was fired at the Legion soldiers as they tried to ride into Nauvoo. Old Uncle John seemed mighty shook up. I s'posed that this meant that Brother Joe and Hyrum was havin' a long talk with the men inside.

Now it's right quiet outside, and all I can hear is the sound of the horses breathin' or eatin' their feed in the stable.

You still awake, Major?

FRIDAY, JUNE 21, 1844

BROTHER JOE RIDES OLD CHARLIE OUT TO REVIEW THE
NAUVOO LEGION – JOHN TAYLOR AND LADY GRAY
RIDE TO CARTHAGE WITH A MESSAGE FOR THE
GOVERNOR – CHARLIE HEARS GUNFIRE IN THE LATE
EVENING

NAUVOO, ILLINOIS – FRIDAY, JUNE 21, 1844

In the morning, Governor Thomas Ford arrives at Carthage and establishes his headquarters in the Hamilton House hotel.[50]

10:00 a.m. Joseph Smith rides out and watches the Legion practicing maneuvers in preparation for defending Nauvoo from attack.

12:00 noon. Joseph sends John Taylor and others with a letter to Governor Ford inviting him to come to Nauvoo to investigate conditions, and telling him that it is much too dangerous for Joseph or any other member of the City Council to go to Carthage. "We have ever held ourselves amenable to the law . . . I am ever ready to conform . . ." Joseph contradicts all the malicious rumors concerning illegal detaining of strangers and illegal imprisonment of citizens, and destruction of property.[51]

2:30 p.m. Joseph Smith receives a message from Governor Ford requesting a representative to give the Mormons' side of the story to him

---

[50] Susan Easton Black, "Artois Hamilton: A Good Man in Carthage?" in *Journal of Mormon History*, Vol. 31, No. 2 (Salt Lake City: 2005) pp. 152-153

[51] HC 6:526-527; HC 7:75-77; Glen M. Leonard, *Nauvoo: A Place of Peace, A People of Promise* (Salt Lake City: Deseret Book, 2002) p. 372.

in Carthage. Joseph orders the City Council to meet to deliberate on an answer.

4:00 p.m. The City Council convenes. Affidavits of twenty or more are prepared and sent to Ford, testifying of threats on the Prophet's life and the extermination of Nauvoo.

10:00 p.m. There are reports of guns being fired two miles from Nauvoo.

11:00 p.m. John Taylor arrives at Carthage and witnesses crowds of drunk and vociferous mobbers.[52]

You hear that sound, Major? It was the bang of a gun out there in the dark, sure thing. You didn't hear it? No matter, I heared it plain as plain, and I knowed the other horses here in the stable heared it, 'cause Tom and Joe Duncan and the others pricked up their ears. Guess you don't know how much we horses can hear. We can hear the sound of hooves a-comin' long before a man or even a dog can hear. It's part of our nature. I guess you don't know that we can point our ears in any direction we want. When a horse hears somethin' interestin', he will swing his head around, or even his whole body, to listen right intent like. Well, I heared a bang outside in the dark, sure as daylight.

Well, with the bangin' already started around Nauvoo, I'm right glad Brother Joe's got the Legion all organized. They been out in the city day and night, a-marchin' up and down the streets.

This mornin' the fog rolled in from the Big River, so I couldn't see across the pasture. I wandered out in the pearly light to stand in my usual spot to look and listen—as there's always plenty to hear, like the chug chug of a big boat slidin'

---

[52] HC 6:521-524; 7:71-74

up the Big River, and the neighbor horses makin' their mornin' sounds up yonder. Soon I heared the back door to the Mansion slam shut and see'd the figure of Lorin appearin' through the fog on the street. He'd come to saddle me all up for Legion business, fog or no.

Brother Joe and me rode up through the fog on Main Street to the hill and then up to the white walls, and sure enough we walked right out of the fog into the mornin' sun, which was glintin' off all the shop windows.

We passed all the Legion cavalry a-ridin' in formation on Mulholland Street, and they all brung up their hands to their caps when Brother Joe passed. They follered us on into the parade ground. All durin' the ride, I had heared plain the sound of the musketry, and I figured it must be the Brigadier and his First Cohort fellers firin' out over the open field toward the river. When we rode into the open parade ground, I see'd the Brigadier astride True Blue. He and his officers—what Brother Joe calls the colonels and majors and captains—was jest standin' in the field behind all the infantry of the First Cohort, who was lined up as far as you could see. The Brigadier had his sword in one hand, raised high up in the air. He jest sat there still for a jiffy, with no one sayin' a word, and his sword kinda shinin' in the sunlight. And then suddenly he swiped the sword down real fast and yelled "Fire!" and all the muskets crackled off at once.

Brother Joe and me settled down to watch all the firin', and meantime General Dunham rode up on Rambler. He was follered pretty quick by Hyrum on Sam and John Taylor on Lady Gray. The four of 'em talked back and forth. They was mostly talkin' about a man called the Gov'nor, who as near as I can tell was in charge of the whole country 'round about. Brother Joe said that he hoped the Gov'nor would come to Nauvoo to help us fight off the men with guns, what was tryin' to take Brother Joe to Carthage and shootin' at the Brethren and tryin' to drive us out of Nauvoo. Brother Joe was sayin' that he wanted to send Lady Gray to Carthage with John Taylor to talk to the Gov'nor in Carthage.

Then the Brigadier rode up to Brother Joe and said he wanted to take his Cohort out on the road for a march, so Brother Joe and the others decided to foller along. We soon lit out and follered the Brigadier and his men. Major, you should'a see'd the way that First Cohort was marchin' along in one great block of soldiers, fillin' up Mulholland Street from side to side. They was stretched out 'bout half a mile, but their feet all jest hit the ground at the same time. Brother Joe rode along behind, and we went out four, five mile, past the hill where our fellers was standin' at attention by our cannon, and past all the ditches where some of our other fellers was standin' ready with their rifles and pistols. When they see'd the First Cohort go marchin' by, you better b'lieve that they stood right straight and brung their hands up to their caps. You should'a see'd how the First Cohort was jest eatin' up the miles! Each of the fellers had his musket or rifle restin' on one shoulder, and they was swingin' the other arm as they marched. They warn't singin' or talkin' at all, jest marchin' along in dead silence with their thousands of feet all hittin' the road all together and their belts and muskets and 'quipment all jinglin' as they went.

After a spell, the Brigadier called a halt, and the men stood with their guns restin' 'longside of 'em. Brother Joe and me and all the other officers rode on past 'em on the side of the road, and the fellers cheered Brother Joe like you never heared in all your born days. Brother Joe seemed right touched, and then he lifted his General's hat to 'em and held it high above his head. Then all the fellers jest went wild. They was shoutin', "Hallelujah! God bless you, Brother Joseph!" and lots of other things I didn't rightly understand. But I knowed at that moment that all the fellers, from the Brigadier down to the dirtiest soldier standin' in the dust, was ready to go anywhere with Brother Joe, they loved him that much.

When the Brigadier had the First Cohort turn around and march on back to Nauvoo, Brother Joe had all the officers halt on the side of the road to stand and watch 'em go by.

Before lunchtime, Brother Joe and me rode back to the Mansion House with John Taylor, and when we got there, Lady Gray waited in the pasture while John Taylor went inside with Brother Joe. Lady Gray seemed mighty calm, and jest had herself a long drink in the trough. I stood by drinkin' myself wonderin' how long Lady Gray would be fixed up with us in the stable, but soon John Taylor come out of the house with a leather pouch in his hands. Lorin Walker come and fetched Lady Gray and led her over to John Taylor. I heared him tell Lorin that he was ridin' off alone to Carthage to take somethin' to the Gov'nor. Then he got right up in the saddle, and he and Lady Gray rode off. It was jest the two of 'em, without no Cohort or Legion soldiers, and so I kinda wondered if they was goin' to be all right.

And so here I waited all the rest of the day and evenin', Major, listenin' and thinkin'. I been listenin' to the sound of boats out on the Big River, to the feet of the Legion soldiers walkin' up and down the streets, and to the sound of guns a-bangin' out in the dark. And then I been thinkin' about Brother Joe and the Legion. But mostly every time I hear the sound of a bang out on the Carthage Road, I been thinkin' about John Taylor and Lady Gray ridin' alone in the dark.

SATURDAY, JUNE 22, 1844

BROTHER JOE AND OLD CHARLIE WORK WITH THE
LEGION – BROTHER JOE SPEAKS TO THE MEN – A LARGE
COMPANY OF HORSEMEN RIDE INTO NAUVOO AFTER
DARK

NAUVOO, ILLINOIS – SATURDAY, JUNE 22, 1844

Morning: The Legion meets and goes through military drills.

Joseph Smith prophecies to the men: "You will be called the first Elders of the Church, and your missions will be to the nations of the earth. You will gather many people into the fastnesses of the Rocky Mountains as a center for the gathering of the people." Orders are given to take measures to protect the city and the saints in case of attack, and then Joseph Smith dismisses the troops.[53]

Joseph Smith tells his scribe, William Clayton, to hide the records of the Kingdom to protect them from destruction at the hand of the enemy. William Clayton buries them.[54]

In Nauvoo, Luman Calkins gives testimony under oath that a conspiracy to kill Joseph has been underfoot since May, that men plan to kill Joseph by the first of July and then exterminate the saints in Nauvoo.[55]

6:00 p.m. Joseph Smith prophesies that sickness would enter the houses of the mob.

---

[53] Diary of John E. Forsgren, cited in N.B. Lundwall, *The Fate of the Persecutors of the Prophet Joseph Smith* (Salt Lake City: Bookcraft, 1952) 123
[54] JWC 135
[55] HC 6:531-32

7:00 p.m. Joseph Smith receives a letter signed by eight captains of the Nauvoo Legion, asking Joseph to preach tomorrow, "inasmuch as we have an opportunity to hear [you] but seldom."[56]

8:00 to 9:00 p.m. A large company of horsemen, including Captain Yates of the Illinois State Militia, rides into Nauvoo with a letter for Joseph Smith from Governor Ford. Also with the company is John Taylor, just returned from his disappointing interview with the Governor; Constable Bettisworth from Carthage, who was unsuccessful in arresting Joseph on June 12; and "a company of mounted men, who came for the purpose of escorting Joseph Smith and the other accused to Carthage."[57]

It is nighttime when they arrive. Joseph, surrounded by his friends, refuses to be taken into custody, but welcomes the Constable, feeds him and the members of the posse, and provides food for their horses. Joseph promises to travel to Carthage with them the next morning, if they will return in the early morning.[58]

A short time later, two men arrive at the Mansion House, one of them a son of South Carolina senator John C. Calhoun. They are anxious for an interview with Joseph Smith concerning his candidacy for president of the United States. Joseph speaks with them for some time.[59]

10:00 p.m. Joseph and his friends carefully read the letter from Governor Ford. Ford enters upon a discussion of the legality of the City Council's order to destroy the press. He claims that Joseph has violated the Constitution in four particulars: freedom of the press has been obstructed; unreasonable search and seizure has been inflicted; the

---

[56] HC 6:532-33

[57] HC 7:78

[58] Dan Jones, "Hanes Saint y Dyddiau Diweddaf" (Wales, 1847) 85, (translation in *BYU Studies* 24, no. 1 (1984) (hereafter "Jones"). While Dan Jones claims the officer seeking arrest was the "Sheriff," it is clear from Governor Ford's letter that it was "the same constable" who came to Nauvoo on the 12th of June. *See* HC 6:536.

[59] HC 7:78

Nauvoo Council, assuming judicial powers where it does not have any, has combined the legislative and judicial powers into one; and Joseph Smith has forcibly detained people and their property in declaring martial law.[60]

Governor Ford claims that in destroying the Expositor *press the Nauvoo City Council combined their legislative and judicial powers, becoming a "tyrannical power." Ford attacks the habeas corpus power as exercised in Nauvoo and concludes by demanding that they undergo judicial review. Ford says he will not protect Nauvoo with a militia until they submit to the law. "You know the excitement of the public mind," he wrote. "Do not tempt it too far. . . . I would say that your city was built, as it were, upon a keg of powder which a very little spark may explode."*[61]

The Governor demands that Joseph and the other accused "submit yourselves to be arrested by the same constable, by virtue of the same warrant and be tried before the same magistrate whose authority has heretofore been resisted."[62]

Joseph immediately holds council with his friends and the City Council members and expresses his dissatisfaction with the Governor's letter.[63]

Joseph tells the men around him that, "these facts show conclusively that he is under the influence of mob spirit, and is designedly intending to place us in the hands of murderous assassins, and is conniving at our destruction, or else that he is so ignorant and stupid that he does not understand the corrupt and diabolical spirits that are around him."[64]

Joseph dictates a response to Ford's letter: The authority of the Nauvoo charter, which was approved by the state legislature and is the

---

[60] "Thomas Ford to Mayor and City Council," June 22, 1844, published in *Warsaw Signal*, June 29, 1844; HC 6:533-37

[61] Joseph Smith Papers, MSS 155, Box 3, Folder 8; HC 6:533-537

[62] HC 6:536

[63] HC 7:78

[64] HC 6:542

same as Springfield's, gives the council the power to declare and rid the town of a nuisance. If they have erred, the Supreme Court must correct the problem. Furthermore, Joseph cites William Blackstone's canonical Commentaries on the Laws of England: "Scurrilous prints may be abated as nuisances." Joseph continues that "it is not unreasonable to search so far as it is necessary to protect life and property from destruction," which destruction these libelous prints have been urging. He beseeches the governor to disperse the mob in Carthage and says he is willing to stand trial for the third time, for the same offense. Joseph responds to Ford's attack on the city's use of habeas corpus by explaining that they have strictly followed the usual customs in exercising the right of habeas corpus. Joseph repeatedly tells the Governor that they "dare not come," that the presence of enemies and mobs prevent them from coming to Carthage, that they will go anywhere to submit to a trial if the lives of their families in Nauvoo will be protected.[65]

At first Joseph determines to lay his case in person before President Tyler, but this project is soon abandoned because of an inspiration he receives. "The way is open. It is clear to my mind what to do. All they want is Hyrum and myself; then tell everybody to go about their business, and not to collect in groups, but to scatter about. There is no doubt they will come here and search for us. Let them search; they will not harm you in person or property, and not even a hair of your head. We will cross the river tonight, and go away to the West."[66]

I been wonderin' where you was, Major. Thought you wouldn't be comin' over to the stable to sleep tonight, what with all of the strangers comin' and goin' on over to the Mansion House. We had a stable full of strange horses, too, until a short time ago. 'Bout twenty, thirty of 'em was here jest before you walked over, but they've ridden off into

---

[65] HC 6:538-41

[66] HC 6:545-46

the dark night. It's right dark outside tonight. In fact, there been awful dark nights this whole week, Major, with nary a bit of moonlight out, and tonight seems the darkest of 'em all. Well, lay yourself down on the straw, and I'll tell you what happened, so that I can sort it all out proper like.

The mornin' started clear and calm enough. The Legion was out again as usual, and in the mornin' Lorin fancied me all up with the Legion saddle and leathers and all, and I rode out at the head of the column of horses with Brother Joe, as usual. It always makes me feel good to be with Brother Joe at the head of the troop, with all of the finest horses of the big city of Nauvoo, but knowin' inside me that Brother Joe and me could outrun 'em all if it ever come to it. So, even walkin' slow, steppin' high, I knowed both he and me felt a kinda pent-up life, which we could open up and let burst forth at any moment.

It was bright daylight, and Brother Joe and me first rode down with his bodyguard on horseback to fix up all the guns along the Carthage Road, makin' sure all was set to rights, jest to give a few s'prises to any of the Carthage army if they happened to try anythin'. Then we rode back and watched the infantry march around and shoot their guns, then watched some more while the cavalry of the Second Cohort rode up and down the parade ground. There warn't no shootin' of the 'tillery, mostly 'cause the cannons has been set up down on the Carthage Road.

After a couple of hours, Brother Joe rode over to the soldiers and said he wanted to say a piece to 'em. They all crowded around to listen while Brother Joe sat in the saddle. He was right quiet at first, and I could tell he was touched, 'cause his voice quavered some as he started speakin'. He talked some about the Legion and all the men what served in it. I looked around as Brother Joe spoke, and there was 'bout a thousand eyes clapped right on Brother Joe, watchin' him, and they was listenin' real quiet like to every word he said. I didn't properly understand everythin' Brother Joe said, but I do remember that he said that sooner or later the Legion fellers would travel out one by one to jest 'bout every spot in the world, and then they would all muster back together in a place called the Rocky Mountains. He then told 'em to be ready for the enemy to attack the city, then he dismissed 'em all for the day.

The rest of the day was pert' near standin' in my spot in the pasture and watchin' all the comin's and goin's at the brick stable. There was more hotel guests with their horses than I ever remember—'bout fifteen, twenty visitin' hotel guests and their horses all together. Two of 'em rode in durin' the afternoon on fine black walkin' pacers, with bells on their harness and their tails high up in the air. Lorin took their mounts to feed and rest 'em, and the men said they was from a place called South Carolina.

Then all afternoon, the horses of the different Brethren of Nauvoo was comin' and goin', and I had time to see each of 'em. In particular, Brother Hyrum's Sam come in and out at least three times, I s'pose while his master was over at the Mansion House with Brother Joe.

Then in the evenin', the trouble started.

'Long 'bout early dusk, Lorin saddled me up in the everyday tack for a ride with Brother Joe, then took me around to the front of the Mansion House to be ready when he come out. There was 'bout seven, eight other horses, all from captains in the Legion, includin' white Sam, tied up to the long hitchin' post on the big street which runs down to the Big River. Presently, Brother Joe and Brother Hyrum come out of the house in their everyday clothes, and follerin' them was a group of Brother Joe's generals and officers in their Legion uniforms, with swords at their sides. They all come out of the house in the dusk and stood around talkin' real quiet like, not laughin' or jibin' or jokin' like usual. In fact, it seems like it's been days and days since I heared Brother Joe laugh or jibe. Then Brother Joe and the rest all mounted up, and then the hullabaloo started.

First, I heared the sound of gallopin' hooves comin' down the big street and see'd a Legion cavalry officer on a small bay horse, all lathered up from the run. He called out, "Constable comin'!" and then he shouted somethin' to Brother Joe that I couldn't understand. Then I heared the sound of a mighty number of hoofbeats on the road and looked up to see the street filled with runnin' horsemen, twenty, thirty of 'em at least, strangers mostly, with lots of Legion horses and riders follerin' along. I see'd Long Whiskers in the front of the bunch of foreign riders. In a jiffy they all pulled up in front of the Mansion House, and Long Whiskers and his men surrounded Brother Joe and me. All the Legion men and their horses circled around Long Whiskers' fellers in a bigger circle, so that Brother Joe and me was in the middle of a whole bunch of horses and riders. Long Whiskers was on a dappled mare, and he reached out a paper towards Brother Joe and said, "Joe Smith, you're under arrest! And this time no legal tricks. You're comin' to Carthage with me! That's that."

Then Major, you never seen such a commotion of men and horses. The Legion men tried to ride up between the dappled mare and me, but Long Whiskers and his men boxed us in, and they all drew out their guns. Then the Legion men all around all drew out their swords and guns, and it looked to be a fight. There was a scuffle between one of the strangers and a Legion man, and the strange man was pulled off his horse, bangin' his gun into the high branches of the tree. I could hear the sound of the leaves and branches crackin' and rippin' up in the tree. Well, that set most of the horses to rearin' up and screamin'. It was a ruckus, let me tell you, with me and Brother Joe right in the middle of it all.

My blood was coursin' through my body, and every thought of my mind screamed out, "Run! Run away!" So I jest tensed up and waited for the signal from Brother Joe and was ready to go like lightnin'. I see'd a gap in the circle of horses and knowed that we could escape the bunch, and I knowed that once out of the circle, we could outrun Long Whiskers' mare and every single one of 'em.

But then, as I waited for Brother Joe to kick in his heels and give me the reins and the direction to run, I suddenly felt him jest relax in the saddle, and he dropped the reins. I turned my head and see'd that he kinda stretched up his hands. He was right calm, and jest said, "I submit."

And then Brother Joe climbed down from off my back, and stood quietly while two of the riders from Carthage held his arms. Then he said quietly, "Constable, you and your men have ridden far tonight. Your horses are tired. Let me feed you all some supper and give something to your horses."

"None of your legal tricks, Joe Smith," said Long Whiskers. "My orders from the Carthage court and from the Governor himself are to bring you back to Carthage. And I aim to take you back to Carthage, whether you are willing or no."

"I'll go," said Joseph. "But it's too late tonight to ride to Carthage. It's almost dark, with almost no moon to ride by."

"I suppose," said Long Whiskers. By this time the sun had gone down, and the shadows was lengthenin' in the street, and I see'd how the little lights was flickerin' on here and there in the houses in Nauvoo.

Brother Joe spoke up again to Long Whiskers: "I promise you that I will willingly ride with you to Carthage, but wait overnight. We can ride at first light. Meantime, I'll feed your men and horses."

Long Whiskers looked around at the other riders. The men was right tired in the saddle, plain as plain. And some of the Carthage horses looked right tuckered out and was almost asleep on their feet. I know what it's like to ride all day, Major. There been times after long journeys with Brother Joe when I felt like I was dreamin' on my feet, and I was sure hankerin' for a nice feed and a sleep. I see'd that those Carthage horses was 'bout dead on their feet.

I was sure that Long Whiskers was tired hisself, and seein' the weariness of his men and their mounts, he finally nodded his head. Then things happened very strangely, Major. I'm sure you see'd it over to the house, how the whole bunch of fellers from Carthage went into the Mansion House. Brother Joe jest takes 'em all inside the Mansion House, like they was great friends or somethin'. Well, Lorin and some of the Legion soldiers and two or three of the Carthage fellers brung the horses into the stable yard and give 'em water and feed. Brother Joe's other horses, Tom and Joe Duncan, was restin' real quiet like in their boxes, but I could tell that the strange horses from Carthage was fidgety and agitated. Finally they settled down. They was here one, two hours, and then the Carthage men all come out of the house and mounted back up. They talked about sleepin' out in the prairie grass below the hill and returnin' first thing in the mornin'. I felt sorry for Long Whiskers' horses, as they was clearly tuckered out and ready for a long sleep. Now I 'spect they is sleepin' out on the prairie yonder, waitin' to come back in the mornin'.

After Long Whiskers and his fellers rode off, I knowed there was still plenty of Brother Joe's friends over to the Mansion House, 'cause I see'd the lights a-blazin' in the windows, and lots of their horses was waitin' here in the stable and in the pasture. There was Sam, of course, and the Big Doctor's poor old paint, Saucepan, and Porter's scrappy little Jack. In fact, they all is still here, waitin'.

I can hear the Carthage horses right now, Major, can you? They's a-makin' their soft night sounds up yonder in the prairie grass, as they is not a mile from here. And I can hear the sounds of the Legion men walkin' around in the street and talkin' quietly to theirselves. With all that ruckus, I don't 'spect I'll get a wink of sleep tonight, nor you neither. So I'll jest keep you company through the dark night.

Where you off to, Major? You goin' back across to the Mansion House? Well, it's all for the best, I 'spect, as you'll get no sleep here. Goodnight, old friend.

SUNDAY, JUNE 23, 1844

OLD CHARLIE SEES BROTHER JOE CROSS THE BIG RIVER IN THE NIGHT – OLD CHARLIE RIDES TO HYRUM'S FARM AND BACK

NAUVOO, ILLINOIS – SUNDAY, JUNE 23, 1844

2:00 a.m. Joseph, Hyrum, Orrin Porter Rockwell, and Willard Richards cross the Mississippi River in a small rowboat; the boat is leaky and three men bail water out with their boots while one rows.

Daybreak: Joseph and his three companions arrive on the Iowa side of the river. He sends Porter Rockwell back to Nauvoo with instructions to return the next night with Joseph and Hyrum's horses and to pass them over the river in the night secretly, so that they might be ready to start for the Rocky Mountains.[67]

Early morning: Constable Bettisworth's posse arrives back at the Mansion House to take Joseph to Carthage. Finding Joseph missing, they start immediately for Carthage to report his disappearance to the Governor and the other officials in Carthage.[68] *Back in Carthage, Bettisworth tells the Governor that Joseph refused to turn himself into official custody and that "they had barely escaped with their lives from the city."*[69] *The Governor orders that if Joseph and Hyrum do not appear*

---

[67] HC 6:548

[68] HC 6:548-49

[69] Dan Jones, "Hanes Saint y Dyddiau Diweddaf" (Wales, 1847) 85, (translation in *BYU Studies* 24, no. 1 (1984) (hereafter "Jones"). While Dan Jones claims the officer seeking arrest was the "Sheriff," it is clear from Governor Ford's letter that it was "the same constable" who came to Nauvoo on the 12th of June. *See* HC 6:536.

in Carthage by 10:00 a.m. Monday morning, he will order the state militia to destroy Nauvoo and "all the men, women and children that were in it." [70]

Mid-morning: Some of the Brethren persuade Emma to send a letter to Joseph, entreating him to return. She sends the letter back across the river with Porter Rockwell. Emma insists that the Brethren try to persuade Joseph to return. The Brethren find Joseph and Hyrum in a room by themselves, packing flour and other provisions for the trip to the Rocky Mountains. [71]

Joseph reads the letter from Emma, hands it to Hyrum, and says, "I know my own business." Two brethren present accuse Joseph, "You always said, if the Church would stick to you, you would stick to the Church, now trouble comes you are the first to run." They accuse him of deserting the flock when the wolves come, as in the fable. Joseph makes no reply. Joseph asks Rockwell, "What shall I do?" Rockwell replies, "You are the oldest and ought to know best; and as you make your bed, I will lie with you." Joseph then asks Hyrum, "Brother Hyrum, you are the oldest, what shall we do?" "We had better go back," says Hyrum, "and if we die, we will die like men." At length Joseph replies, "If they had let me alone, there would have been no bloodshed, but now I expect to be butchered." Hyrum responds, "No, no; let us go back and put our trust in God, and we shall not be harmed. The Lord is in it. If we live or have to die, we will be reconciled to our fate." [72]

4:00 p.m. Joseph decides to return to Nauvoo. At some point he says, "If my life is of no value to my friends, it is of none to myself." Later, while walking towards the river where he and Hyrum will board a boat to cross the Mississippi, Joseph says, "It is of no use to hurry, for we are going back to be slaughtered."

---

[70] HC 6:550-52

[71] HC 6:549

[72] HC 6:549-50

5:30 p.m. Joseph and Hyrum land north of Nauvoo after crossing the river. Hyrum's family is watching from a chamber window in Hyrum's farmhouse as the skiff nears the riverbank. As they near the shore, Hyrum's five-year-old son, Joseph F. Smith, is playing on the bank of the river and sees the skiff land on a sandy spit which extended some distance out from the shore. The boy recognizes his father as they disembark, and the boy runs to Joseph and Hyrum. Hyrum takes his son by the hand as the three of them walk to Hyrum's farm. Joseph seats himself in the kitchen at the farm while Hyrum shaves and freshens up.[73]

According to family tradition, when Hyrum's oldest daughter, Lovina, greets her father, he asks when she plans to be married to her beau, Lorin Walker, who serves as Joseph's groom and horseman. She tells Hyrum that they have been waiting for him to perform the ceremony. Hyrum tells her that if she wants him to marry them, it will have to be that day. So Lovina removes her apron and goes out to find her lover, Lorin Walker. They are married at Hyrum's farm with only Joseph and the family as witnesses, only four days before Hyrum and Joseph's deaths in the Carthage jail.[74]

Hyrum's sister-in-law wrote, "Although I did not know that the brothers had returned home to be taken as 'lambs to the slaughter,' my feelings were indescribable, and the very air seemed burdened with sorrowful forebodings."[75]

---

[73] Joseph F. Smith recollection, as told to his descendants and quoted in Pearson H. Corbett, *Hyrum Smith: Patriarch* (Salt Lake City: Deseret Book, 1963) 389-90

[74] Corbett, 389-90; Mary Audentia Smith Anderson, ed., "The Memoirs of President Joseph Smith (1832-1914)," in *The Saints' Herald*, (Independence Missouri), December 18, 1934 p. 1614, quoted in *The Memoirs of Joseph Smith III* (Price Publishing Company: Independence, Missouri 2001) p. 22 (hereinafter referred to as "JSIII Memoir")

[75] Mercy R. Thompson, "Recollections of the Prophet Joseph Smith," in The *Juvenile Instructor* (Salt Lake City: July 1, 1892) 27:398-400

Joseph is intent on speaking one last time to the people by starlight. Joseph sends a letter to Governor Ford announcing that he will come to Carthage if the Governor will send a posse and if he will guarantee their safety.

Joseph spends his last night in the Mansion House with his family. He is persuaded not to give a last sermon. [76]

You jest waked me up, Major. I'm that tired, standin' in my box dozin'. Didn't sleep a wink yesterday, what with all the goin's on. After you left the stable in the pitch black and wandered back over to the house, I had the strangest night I seen in many a year.

Last night, after Long Whiskers and his men rode out to camp on the prairie, the other horses finally settled down, and the darkness kinda crept up in the stable. It was warm and sultry. Lorin come out to hang up a bridle on the hooks, and he opened up all the shutters in the stable and left the door wide open to get some sorta breeze to cool off the horses. I walked out of my box into the open pasture, which was kinda glimmerin' in the starlight, and walked over to my reg'lar spot in the pasture. I jest stood there for a bit, lettin' my eyes clear up so I could see things in the dark. Off to one side was the Mansion House, with a few lights still glowin' real dim like, and off to the other side was the Big River. A bit of a moon come up and was fallin' real soft on the water so that I could see the waves kinda flashin' in the dark. There was a little breeze, and it felt good to be out of the stable.

Then I see'd the side door to the Mansion House open real slow like, sendin' a yellow light on the ground. And

---

[76] HC 6:549-50

then I see'd you, Major. You was layin' on the side porch as the door opened wide, and you stood up to let Brother Joe and Hyrum walk past, with Lorin Walker behind 'em. They warn't talkin', but walked calm and steady across the street. Brother Joe had his saddlebag slung over his shoulder, so I figured we was goin' out ridin' in the dark. I watched 'em both walk real quiet and come over to the pasture fence. I wandered over to see what was what. Brother Joe come up and gave my ears a nice scratch and patted my neck, then he reached in his pocket and brung up a little piece of sugar bread, which I ate clean off his hand.

Then up come two horses in the dark, ridin' in slow and calm. It was Saucepan and Jack, carryin' the Big Doctor and Porter, of course. And I thought to myself, what in the dadgummed world is they two doin' out ridin' in the middle of the night, with the stars peepin' out overhead. Well, then the strangest thing of all happened. Lorin Walker opened the pasture gate and led Saucepan and Jack into the pasture and unsaddled 'em both. Then out of the stable, Brother Joe and Hyrum carried the little skiff held high over their heads. Porter run over to help 'em lift it, but he is so short, he warn't much help, so he carried the long poles in his arms, and the Big Doctor scurried on behind, carryin' Brother Joe's saddlebag.

'Course it was pitch black, and there warn't any folks out in the streets, 'cept for a soldier in Legion get-up here and there on the corners. But I stood in my special spot in the pasture and watched as Brother Joe and Hyrum carried the little skiff on their heads past the scaffoldin' and past the Nauvoo House, and come out on the other side, right down by the Big River by the water's edge. I then heared how they dropped the boat quietly in the water, with a little splashin' sound. Then Brother Joe and Brother Hyrum climbed theirselves into the boat, follered by Brother Porter and last of all the Big Doctor, and they shoved off. Brother Joe picked up the long poles and set 'em in the water and started paddlin' back and forth, and the skiff kinda scooted out into the blackness of the flowin' river. I see'd that they was ridin' real low in the skiff, I 'spect 'cause the Big Doctor is a heavy sorta feller.

They got smaller and smaller so that pretty soon I couldn't see 'em at all on the water, but for a long piece I heared the sound of the wooden paddles splashin' in the water. Then I see'd 'em again out on the Big River. I stood and watched as the skiff kept on movin' slowly over the water with Brother Joe pullin' on the long poles, strokin' 'em back and forth, back and forth over the water. The little sliver of moon was all the way up in the sky, and I jest stood a long time in the dark watchin' Brother Joe's little skiff disappear over the Big River, like a skeeter dancin' over a little stream of water.

Well, so I thought to myself, Brother Joe is off on one of his preachin' trips, so I figured that was that and settled in for a quiet day. But it turned out anythin' but quiet.

At early light, I heared a troop of horses comin' from the direction of the sunrise and pretty soon see'd Long Whiskers and his men ridin' up to the Mansion House. They stopped in the street, all saddled up, the horses lookin' tired, and the men not sayin' much. There was a Legion feller standin' on the corner, and he looked a mite perplexed when the horsemen rode up. Then I see'd from the pasture how Long Whiskers climbed down off of his big blood bay stallion, and two or three of his fellers with him. They spoke a word or two to the Legion feller, and then walked up to the front door of the Mansion House. 'Course I can't see the front door from the pasture, but I heared a rappin' and figured he was knockin' at the front door. There warn't no other sound that time of mornin', only the sound of Long Whiskers a-knockin' then a-poundin' on the Mansion House door.

Then I see Long Whiskers walk around to the side door across from the stable, with his two fellers and the Legion guard follerin'. The other Carthage men waited on their horses in the street, lookin' back and forth between each other and talkin'. Long Whiskers kinda marched around to the side porch of the house, where you like to lay in the sun durin' the day, Major. You was barkin' some by this time, but Long Whiskers didn't give you no nevermind, and he walked right up to the side door and started poundin' with his fist. Pretty soon, I see Lady Emma open up the door, wearin' her sleepin' gown, and I hear her voice, right agitated, speakin' angry like at Long Whiskers. Then I heared Long Whiskers' deep voice, soundin' real angry hisself. By this time all the Carthage horsemen in the street had ridden over to the side door and was talkin' loud amongst theirselves. And then Lady Emma walked out on the porch holdin' little Alex by the hand, and she held the door open wide, and Long Whiskers and two other fellers went right inside the Mansion House. Then I see'd how Little Joseph and Julia and Fred come out on the side porch to stand with Lady Emma, and I see'd Lorin Walker and two or three of the hotel helpers out talkin' to Lady Emma.

Then, after twenty, thirty minutes, I see'd Long Whiskers come back out into the street. By this time, there was several of the Brethren gathered in the street, includin' John Taylor and Markham and Phelps. There was some shoutin' back and forth between them and Long Whiskers, and Lady Emma put in a lick or two of her own. Then, finally, Long Whiskers jest mounted right back up on his big blood bay stallion, shouted out to his men, and they all rode off lickety-split in the direction of the Carthage Road. Lady Emma then shut the door tight, and it got quiet in the street, 'cept I could hear the sound of the hooves of the Carthage fellers' horses for a piece.

The rest of the mornin' there was more comin' and goin' at the Mansion House than I see'd in a long while. Men and women a-comin' and goin' all mornin'. Then, 'bout noontime, I was out in the pasture enjoyin' the sun with the other horses. There was me and Tom and Joe Duncan, of course, and then there was Sam and Jack and Saucepan. We was all jest standin', when I see'd Brother Joe's little skiff comin' back across the Big River, but Brother Joe warn't in it, nor Hyrum, nor the Fat Doctor, only Porter. He was sweepin' them poles back and forth like his life depended on it and finally dragged the skiff up to the Nauvoo House landin'. Pretty soon he walked right up to the gate and spoke to Lorin Walker, who was workin' inside the stable. I walked over to 'em and heared Porter say, "They want their horses brung over tonight on the ferry." Then they talked back and forth a bit, and I heared Porter say somethin' about Brother Joe ridin' to the Rocky Mountains. So I perked right up, thinkin' I'm 'bout to go on another long journey with Brother Joe, and I was ready.

Porter then run across the street to the Mansion House with a paper in his hand, and I wondered what would happen next. Then, sure enough, Lorin took me and Sam into the stable and got us both all saddled up and then led us around to the pasture gate, where we waited.

'Cept nothin' happened then. Porter was a long time inside the Mansion House, and meantime ten, fifteen other men rode up and went inside. Lorin kept goin' back and forth to the house, and then finally, he jest unsaddled Sam and me. So I guessed the trip to the Rocky Mountains warn't happenin' today after all. Then I see'd Porter and another man—his name is Cahoon—head back down to the landin' and get into Brother Joe's little skiff and head out on the Big River again. I watched 'em a long time on the water. 'Course the river is mighty wide—a mile or more—and finally they was out of sight over agin' the far shore.

All through the rest of the afternoon I stayed in the stable and the pasture, jest restin' and eatin' and watchin' and wonderin' why Sam and me warn't goin' on the journey to the Rocky Mountains after all. 'Bout late afternoon or early evenin', I was enjoyin' the fine weather and watchin' Lorin Walker fix up the evenin' feed for all the horses. Little Joseph was with him, helpin' with this and that.

Little Joseph is like a small version of his Pa, though he don't talk as much as Brother Joe. He was carryin' a bucket of oats in his arms, strugglin' with it, but wantin' no help from Lorin. Well, then suddenly I look up and who do I see, but Porter walkin' up to the stable gate on foot from the direction of Main Street. I looked around for Brother Joe and Hyrum, but Porter was all alone, and he looked mighty winded, right tuckered out. Lorin Walker and Little Joseph went right over to the fence, and the three of 'em talked real short while they stood by the fence. I didn't hear what they said, but suddenly Little Joseph gave a little yell and brightened right up and run right quick across the road to the Mansion House. Then, Porter saddled up Jack and rode off, while Lorin saddled me and Sam all up.

I was right jittery, let me tell you, feelin' like I was ready for a long journey to the Rocky Mountains, and Sam stepped lively hisself. Then Lorin took us out of the gate into Water Street, swung up into my saddle, and leadin' Sam by the reins, rode off into the city. I see'd as we passed the Mansion House that Lady Emma and Little Joseph was standin' in the doorway watchin' us go.

We rode up Main Street, past the shops, past the clump of trees where Brother Joe preaches, then on up the big hill and past the white walls where the Stone Men was workin' away, a-clinkin' on the white stones with their hammers. Everywhere we went, folks jest stopped what they was doin' and stared at us ridin' by.

Up on Mulholland Street, we rode past the crossroads and then north to Hyrum's farm. As we rode in, I see'd Brother Joe and Hyrum right off. They warn't out on the Big River in a skiff, but back all safe and dry in Hyrum's farmyard, jest settin' on Hyrum's front porch. After they see'd us pull in, Brother Joe come over and talked with Lorin, then went into the house with Hyrum for a long spell while I waited outside with Sam and Lorin Walker.

And then somethin' strange happened, Major. Suddenly the farmhouse door swung open, and there was Hyrum and Hyrum's daughter, Lovina. She run right up to us, and said to Lorin Walker, "Let's go talk!" Then Hyrum kinda wandered up to us, smilin', and then the three of 'em jest went walkin' off into the field.

I was jest waitin' in Hyrum's pasture with Sam, wonderin' what was comin' next. Then Brother Joe come out of the house and sat hisself down on the bench, stretchin' his boots out on Hyrum's porch, and actin' like he had all the time in the world, but I noticed that he was mighty quiet. I know when Brother Joe is quiet, that he is full of his own thoughts. No one 'cept me would understand that, but I spent more time with Brother Joe than any creature on earth, maybe more than he's spent with Lady Emma and the young'uns. But, anyhow, I got the feelin' like Brother Joe was thinkin' awful deep about somethin', and he also looked mighty tired to me.

After settin' a while, Brother Joe stood up and walked over to the fence. I went over to him, wonderin' what he wanted me to do, but he jest stroked my head, real slow like, but all the while he was lookin' off yonder at I don't know what. We stood there like that at the fence a while, when through the trees and over the prairie come Hyrum with his girl Lovina and Brother Joe's horseman, Lorin Walker. 'Cept it didn't look none like the Lorin I knowed. For one thing, he was grinnin' from ear to ear.

Lorin's never been much for smilin'. He's not like Brother Joe, who can smile all the day long, and when he smiles, he sets the fellers around him to smilin', too, so pretty soon there are laughs and jokes and jibes goin' back and forth. But Lorin would always do his work and stand silent, but was never one to pitch hisself into the conversation. But here he walked, grinnin' like no man I ever see'd. And another thing, Major, if you can b'lieve it, he had Hyrum's daughter Lovina right by the hand. He was pullin' her gently along by the hand, which is odd, as I seldom ever see'd Lorin that close to a girl.

Well, they walked back out of the field to Hyrum's farmhouse, and Hyrum and Brother Joe had a quiet talk while Lorin and Lovina stepped inside. Then I heared lots of voices from the womenfolk comin' through the doorway, and pretty soon Hyrum's wife, Lady Mary Fielding, come out of the door and stood there in her apron, her hands on her hips, jest lookin' at her husband.

"Right now?" Lady Mary asked.

Hyrum said, "Well, why not right now, Mary? It has to be now."

So, after that, Brother Joe and Hyrum went back into the house for a long spell, and Sam and me jest waited outside. Then finally Brother Joe and Hyrum come outside again. Lorin Walker then come out of the house holdin' Lovina's hand. Then he leaned down and kissed her right on the mouth. Hyrum's little girls laughed, but their brother John soon shushed 'em.

Then, jest like that, Brother Joe and Hyrum mounted up on Sam and me. Lorin Walker kissed Lovina one more time and then climbed up on me behind Brother Joe. I was ready for a long ride, rememberin' what Porter had said to Lorin about the Rocky Mountains. But 'stead of headin' out of the city, we jest rode back down here to the Mansion House.

And so here I set, Major. I can't rightly understand whether we is goin' on a journey or not. But I'm ready, if Brother Joe is ready. I been ready to ride with him my whole life.

LATE FRIDAY NIGHT, JUNE 28, 1844

NAUVOO, ILLINOIS – LATE FRIDAY NIGHT, JUNE 28, 1844

Hey there, Major. Bless me, how long is it since we see'd each other? It's been days and days since I rode off with Brother Joe to Carthage that early mornin'. I take it real kind you droppin' in to set a spell with me the first night I been back.

Well, lay down on your bed of straw and listen a spell. I can't sleep none, for all the thinkin' of what's transpired.

Fact is, I been mighty confused. I wonder where Brother Joe has gone off to. He warn't in today for a ride, though I 'spected he would be, since Sam and me got back safe from Carthage yesterday. I 'spect he's gone off on one of his preachin' trips in the stagecoach or out on a riverboat. Anyway, I ain't see'd him since the day after we rode to Carthage.

Well, you lay in your spot while I tell you about what I see'd and heared these past days.

I'll start with the mornin' we rode off to Carthage.

MONDAY MORNING, JUNE 24, 1844

BROTHER JOE RIDES OLD CHARLIE FROM NAUVOO TO CARTHAGE WITH THIRTY MEN – CAPTAIN DUNN AND HIS CAVALRY SURROUND THEM

NAUVOO TO CARTHAGE – MONDAY MORNING, JUNE 24, 1844

4:30 a.m. Brothers Grant and Turley arrive with a message from Governor Ford. They warn Joseph not to go to Carthage and of the Governor's animosity and the dangers, but Joseph refuses to listen. [77]

6:00 a.m. About to depart from Nauvoo, Hyrum reads from Ether 12, including: "I prayed unto the Lord that he would give unto the Gentiles grace, that they might have charity. And it came to pass that the Lord said unto me, if they have not charity, it mattereth not unto thee, thou hast been faithful."

6:30 a.m. Joseph rides out of Nauvoo bound for Carthage with his co-defendants, Hyrum Smith, Samuel Bennett, John Taylor, William W. Phelps, John P. Greene, Stephen C. Perry, Jonathan Dunham, Dimick B. Huntington, Stephen Markham, William W. Edwards, Jonathan Holmes, Jesse P. Harmon, John Lytle, Joseph W. Coolidge, David Harvey Redfield, Orrin Porter Rockwell, and Levi Richards. Several others accompany the Prophet, including Willard Richards, Dan Jones, Henry G. Sherwood, Alfred Randall, James Davis, Cyrus H. Wheelock, A. C. Hodge, and several other brethren, together with James W. Woods, as counsel accompanying them.

---

[77] Corbett, 389

Hundreds beg Joseph not to go. "No," Joseph says to the people around him, "it is better for your brother, Joseph, to die for his brothers and sisters, for I am willing to die for them. My work is finished; the Lord has heard my prayers and has promised that we shall have rest from such cruelties before long, and so do not prevent me with your tears from going to bliss."[78]

Joseph's mother, Lucy Mack Smith, entreats, "My Son, my Son, can you leave me without promising to return? Some forty times before have I seen you from me dragged, but never before without saying you would return; what say you now my Son?"[79]

Joseph embraces his children, wife, and mother.

7:00 a.m. Joseph pauses at the temple, then looks upon it, then the city, and says, "Oh, city, once the most blessed, but now the most pitiful in sadness. This is the kindest and most godly people and most beloved by Heaven of all the world. Oh, if only they knew what awaits them."[80]

9:50 a.m. Joseph and his fellow riders arrive at Fellows' farm, four miles west of Carthage. There they meet Captain Dunn and his sixty mounted militia. He says to those who accompany him: "Dear Brethren, you cannot come with me any further; retreat for your lives and let them pour out all their vengeance upon my head; I shall suffer it, for I am going like a lamb to the slaughter with a conscience void of offense toward God and men."[81]

Captain Dunn and his men surround Joseph and take him into custody. Joseph asks them for a favor: that they defend his life, "so that I shall have a fair trial before the court of my country. I do not fear the consequence, be it even the most horrible death, as much as I fear dying with a blemish on my character, or for the world to disgrace the religion, which I profess. Will you promise this?" Captain Dunn, impressed by this request, promises to protect him, as do his men. Dunn shows them a

---

[78] Jones 85

[79] Jones 96

[80] Jones 86

[81] Jones 80; AWM 145

letter from Governor Ford demanding the people of Nauvoo to surrender their arms. All the men return with Captain Dunn to Nauvoo to comply with the order.[82]

Of all the long days of my life, Major, that day we rode to Carthage was the longest.

It began with a hundred horses all standin' in the street in front of the Mansion House.

I didn't sleep much, as there was comin' and goin' all night long. I remember in the dark of night, under the stars, two riders rode up to the stable—messengers for Brother Joe. I heared 'em say so to Lorin Walker. Their horses was 'bout dead from ridin'. I heared they had ridden in the dark all the way from Carthage with papers from the Gov'nor.

Well, Lorin was up and with me right early in the stable, before the sun even peeped over the hills, pullin' me out of my box and fixin' me up in my saddle and bridle for ridin'. At first I stepped right out, not knowin' what was in store or about all the miles between me and my next sleep. I was all frisky and excited, thinkin' at that time that Brother Joe and me would be headin' out for the Rocky Mountains. Or, if it warn't the Rocky Mountains, I was at least hopin' that Brother Joe and me would be havin' a fine ride out to the farm and back, or at least up to the white walls on the hill to see how the men was liftin' the big rocks up on the walls and a-poundin' and clinkin' away with their hammers.

Lorin tied me up to the hitchin' rail out front of the Mansion House. It was real peaceful. I heared the sound of the birds up in the trees. Then I waited a spell in the street as

---

[82] Jones 86-87

the early light crept underneath the trees real peaceful like. Then the horses started arrivin' in the street. First off there was Sam bringin' Hyrum. Sam nickered at me, all friendly like, and then the others started arrivin'. There was Lady Gray bringin' John Taylor, and Saucepan carryin' the Big Doctor. They was hitched up while their riders went into the Mansion, and we jest stood together, companionable like, since I knowed these horses for so many years. Then Porter rode up on Jack. Jack's saddlebags was slippin' off, so Porter settled 'em all in and then went inside the Mansion. Then a whole herd of horses come up with riders, includin' Markham ridin' on Pickwick and Blue Dan ridin' on Tramp. Then last of all the man with the big voice they call Squire Woods. I could hear his voice a-talkin' right out loud as he come down Main Street on his stout seal brown mare called Gypsy Queen.

Little Joseph come out of the house to watch the horses all comin' in, and he come over and stood by me, jest strokin' my neck and pattin' my nose. Before you knowed it, there was more men in the street than horseshoes hangin' in a blacksmith shop. And not jest men, but ladies and children, too. It was a reg'lar meetin'. A lot come in on horseback, but others come walkin' up and stood in the street, under the trees, around the house while it was jest gettin' light outside.

After a bit, the whole bunch come outside—Brother Joe, Lady Emma, Julia, the little boys, all the people from 'round about the house, 'cludin' all the hotel helpers and the guests. Lorin and Lovina was there, standin' side by side, and all of Hyrum's family, and even Old Lady Lucy from next door. I see'd how she come amblin' 'round the corner of the

Mansion real slow like with one of her daughters—it was Lady Katherine. Lady Lucy was jest leanin' on her stick. She looked right small in the middle of so many big men. There was a good deal of talkin', and it looked like some serious discussion involvin' Brother Joe. I heared one of the men suddenly call out to him from the crowd, sayin', "Don't go!" then a bunch of others picked that up and called out, "Don't go, Joseph! Don't go!" over and over in one big chorus.

Brother Joe was a-standin' on the porch with Lady Emma on one side of him, Julia on the other, and the little boys in his arms. Little Joseph left me and run up to hug his father, and there was water a plenty on everyone's faces. Then Brother Joe looked up and see'd Old Lady Lucy, and then he goes to her and takes her in his arms, he so big and she so stooped over and tiny. There was a kinda hush amongst the crowd, and I heared Old Lady Lucy say in her weak and raspy voice, "My son, my son!" and he hugged her again, but she kinda pushed him up and off and said, "Can you leave me without promising to come back?" But Brother Joe was real quiet and didn't say nothin'. Then the old lady said, "Forty times I have seen you dragged away from me, and every time you promised me you would come back. Now, what say you, my son?"

And Brother Joe was as silent as midnight, and no one said a word. There was no sound, 'cept the snuffle of a horse here or there or the jingle of a bridle.

Finally, Brother Joe said to his mother, "No. I can't promise that I'll return. It is better for your son to die for his brothers and sisters, for I am willing to die for them. My work is finished!"

And then I heared a bunch of folks shoutin', "No! No!" or "Don't go!"

But presently, jest as the sun was a-gettin' fixed to peek up over the land, Brother Joe kissed Lady Emma one more time, put down his little boys and come over to me, and mounted up in the saddle. There was a big hush while he settled down in the saddle, and then we rode out into the middle of Main Street. Then, 'bout twenty, twenty-five others mounted up on their horses and gathered around us in the street. Then Brother Joe clicked at me, and we headed on up Main Street, with the whole passel of horses and men and women and children jest follerin' us up the street a long, long ways.

We left behind most of the crowd of people in Lower Nauvoo as we climbed the big hill past the trees and on up to the place of the white walls, and we slowed down a bit as we went past. Brother Joe jest rested in the saddle for a spell. I guess he wanted to look at the walls. There warn't any workmen that time of the mornin', but Brother Joe seemed to look it over real good.

Then Brother Joe turned around in the saddle, kinda lookin' down over the rest of the city below the hill, with the Big River spreadin' out in the mornin' light beyond. He jest sat there for a minute, and then real quiet like he said, "Oh, city!" Well, I didn't know who he was talkin' to, but then he said, "You are the kindest people in all the world. Oh, if only you knew what awaits you."

All the other horses and riders was jest watchin' and listenin'. Then Brother Joe kicked me up a bit, and we rode on out of the city.

We passed the crossroads and the Cemetery and Brother Joe's farm and then headed down the Carthage Road. There was Legion fellers here and there along the way, and they all snapped their hands right up to their caps as we passed by.

By this time the sun was out proper, and we made real good time on the Carthage Road, it bein' dry and clear. And for a bit it felt like old times, havin' a rare old gallop out in the open. Brother Joe rode me out in front, with Brother Hyrum on Sam at our side and all the other men follerin' us behind.

At first, I was havin' a grand ride, out like old times with Brother Joe and the Brethren he loves to be with, kickin' up my heels along a clean stretch of road. I always love to be out ridin' in the cool of the mornin' in the summertime, before the sun creeps up and it gets to be a real hot day. Robins and meadowlarks singin', sparrows flitterin' in the branches overhead, dew still shinin' on the grass, Brother Joe talkin' quietly now and again from the saddle to the other men, hooves drivin' steady on a good, dry road, easy goin', other horses around. That's what I love, and that's the way it began on the Carthage Road this mornin'. But there warn't no laughin', like Brother Joe usually does. Brother Joe was mostly quiet, I guess filled with his own thoughts, and the other riders was mighty quiet as well. There warn't no skylarkin' around or jibin' or jestin', jest steady ridin'.

Usually when we is out for a run, Brother Joe is in the best of spirits. I can feel it through his legs, almost like happiness is flowin' through him from his heels all the way up through his body to his hands on my reins, and his cheerful voice always a-callin' to me or cluckin' at me or soothin' me with his talk. But today, even though we was ridin' through a beautiful prairie, with the flowers bloomin' on the roadside and the birds flyin' here and there and the sunshine warm in our faces, I could tell by Brother Joe's every movement that he was right sad. And with each passin' mile he got sadder and sadder, I could feel it. I got the feelin' Brother Joe'd ruther be anywhere on earth but out ridin' with me and the Brethren on the Carthage Road.

So we jest rode most of the mornin'. And then after eighteen, twenty mile we come up towards Fellows' farm, jest a ways out of Carthage. I knowed we was close, jest beyond the turn in the road. One side of the road was prairie and the other open woodland. It's a real fine house, the Fellows' place, with a line of trees along the road and the air always smellin' of sweet grass and lilacs. There's a real nice pasture and clean water. Brother Joe and me stopped there many a time before, so I knowed it, as there are brethren and sisters from the Church livin' there.

As we got close up on Fellows' place, I suddenly felt uneasy, smellin' that there was lots of horses up ahead, and then I heared the poundin' of hooves on the road, felt it through my feet and legs, so I pointed my ears in the direction of Carthage, and then I heared 'em, clear as clear, though neither Brother Joe nor none of our fellers ridin' had heared anythin' yet. But I heared it, and Sam heared it, and I suspect most of our horses knowed it, too. But presently Brother Joe could tell that I was hesitant, and he asked me, "What's wrong, Old Charlie?"

Then suddenly, jest 'round the corner of the road we see'd a big bunch of cavalry soldiers ridin' hell-bent toward us, all fixed up in their uniforms and guns in their hands. They sure enough looked like they meant business! Two or three of the cavalrymen called out, and they started to gallop up towards us. Brother Joe pulled me right up, and our bunch of horses all stopped, Sam and Jack and Tramp and Pickwick and all the rest with their riders. Our horses was a bit skittish with all the cavalry ridin' pell-mell toward us, and some of 'em kinda reared up and pulled in the harness.

One of the cavalry horses neighed to ours, the kinda neigh a horse gives to a stranger, like he was sayin', "Who the heck are you?" and I could tell it was from a stallion as he put a kinda grunt in at the end. As they rode closer, Brother Hyrum's Sam answered him with his own neigh, like, "This is our road, and who are you?"

And then Brother Joe stood up in the saddle and turned, so all his fellers could hear, and he called to 'em real urgent like. I didn't understand everythin' he said, but he told 'em, "Go back, Brethren! Go back!"

"No," said Hyrum.

"Go back, Hyrum," said Brother Joe. "All of you go back. You can't come with me any further. I'll meet the soldiers alone, and I'll die if I have to. But you go back."

But none of the riders went back, like Brother Joe told 'em to, but they jest pulled right up and around Brother Joe and me, as if to protect us from the cavalry riders. One or two of our boys pulled out their rifles, and Porter Rockwell on his scrappy little Jack rode right out in the front, facin' the cavalry, and whipped out two horse pistols from his belt, as if he was ready to fight the world.

Lickety-split the cavalry horses was all around us. They formed up into two groups and circled us around, the first goin' one way around us, and the second goin' the other way, so we was shut up in two movin' circles of horses.

There was some mighty fine horses in the bunch, maybe sixty or seventy of 'em. One of the cavalry fellers was carryin' a scrap of colored cloth on a pole, and right behind him was a real impressive lookin' feller ridin' on a gold champagne stallion. He was wearin' a big officer's hat with a feather in it, so I reckoned he was in charge of the whole bunch. He had his sword out in his hand, and all of his men had their guns ready, so I reckon Brother Porter and Jack warn't much of a match agin' 'em all with his two horse pistols.

The officer in the hat then come ridin' right up to Brother Joe and me with one or two others, while the others stood in a circle around us, right there on the road. Brother Joe said, "Howdy," to him, and the officer said his name is Captain Dunn, and he saluted Brother Joe real smartly and respectful like. But then he said, "I have orders to arrest you." I could see that the gold stallion he was ridin' had right powerful legs and a spirit and life in his step.

Then Brother Joe said, "Will you kill me or defend me?"

I could tell that this kinda s'prised Captain Dunn. Then Brother Joe said, "Will you defend me so that I can have a fair trial? Even if I die in the end? Will you promise me, Captain?"

And Captain Dunn saluted real smartly, and he said, "I promise. I'll defend you." And then Captain Dunn pulled a piece of paper out of his leather ridin' pouch and said, "This is a letter from Governor Ford," and he handed the letter to Brother Joe, who set atop me readin' it.

"What is it?" Brother Hyrum asked, ridin' closer on Sam.

"It's an order for the Nauvoo Legion to surrender all of their guns to me," says Captain Dunn.

The Brethren with Brother Joe talked amongst theirselves all at once. I could tell they warn't happy.

"They'll never give up their guns," says Porter, kinda nudgin' Jack up close to Brother Joe and Captain Dunn. "Not without a fight. And then you'll have more fight than you want, Captain! I promise you that."

Captain Dunn's horse snorted at Jack in challenge as he kinda bumped up agin' him. "Steady, Caesar," said Captain Dunn. Captain Dunn was a whole lot higher than Porter, him bein' a short man and ridin' Jack, who is jest a scrappy little horse. "Steady."

"I think he's right," said Brother Joe. "The Legion won't give you their guns, though the President of the whole United States orders it."

"Then we'll take 'em," said one of the cavalrymen out loud, but Captain Dunn held his hand out toward his feller, like he wanted him to pipe down.

So we sat there for a minute, and then Brother Joe and Captain Dunn rode off the side of the road for a stretch, away from Brother Joe's fellers and Captain Dunn's cavalrymen, and they started talkin' jest the two of 'em, while all the others waited. Captain Dunn, turns out, was a right friendly feller, and I could tell he took a likin' to Brother Joe. He warn't 'bout to shoot Brother Joe and the Brethren after all. Brother Joe and the Captain decided to ride on down around the bend a short ways to the Fellows' place to talk some more. We pulled up and s'prised the family, and all hundred horses was let out to graze on the prairie grass while Brother Joe and Captain Dunn dismounted and talked some more.

I watched Brother Joe and Hyrum under the trees by the house, havin' a drink of cider and talkin' with Captain Dunn. All of the cavalrymen was restin' on one side of the house and Brother Joe's fellers on the other. But after talkin' and restin' a half hour, Brother Joe gave the signal to the Brethren, and everyone mounted back up. Captain Dunn called out to his fellers, too, and they all mounted up.

Then we headed back up the Carthage Road toward Nauvoo, with Captain Dunn and his whole durned cavalry follerin' right along with us.

MONDAY AFTERNOON, JUNE 24, 1844

BROTHER JOE RIDES OLD CHARLIE BACK TO NAUVOO –
THE LEGION GIVES UP ITS GUNS TO CAPTAIN DUNN –
BROTHER JOE SAYS GOODBYE TO HIS FAMILY A SECOND
TIME AT THE MANSION HOUSE

CARTHAGE TO NAUVOO – MONDAY AFTERNOON, JUNE 24, 1844

2:30 p.m. Joseph and his fellow defendants arrive back in Nauvoo with Captain Dunn and his cavalrymen as escorts.

3:00 p.m. The officers of the Nauvoo Legion and the enlisted men are unwilling to surrender their guns. Joseph spends the afternoon persuading them to comply with the State's order.

6:00 p.m. The order to surrender all arms is complied with at Joseph's insistence. Joseph says to the officers of the Legion, "These men are too good, too quiet and law abiding for this rough generation." Then to the privates he says, "Boys, don't be cast down, I will come back again—as soon as I can."[83]

The Nauvoo Legion is disbanded.

Early evening: The Prophet rides twice to his house to bid farewell to his family. Three times he says, "Emma, can you train my sons to walk in their father's footsteps?" Three times Emma responds, "Oh, Joseph, you are coming back."[84]

---

[83] AWM 145-146

[84] Edwin Rushton journals, n.d., p 3 (copy in possession of author)

Joseph gives Emma a final blessing before departing the Mansion House for the last time. "Thou shalt bear a child," he tells her in the blessing, "and though he should be incarcerated in solid rock, yet shall he come out and make his mark in the world. Call his name David." Before Joseph rides off, Emma says to him, "Suppose it be a girl?" Joseph answers, "Call him David!" and then rides off.[85]

On their way out of town, Joseph repeatedly looks upon his own farm and, when noticed by others, says, "If some of you had got such a farm and knew you would not see it any more, you would want to take a good look at it for the last time."[86]

You know, Major, that Carthage lies more than twenty mile from Nauvoo, and so by the time we rode back to Nauvoo, we had ridden near forty, fifty mile for the day. Forty mile ain't nothin' for me, but I could tell it was a lot for some of the other horses, Lady Gray in particular. She was blowin' hard when we rode into town.

Brother Joe and me rode the whole way 'longside of Captain Dunn and Caesar, and the two men talked back and forth all afternoon. Captain Dunn seemed right pleased to make Brother Joe's acquaintance, and he asked him plenty about his life. For a while it seemed that Captain Dunn had taken a shine to Brother Joe. By the time we reached Nauvoo, their speech was right friendly.

It was afternoon before we 'proached the city. There was lots of s'prised looks on the faces of the Legion fellers as we passed 'em on the road. I could see to the top of the little hill

---

[85] Edmund C. Briggs, "Autobiographic Sketch and Incidents in the Early History of the Reorganization, in *The Saints Herald* (Independence Missouri, May 1, 1901) p. 48.

[86] HC 6:558

where the cannon was set up that General Dunham had out his two bottles and was lookin' at us. He come right down from the hill and talked some with Brother Joe and Captain Dunn then mounted up on Rambler and rode with us the rest of the way.

We first stopped at the Legion armory up on the hill, where the guns is all kept. I understood that Captain Dunn was goin' to take away all the guns what belonged to the Legion and haul 'em away in wagons.

Captain Dunn left some of his cavalrymen up there by the armory, and then we all rode down into the city to the Masonic Lodge, where Brother Joe sent out word for all the Legion fellers to bring their guns.

Some wagons was brung around and set up in the street. Our Legion fellers was s'posed to bring their muskets and rifles and pistols and swords and set 'em in the wagons. There was a cavalryman settin' at a table by the wagon with a stack of papers.

Pretty soon a whole bunch of Legion fellers filled the streets, and they lined up from the Masonic Lodge pert' near all the way up to the clump of trees where the preachin' happens. They all had their rifles and muskets and pistols and swords in their hands, but there warn't none who come up to the wagon and gave 'em up. So finally, Brother Joe stood up in one of the wagons and started to talk to the men. As far as I could tell, he told 'em that we got to give up our guns, otherwise the Gov'nor would come in and burn down the city.

I see'd Old Man Lott, the head of Brother Joe's bodyguard. He was standin' in the street and finally walked up to the wagon and laid his musket, pistols, and sword inside. He was the first one. The cavalryman with the papers asked Old Man Lott's name, and then made some scratches on his paper. Then, one after another, all the other Legion fellers did the same.

Brother Joe turned to Captain Dunn and said, "My men are too good for this rough generation."

Then Brother Joe and me rode up and down the street, a-talkin' to the reg'lar Legion fellers who was lined up to lay their guns in the wagon. Brother Joe talked to lots of 'em. I could tell they was sad. Then Brother Joe kinda called out to 'em, sayin', "Boys! Don't be cast down. I'll come back again, as soon as I can!"

After that, Brother Joe asked Captain Dunn if he could ride down to his house to see his family. Captain Dunn said he would ride with him, and so we rode down Main Street together. The streets was filled with people, and everyone took off their hats as Brother Joe and me passed by.

We rode right up to the Mansion House and stopped out front. Brother Joe climbed down from the saddle. The front door opened right up, and Little Joseph come runnin' down the path with Julia and Fred and Alex follerin' right behind. Lady Emma come out and jest stood in the open door, her face all wet for some reason or another. I could see that she was movin' real slow like, and she had both of her hands restin' softly on her stomach.

Captain Dunn dismounted from Caesar and took off his cavalry hat with the feather in it and jest watched Brother Joe huggin' his children and then Lady Emma. Brother Joe turned back from the doorway and called to Captain Dunn to come in. That left me tied up out front with Caesar.

By this time Lorin Walker had run around the corner, and he led me off to the stable, where he took off my saddle and gave me a nice rubdown, which felt mighty good after a forty-mile ride. He then gave me water and feed and let me out into the pasture. I went over to my spot to watch things and see'd him bringin' Captain Dunn's Caesar around for a feed and rest of his own.

I figured we was home and for good, but after a short while, Lorin come out and fetched me, put a new blanket on my back and saddled me up one more time. Captain Dunn come over from the Mansion and saddled up Caesar. After I was all ready to go, Lorin led me around to the front of the Mansion House again.

There was all the horses I had ridden with all day—Sam and Jack and Pickwick and Saucepan and Tramp and all the rest—and all of Captain Dunn's cavalry, jest a-waitin' in the street. John Taylor was ridin' on Lady Gray, and she looked ready for the pasture and a long sleep. We all jest stood in the street in the front of the Mansion House.

Finally, the front door opened and Brother Joe stepped outside, with his four young'uns holdin' his hands and follerin' along. I see'd that Lady Emma was seated at the window facin' Main Street. She had the curtain parted with her hand and watched from inside as Brother Joe kissed his children then mounted up on me.

I was 'spectin' to ride out straightaway, but Brother Joe jest sat in the saddle for a time, while all the horses and riders stood around waitin'. We was waitin'. We was waitin' for somethin' to happen before we rode out, I knowed that much. Brother Joe seemed to be deep in thought about somethin'. He kept tap-tappin' one of his hands agin' his leg, but no one else could see, and I was the only one who knowed.

Finally, Brother Joe dismounted and walked right on back into the Mansion House, then come back out and looked all around, like he had forgotten somethin'. Then he mounted right back up, but we didn't move. I could feel that he was thinkin' about somethin' and seemed perplexed somehow. I was wonderin' when we would ride off, when he got down out of the saddle once more and went back into the house. I see'd through the open curtain that he walked right up to Lady Emma, who was settin' in a chair by the window. Then I see'd how Brother Joe laid his two hands on Lady Emma's head and started to speak to her real softly. Finally, Brother Joe come outside a third time and mounted up in the saddle. I looked over, and Lady Emma was standin' in the doorway again, her hand restin' on her stomach.

"Suppose it be a girl?" said Lady Emma.

"Call him David!" said Brother Joe. Then we rode off.

It was gettin' on toward evenin' by the time we rode out of Nauvoo, a hundred horses or there'bouts turnin' at the crossroads down the Carthage Road. As we rode past Brother Joe's farm, he slowed me down and kept a-lookin' at his fields and his fences. The others slowed down, too, and soon we was walkin' slowly along the road. Brother Joe turned to the other riders and said, "If you had a farm like that and you knew you wouldn't see it again, you would want to take a good look at it for the last time."

Brother Joe then nudged me with his boots and shook the reins, and we started off toward Carthage.

MONDAY EVENING, JUNE 24, 1844

NAUVOO TO CARTHAGE – MONDAY NIGHT, JUNE 24, 1844

9:00 p.m. Joseph and his party return to Fellows' farm, dismount from their horses, and eat. Then Captain Dunn and his troops escort Joseph, Hyrum, and the other prisoners to Carthage.

11:55 p.m. They arrive at Carthage. Hundreds of hostile militiamen surround and throw insults and threats at the prisoners. Governor Ford pacifies the troops by promising them a closer view of Joseph the next day. The troops yell, "Hurrah for Tom Ford."[87]

Joseph and his companions spend the night at the Hamilton Hotel. Many of the apostate Mormons also stay at the same hotel that night.[88]

So we kept on ridin', goin' back again to Carthage. Seems like all of the ridin' and goin's on have been in the pitch black of nighttime, and all of the days, quiet and somber like. Ridin' through the night is not the best for a horse on a strange road, as there are holes to step in and roots to trip over. But with Brother Joe ridin', I still feel a peaceful strength and am willin' to go wherever he needs to go.

On our second journey to Carthage, we stopped at a little wayside by some trees. Captain Dunn and his horse

---

[87] HC 7:83
[88] HC 6:560

soldiers was ridin' with us. Here we met some messengers on horses, comin' from the way towards Carthage. They rode up and spoke low to Brother Joe and Hyrum. I heared some of their words. "You'll be killed," one man whispered to Hyrum. "You'll both be killed, as sure as you get to Carthage." He then pointed to the soldiers on horses around us. "Those are the boys that will settle you up, Hyrum. Those are the men who will kill you. Don't go another foot, or they say they will kill you if you go to Carthage."

We rode on and headed for Carthage the second time. We rode on in the darkness without so much as a light to see by. Every horse jest follered along the sound of hooves ahead. The whole way Brother Joe was real quiet, which was not like him, as he was always talkin' to this man or that, tellin' his jokes, or makin' 'em feel good about theirselves. But the closer we got to Carthage, the quieter Brother Joe become.

But Brother Joe did talk to me a bit, as we rode. "Good boy, Charlie," he kept sayin'. "Good boy! Good boy! It's all goin' to be good, old son! Steady on! Steady on!" and he patted my neck a good bit, and it made me feel right safe and under control to be ridden by him, 'specially with the darkness and the feelin' that we was enterin' into somethin' we had never seen before.

Then we come into the town. I could hear the hubbub from the soldiers a mile out. It sounded like ten thousand man voices, all yellin' and screechin' and callin' at once, and here and there I could hear the muskets goin' off. From the sound, I could tell where the men with the guns was and where the bangs was. Sam was right steady, but a few of the younger horses, Lady Gray in particular, was right skittish by all the noise. She screamed some jest out of fear.

Then we rode into the town proper, and you should'a seen the lights. A hundred men carryin' torches and then runnin' 'longside us as we moved from street to street. I kept turnin' my head when I see'd more and more men runnin' beside me and Brother Joe. They was laughin' and hootin' and hollerin' like tomcats in the nighttime. The soldier men—you should'a jest seen 'em comin' on. More soldiers that you would think there was in the world. They jest kept comin' down the side streets, a-runnin' and a-jumpin' along like leaves blowin' in the wind.

From the way Brother Joe held hisself in the saddle, kinda quiet and rigid like, I could tell that he was wonderin' how it was goin' to turn out. The whole feel of him was tense—his knees, his hands, his seat. I could tell that, though I'm sure no one else ridin' in with us knowed it, either man or horse. I knowed that Brother Joe was worried about what was goin' to happen, and that made me worried.

Then we rode into the main part of town to the big hotel, where Brother Joe had been with me a time or two. It's called Hamilton's, and it's a proper hotel with plenty of space for men and horses. Well, in front of Hamilton's the street was jam packed with men. There was a good bit of scufflin', too, jest as we pulled up. A big circle of soldiers stood all around us, and they was yellin' and shoutin' 'til I could hardly hear nothin'. I pulled up and stood pantin', tuckered out through and through. I stood there, hangin' my head down, jest like an old donkey under two grain sacks.

Brother Joe dismounted, patted my neck and spoke to me real soft like. He said, "Easy Charlie, easy! Been a long day. Soon be done now, old soldier. We'll rest a spell now, you and me together."

Brother Joe stood a minute holdin' me by the reins. Hyrum and Blue Dan and Porter and Markham and all the rest had dismounted theirselves. Then a young feller come up and told Brother Joe his name was Will. Said he was the son of the innkeeper and would be pleased to take charge of the horses.

Brother Joe patted my neck one more time and handed the reins over to Will. Hyrum did the same, handin' over Sam's reins to the young feller. Then Will walked us across the street to a stable, pullin' Sam and me right along.

I turned and looked back at Brother Joe. He and Hyrum walked past all the shoutin' soldiers and went into the hotel.

TUESDAY, JUNE 25, 1844

Old Charlie waits in the Hamilton House stable with the other horses – he sees Robert Foster's and the Governor's horses – Porter Rockwell rides home with messages – soldiers come in and out of the stable all day and night

CARTHAGE, ILLINOIS – TUESDAY, JUNE 25, 1844

8:00 a.m. Joseph and Hyrum are arrested for treason at the Hamilton House Hotel in Carthage.

8:30 a.m. Outside the hotel, Governor Ford musters the troops, mounts an old table, and incites the crowd with inflammatory language.[89]

9:15 a.m. Ford asks Joseph to present himself before the troops. Joseph asks for a private interview. Ford denies it, while looking down at his shoes ashamedly.[90]

9:53 a.m. Ford makes Joseph and his comrades pass through the midst of the troops, acceding to the request of the soldiers to see Joseph. He introduces them to the troops as "Generals," which crazes them. Joseph and Hyrum walk through the midst, receiving insults the entire time.[91]

---

[89] William R. Hamilton letter, December 24, 1902, copy in possession of author (hereafter "1902 Hamilton Letter")

[90] *Deseret News*, No. 35, November 4, 1857, p. 274; HC 7:83-84

[91] Jones 87; "To Mrs. Emma Smith," in *Times and Seasons* (July 1, 1844)

10:30 a.m.   The Carthage Greys clamor for the blood of Joseph and Hyrum Smith. Ford appeases them by promising them "full satisfaction."[92]

11:15 a.m.   Troops from the nearby town of Warsaw arrive outside of Carthage.[93]

12:48 p.m.   Joseph is told that the Higbees, Laws, Fosters, and other apostates are returning to Nauvoo to plunder the city. Joseph asks the Governor, who happens to pass by, to please send a guard to protect the city.

2:30 p.m.   Ford sends a company of men to protect Nauvoo and informs Joseph. Joseph writes a letter to Emma, speaking respectfully of the Governor: "I think the Governor has and will succeed in enforcing the laws. I do hope the people of Nauvoo will continue pacific and prayerful."[94]

3:00 p.m.   Militia officers have an interview with Joseph in the Hamilton Hotel. Joseph asks them if he appears to be the "desperate character" his enemies have portrayed him to be. "No, sir, your appearance would indicate the very contrary, General Smith; but we cannot see what is in your heart, neither can we tell what are your intentions." "Very true, gentlemen," Joseph answers, "you cannot see what is in my heart, and you are therefore unable to judge me or my intentions; but I can see what is in your hearts, and will tell you what I see. I can see that you thirst for blood, and nothing but my blood will satisfy you. . . . and inasmuch as you and the people thirst for blood, I prophesy, in the name of the Lord, that you shall witness scenes of blood and sorrow to your entire satisfaction. Your souls shall be perfectly satiated with blood, and many of you who are now present shall have an opportunity to face the cannon's mouth from sources you think not of."[95]

---

[92] HC 6:564

[93] HC 6:564-66

[94] HC 6:564-65

[95] HC 6:566

3:48 p.m. Joseph is informed that the apostates were overheard saying, "there was nothing against these men; the law could not reach them but powder and ball would."

4:00 p.m. Porter Rockwell, in a scuffle with Francis Higbee at the Hamilton House, discovers papers that drop from Higbee's hat which tell of a mob that intends to attack Joseph that evening.[96] Porter Rockwell returns to Nauvoo with messages. Joseph orders him not to come back to Carthage, but to stay in Nauvoo and not let himself be taken alive by anyone. [97]

4:00 p.m. Joseph and Hyrum and thirteen other men are taken before justice of the peace Robert F. Smith on charges of riot when destroying the press. Prosecution moves for an adjournment for the day. Defense objects. After much legal wrangling, the defense decides to let the matter drop and to bind it over to the next day.[98]

6:30 p.m. Wilson Law declares in court that he once heard Joseph preach a sermon from Daniel 2:44, saying that the kingdom referred to was already set up and that he was the king over it. Based upon this sermon, treason charges are written up against Joseph.

8:00 p.m. A false mittimus is produced, requiring Joseph and Hyrum to go to jail. John Taylor hears of it and immediately informs Ford that the charge is illegal, that Joseph and Hyrum are innocent. Ford tells him that it is best to let the law take its course. John Taylor responds that they had satisfied the exigencies of the law and could not reasonably satisfy the prejudices of the people. Ford says he does not have the power to interfere. John Taylor lets him know that he has given his word to protect them, but that now it is clear that his "protection availed very little."[99]

---

[96] "To Mrs. Emma Smith" in *Times and Seasons* (July 1, 1844)

[97] HC 6:564-65

[98] Statements of H.T. Reid and James Woods in "State of Illinois," *Times and Seasons* (July 1, 1844)

[99] "State of Illinois," *Times and Seasons* (July 1, 1844)

Joseph and his companions protest against such illegal proceedings and refuse to go until they hear from Ford. When Robert F. Smith, the justice of the peace who made the false mittimus, appeals to Ford as to what he should do, Ford responds, "You have the Carthage Greys at your command."

10:00 p.m. Joseph and Hyrum are dragged from the courthouse to the jail, enduring violent breathings out against them by many men, and Dan Jones parries the bayonets that are stuck out to stab Joseph.[100]

They spend the night in a room ten feet square, speaking of the "secret of godliness." Both Hyrum and Joseph are cheerful, but predict their deaths.[101]

The last words from Joseph before the prisoners fall asleep in the jail are, "For the most intelligent dream tonight brethren."[102]

The night after we rode into Carthage I couldn't sleep much, Major. That's the funny thing. I was practically a dead horse after ridin' the whole dad-burned way from Nauvoo to Carthage three times that day. I figure we rode sixty, seventy mile for the day. I tell you, I was a dead horse what couldn't sleep proper for a long time. No way. I was that strung out for all the thinkin'.

Sam and me and all the other Nauvoo horses was fixed up nice and proper in the big stable across the street from Hamilton's in Carthage. Will and Dallas, two young fellers what lives in the hotel, got us all situated proper. Blue Dan and Markham helped 'em bring over all the Nauvoo horses from off the street.

------

[100] To Mrs. Emma Smith" in *Times and Seasons* (July 1, 1844)
[101] Jones 88
[102] Jones 98

It was a big stable with a low ceilin', and they set us up in a couple of big, loose boxes. There was 'bout twenty or twenty-five of us horses from Nauvoo, all stuck together. Me and Sam was took care of first off. Will got our saddles and bridles off and hung em' up and set out some fresh water and feed. Then Blue Dan and Markham brung in the rest. Lady Gray? She had ridden herself to a frazzle and was plumb tuckered out, let me tell you. When we rode into Carthage, she seemed right skeered by all the shenanigans of the soldiers out in the streets—shoutin' and shootin' off guns and whatnot. She jest stood there a-tremblin' for a spell while Blue Dan got her unsaddled. The rest of the horses was jest 'bout done in too—Saucepan and Jack and Pickwick and Tramp and all the rest of 'em. General Dunham's big Rambler was there, too. Took us all a spell to settle down after we was brung in off the street into the stable. We was all short on sleep and stumblin' around on our feet. We was packed in all snug in the box, right up agin' each other, but we didn't care none—we was that tired.

While the young fellers Will and Dallas was settin' out feed, Will was talkin' with Blue Dan and promisin' to keep a careful eye out for the horses of all the fellers from Nauvoo. There was a lantern hangin' from a rafter so Will and the men could see their work. Dallas was a friendly young feller, but kinda quiet. I reckon Dallas was not much older than Little Joseph and Hyrum's boy John. The other feller, Will, was older. Will sure enough seemed to know horses. He was also a talker and kept up a steady stream of speakin' to Blue Dan as they hung up our saddles and rubbed us down and set out feed.

"You sure our horses will be all right?" Markham asked Will as they worked.

"Yes sir," said Will. Then he told 'em that he and Dallas was the sons of Old Hamilton, what owns the hotel, and that it's his proper job to look out after the horses. "We lock 'em all up safe every night, then in the mornin' we let 'em out into the stable yard. During the daytime they is out in the yard where Pa and I can keep a close eye on 'em all, and then every night we lock 'em safe and sound back up inside."

"We're used to takin' care of valuable horses here," Will told Markham. "For instance, that's Governor Ford's horse in the next box. His name is Napoleon. He's the finest trotter in the state, they say." I see'd that Will was pointin' over yonder in the stable. I looked jest over the railin' and see'd a bunch of other horses, standin' quiet. The one Will pointed to was a mighty fine-looking dark sorrel, and he flicked his ears when he heared Will say his name, "Napoleon." That was the Gov'nor's very own horse.

As I looked the Gov'nor's horse over a little, I was right s'prised to see close by him a chocolate colored mare. Suddenly I recognized her—it was Charity, the one belongin' to Mr. Robert Foster! Can you b'lieve that? Robert Foster's horse was right there in that same stable. I recognized one or two other horses I seen up to Nauvoo, besides Charity. They was mostly horses what belonged to men who had been disagreeable with Brother Joe. I wondered what they was all doin' in the same stable where we ended up.

"How old are you boys?" Blue Dan asked Will when they was 'bout finished settin' us up.

"I'm fifteen," Will told 'em. "And my brother Dallas is eleven. But you don't need to have no worry about that. I'm already a soldier, and I know how to use a gun if I need to. See, I'm already a private in the militia. The Carthage Greys." Then he went on to tell Blue Dan how he knowed how to handle a gun, and how he and his Pa and his brothers wouldn't let nobody mess with the horses in the hotel stable, day or night.

Jest then a skinny lookin' feller come into the stable. "Are you finished, boys?" he called out. "I need you inside."

Will turned to Blue Dan and said, "I'd best be gettin' back to work. That's our Pa." So I understood it was Old Hamilton, what owned the hotel, and he had come over to fetch his boys. Blue Dan and Markham left the stable with Old Hamilton. Will and Dallas hurried up and finished feedin' us, then took their lanterns and closed the big stable doors, and we settled in for a rest.

Like I said, tired as I was, I couldn't sleep at first, even with all the hubbub goin' on outside in the street. It was pitch black inside the stable. It was smellin' like rain a-comin', and all night long from the stable I heared some thunder now and again in the west.

I jest stood awake in our box for a long time in the dark. I ought to have been tired. It had been a long day, but my mind was workin'.

There was lots of noises in the night. There must've been two, three hundred men right outside the stable all a-talkin' at once. It was like the buzz from a hive chock full of angry bees. Every now and then, two or three would drift past the door to the stable, and I could hear their words, like, "Damn Mormons," or "Old Joe Smith," or "We got 'em now." I kept hearin' Brother Joe's name, but thought more about the Tar Men who first attacked Brother Joe at the Johnson farm so many years ago, and not of the Brethren. The Brethren always said, "Brother Joe," with such a voice of kindness and peace, but the soldiers saying "Joe Smith," made my fur stand up and filled me with rage.

After a while the voices settled down, and it got quieter.

I finally drifted off to sleep in the dark.

In the mornin' Will come in all cheerful like to feed the horses and let us out into the yard. His little brother, Dallas, was with him and another feller, who they called Marv. Marv was a right stout young feller, who was chawin' on somethin' in his mouth and spittin' now and then. I sniffed one of the spots where he spat. It was tobacco. I understood from how they talked that Marv was Will and Dallas's older brother. He knowed his way around horses, but he warn't friendly like Will.

Dallas swung out two big stable doors on the side, and the early mornin' light shone right into the stable, kinda hurtin' my eyes for a bit. Marv opened up all the loose boxes where the horses had stood all night. I walked out into the yard with the rest. Will gave me a nice friendly pat on the rump as I passed by.

It felt good to get out of that stable and be out where I could see the sky and feel the breeze. The yard was big, but warn't much to look at. No grass to nibble—jest a big open patch of dirt between the stable and a bunch of other buildin's with a rail fence around it. From the yard I could look over yonder and see the street where we rode in the night before—the street what runs in front of the big hotel.

The sun come up pretty soon, and a few other horses wandered out into the yard. Marv was forkin' feed into a pile agin' the stable, and Will was fillin' up the trough, squeakin' the hand pump up and down. I walked over to the rail where I could see plenty of soldiers walkin' up and down in front of Hamilton's. Will set out good horse feed in the feedin' trough.

Pretty soon the big sorrel trotter, Napoleon, wandered out into the yard and went over to the trough for a drink. I wandered closer for a look-see. He was the gelding what belonged to the Gov'nor. I looked him over nose to hoof and went over to sniff me some. His dark sorrel coat was brushed out fine and silky, and he held hisself kinda superior to the other horses. Well, I guess he was superior, belongin' to the Gov'nor and all.

Then Charity, the sweet mare of Robert Foster's come over and stood next to me. It really fazed me to see her, as I hadn't figured on meetin' her ever again, not never; but here she was. I hadn't see'd her since all the burnin' of the sheets of paper up in Nauvoo. She looked like she had settled right into life in the Hamilton stable. She wanted to groom me, comb out my mane with her teeth, but I didn't let her, as I wanted to see all the horses and s'plore the yard and find the best spots to stand durin' the day.

I figure there was fifty, sixty horses out in the yard that mornin', countin' all of us what had rode in the night down from Nauvoo. Will and his brothers, Marv and Dallas, done finished with the mornin' feedin' and walked back across the street to the hotel. Then things kinda settled down in the stable yard. I found a spot over by the fence where I could see the whole get-up—the stable doors, the yard, and the street in front of the hotel, which Brother Joe called Hamilton's. I couldn't see all the ways down the street either way 'cause of the buildin's standin' there, but off to the west I could see a big buildin' made out of stone with lots of windows, and up top of that buildin' there was a tower with a round roof on top, and at the very top of the roof a long pole with one of them colored cloths flappin' around in the wind.

Blue Dan come over from the hotel early on to check on the Nauvoo horses, but he hurried right back over to the hotel. I was 'spectin' Brother Joe to come over, like he usually does most mornin's, to talk to me or give me somethin' special to eat, but he never come. So, I jest stood in the stable yard and watched. I didn't care much for the hotel and the stable, 'specially compared to Brother Joe's place up in Nauvoo. Hamilton's was big, with big pillars out front and a deep porch with lots of steps leadin' up to the front door and lots of windows. But the stable was small and there warn't enough for a horse to do. In fact, there warn't anything to do, since 'parently Brother Joe warn't goin' out ridin'.

There was more and more noise comin' from the street. Lots of men was walkin' back and forth. A few ladies, too. Then I see'd a big troop of horsemen ride by. Then a drum started beatin' from around the corner, and I heared a bunch of men shout "Hurrah!" and then the men all started clappin'. Pretty soon there were soldiers walkin' up and down on the street by the hundreds, 'til they almost filled up the street. I see'd all sorts of uniforms—some gray, some red, some blue, and some of jest ragtag. I could tell they warn't nothin' compared to the Legion fellers, who was always dressed and polished up fine. But these Carthage fellers looked like they knowed how to fight. I see'd a pair of 'em swingin' their arms at each other and shoutin', 'til one of their officers come up and pushed 'em apart.

Well, by the time the sun had cleared the back of the hotel, the different soldiers had lined up proper with their own fellers—red uniforms in one bunch, and gray in another. The drum was beatin' loud and clear, and then suddenly all the men together started to shoutin' and clamberin' together and raisin' their guns up in the air.

Then out the front door of Hamilton's, I see'd a fine lookin' feller step out. He was wearin' a white suit with a red tie, and he stood on the porch and started wavin' to all the soldiers. Then I heared one of the soldiers nearby shout out, "Three cheers for Governor Ford," and then all the men started yellin', "Hip hip, hurrah!" So I figured the feller in the white suit was the Gov'nor, what had left his horse Napoleon in the stable. Well, you never heared such a noise as the soldiers all gave him after their "Hip hips" and "Hurrahs." The cheerin' went on and on, and then I could hear lots of the men beginnin' to shout out Brother Joe's name, over and over. "Joe Smith! Joe Smith!" they was yellin'. "Bring out Joe Smith!" Finally the Gov'nor held up his hands, and then the soldiers quieted down some, and he shouted out, "You'll see Joe Smith! Jest wait!"

Then the Gov'nor walked down the steps of the hotel and then walked right on down the street to the west, so I couldn't see him no more, but I could hear his voice. By that time, more soldiers was pushin' in from all the side streets, and they all jest kinda follered the Gov'nor off westwards down the street. I heared off in that direction the sound of men a-cheerin' and drums beatin' in the distance. And then it got quieter, and I could hear the Gov'nor's loud voice in the distance, shoutin' out, 'cept I couldn't make out anythin' he was sayin'. This went on for a spell, and then I heared a big "Hurrah! Hurrah!" from all the soldiers yonder, and then a band started playin'.

Pretty soon, I see'd the Gov'nor walk back up to Hamilton's again in his white suit with a passel of other fellers with him. Lots of the soldiers follered him, but most of 'em I could hear still shoutin' and cheerin' off towards the west. The Gov'nor was carryin' his white hat in his hands and speakin' with an officer in a gray uniform. Then they all went into the hotel.

Meantime the band kept a-playin' yonder in the west, and every now and then a troop of horses rode by or a passel of soldiers would march along in the street, and always a feller out in front carryin' one of those colored cloths on a stick. I figure that soldiers can't be soldiers without one of them things bein' carried out front. The colored cloths was jest like the ones the fellers in the Legion carried out front up in Nauvoo, with red and white and blue strips of cloth on it.

One of the bunches of soldiers what marched by was all dressed in gray uniforms, and amongst 'em I see'd Will Hamilton, the young feller what had took care of the horses in the night and in the mornin'. He looked right fine in his uniform, with his musket slung over his shoulder, and though he warn't as tall as all the men, he marched right reg'lar, keepin' up with the bunch.

Then, after a while the Gov'nor come back out of the hotel, and with him was a bunch of militia officers all in gray jackets. Then I see'd comin' out of the door Brother Joe and

Hyrum. When they stepped outside I heared a feller yell, "Hey, it's Joe Smith! It's Joe Smith!" and then all the soldiers come runnin', shoutin' out, "Joe Smith! Joe Smith!" over and over. Pretty soon there was hundreds of soldiers in the street, jumpin' up and down for a look-see. Then there was even more soldiers, all runnin' up and carryin' their guns and wavin' their hats and shoutin' all at once. Brother Joe jest looked all around, but he didn't look skeered none. Fact is, he was mighty calm.

Then the Gov'nor shouted out, "Men, I give you General Joseph Smith and General Hyrum Smith!" and the soldiers jest went crazy. They was shoutin' out, "Damned Mormons!" and "They ain't no Generals!" Brother Joe and Hyrum didn't say nothin', but jest stood there with the Gov'nor. Then the Gov'nor stepped down into the street, kinda pullin' Brother Joe along by the arm and Hyrum with him, and they all walked down the street to the west.

Then for a long spell, I heared the sound of shoutin' and guns shootin' and drums bangin' and now and again the voices of some fellers speakin' out, and all the while I wondered where Brother Joe had got to. I felt strung up tight, and you could feel the same thing all over, in the men out in the street, I mean. The way they stood, the way they moved and held theirselves, in the sounds of their voices. They didn't know it, maybe, but I felt it even in the stable yard. And I felt the tension 'specially in the horses around me.

Well, the mornin' sun got real high in the sky, and I started wonderin' if Brother Joe had off and left Carthage, but then I heared a bunch of soldiers comin' from the west, and soon see'd a bunch of 'em march up to the hotel, and with 'em was Brother Joe and Hyrum. They went back inside and stayed there most of the day.

Meantime, there was horses and riders comin' and goin' from the stable. First off, a bunch of officers rode up in the afternoon and left their horses at the stable. Marv and little Dallas brung 'em over with one of the officers, and I heared him tell the brothers that they was from a big bunch of soldiers jest arrived from Warsaw. After they got their horses all situated, I see'd how the officers went over and stood on the porch of the hotel and talked a while back and forth. Then I see'd how a bunch of other officers joined 'em, wearin' different uniforms, and pretty soon there was a right big group of 'em. Then they all went inside the hotel.

Later on, Will Hamilton come over to the stable yard, still dressed in his gray uniform, and he freshened up the water a bit. I could tell he was right proud to be a soldier. He leaned his musket agin' the wall and set his cap on top of it while he did his chores. 'Bout that time, Porter Rockwell come over and told Will that he was ridin' back up to Nauvoo with messages, so Will helped him saddle up Jack, and Porter rode off. Pretty soon after that, General Dunham and four, five of the other Nauvoo Legion fellers come into the stable yard and fetched their horses and started to saddle 'em up. I stood and watched while General Dunham mounted up on Rambler and waited for the other Nauvoo fellers to finish, then lickety-split, they all rode off. So that was the start of our fellers leavin' Carthage, and the rest of the day I was 'spectin' Brother Joe to show up and fetch me so we could ride on home. But he never did come over.

Pretty soon after Porter rode off, I heared fellers raisin' their voices again, and looked over and see'd Brother Joe and most of the Nauvoo fellers all comin' out of the hotel together. There was Brother Joe and Hyrum, of course. Then there was John Taylor and the Big Doctor and Blue Dan and Markham and Phelps. I also see'd Dimick, the stout feller what leads the Legion band up in Nauvoo, and a bunch of others. Pert' near all of the Nauvoo fellers that rode with us to Carthage was there. They all come out of the hotel and surrounded Brother Joe and started walkin' down the street to the west. Next to Brother Joe was Squire Woods, whose mare Gypsy Queen was in the stable yard. I could hear Squire Woods shoutin' out to the soldiers crowdin' around the street, "Make way, gentlemen! Make way!" And I watched as Brother Joe walked out of sight with all the others.

Funny thing, Major, is that late that same night, 'bout dark, most of our Nauvoo fellers come back real sudden like to the stable yard and fetched their horses. Will Hamilton come with 'em and helped 'em get all squared away. The first one to come over was Phelps, who was mighty quiet for a feller what seems to talk all the time. He saddled up Rust and rode right on out. Then Dimick come, and some of the Brethren, Levi Richards and Jonathan Holmes and Jesse Haromon and a bunch more whose names I don't rightly know. They all jest saddled up and rode off into the dark. Pretty much the only Nauvoo horses what was left in the stable yard was me and Sam, John Taylor's Lady Gray, the Big Doctor's Saucepan, Blue Dan's Tramp, Markham's Pickwick, and one or two more. The rest all rode off quick like into the night.

As it got dark outside, and Will Hamilton and his brothers locked us up inside the stable for the night, I kept wonderin' when Brother Joe and Hyrum and the rest would come and fetch us, so we could ride off. But, Brother Joe never did come.

In fact, Major, I ain't seen Brother Joe since.

WEDNESDAY, JUNE 26, 1844

OLD CHARLIE SEES THE HORSES OF MANY VISITORS COME AND GO IN THE HAMILTON HOUSE STABLE

CARTHAGE, ILLINOIS – WEDNESDAY, JUNE 26, 1844

The men awake, and Dan Jones recounts his dream, in which he saw Ford on his way to Nauvoo, and himself sent from Carthage with a letter, racing through the midst of savages and wild men, arriving at Warsaw to a view of "powder, smoke, death, and carnage." Joseph believes the Governor will not allow him to go again to Nauvoo alive.[103]

6:00 a.m. Joseph and the others breakfast. The jailer moves them to an upstairs room with a bed, writing table, and chairs. The Carthage sheriff repeatedly tells the jailer that he must send the men to the courthouse. The jailor refuses to send them out.[104]

7:30 a.m. Joseph sends Jones, Markham, and Wasson to the Governor with messages, but receives no answer.

8:00 a.m. Captain Singleton arrives at Nauvoo with sixty militia to protect city.[105]

8:48 a.m. Ford sends a reply to Joseph's entreaties for an interview, "The interview will take place at my earliest leisure today."

8:50 a.m. Counsel for defense decides to seek a change of venue for trial.

9:27 a.m. Governor Ford has an interview with Joseph at the Carthage jail, accusing Joseph of suppressing the liberty of speech and

---

[103] Jones 98, 104

[104] Jones 88

[105] Statement of James Woods in "State of Illinois," *Times and Seasons* (July 1, 1844)

press, and not complying with the writ, and in general defying the laws. Joseph responds that he has been maligned and persecuted, that he is accused of treason for following the Governor's orders, that he is charged with lawlessness when those that are lawless are not accused, that any city in the United States would have destroyed a press of that sort, that he and the City Council had done all things strictly according to the law; that, on the contrary, he had been dealt with in illegal ways by being forced to come to Carthage, and that Ford and others were feigning to uphold the law when in fact they were carrying out the mob's lawless wishes. Ford responds by accusing Joseph of detaining, arresting, and giving passes to men. John P. Greene, the city Marshall, replies by saying that the city was under duress and to secure protection they must needs have detained and asked questions, but no one had been detained and there were no passes given out, but to strangers who were to avoid being questioned by the city guards. Ford attacks, "Why did you not give a more speedy answer to the posse that I sent out?" Joseph says that Ford's letter showed an antagonistic spirit, and that they needed to consult upon their safety, because Ford demanded they come to Carthage unarmed. They feared for their safety, and the posse returned too quickly. Ford counters with more complaint of the proceeding against the Expositor, *that they combined the legislative and judicial roles in the City Council, and that Joseph should have come with Bettisworth to Carthage when first served the writ, but now that he was in jail he could not interfere. Joseph silences Ford by explaining how the writ came at the instance of a mob, that they had sworn their destruction, that it was a ruse to get him into their hands. Concerning the destruction of the* Expositor, *Joseph agrees to let the courts decide it and to pay the owners of the press for its cost, if found to be in the wrong. He reminds Ford of his promise of protection, and says that if he is going to Nauvoo, he wishes to go with him. Ford promises to take him along when he goes to Nauvoo.*[106]

---

[106] HC 6:577-586; 7:88-96

10:15 a.m. Governor Ford departs.

Alfred Randall overhears a man tell Governor Ford, "The soldiers are determined to see Joe Smith dead before they leave here." Ford responds, "If you know of any such thing keep it to yourself."[107]

Many persons witness Ford's complicity in the mob's intentions.

Joseph is visited by Judge Phelps, J. P. Green, J. S. Fullmore, C. H. Wheelock. Jones and Markham spend the morning carving the warped bedroom door to get it closed and latched.

Joseph is anxious to get Hyrum out of the jail. He speaks of it often, and sends messengers to Nauvoo with testimonies of witnesses to exonerate Hyrum. Hyrum comforts Joseph, reminding him that the Lord will deliver him for the Church's sake. Joseph says of Sidney Rigdon, "I am glad he is gone to Pittsburg out of the way; were he to preside he would lead the Church to destruction in less than five years." The prisoners alternately preach to the guards. Several guards are relieved of duty because, convinced of the prisoners' innocence, they are deemed unfit to guard them. [108]

Joseph recounts two dreams he had had several days before. The first is a dream of a pit and William and Wilson Law being attacked by wild beasts and a snake, recounted by Joseph first on June 13 in the Seventies' Hall. The second dream is of a ship about to wreck, whose sailors were heedless of Joseph's cries of warning. Joseph saw himself wading into the raging sea to guide the ship to safety, away from the rocks, but he was not heeded. The interpretation: the ship was the United States, which rejected a "safe pilot." Joseph, Hyrum, and Samuel all walk on the sea, which has been calmed. Joseph understood that his and Hyrum's walking on the sea meant that they would overcome their adversaries beyond the veil. Joseph could not understand what Samuel's presence in the dream intimated.[109]

---

[107] HC 6:586-87; Randall was deposed before the Salt Lake County Recorder, Thomas Bullock, on February 12, 1855

[108] Jones 99

[109] Jones 99-100

12:00 noon. Joseph remarks, "I have had a good deal of anxiety about my safety since I left Nauvoo, which I never had before when I was under arrest. I could not help those feelings, and they have depressed me."[110]

12:30 p.m. The prosecution demands that the prisoners be brought out for examination on charges of treason. The jailer refuses the demand, claiming that since the prisoners had been committed without examination, the prosecution has no further jurisdiction. Joseph, seeing the Carthage Greys gathering because of the dispute, and the jailer, receiving many threats, gives himself up.

3:40 p.m. Joseph and Hyrum march through the middle of the Carthage Greys. While walking through the middle of this hostile crowd, Joseph locks arms with the "worst mobocrat he can see" and then locks arms with Hyrum.[111]

Murder seems imminent.

4:25 p.m. Subpoenas are granted to get witnesses for the defendants for the next day.

5:30 p.m. Joseph and Hyrum are returned to jail. Joseph's uncle John Smith visits him at the jail. The guard refuses entrance, to which Joseph says, "You will not hinder so old and infirm a man as he is from coming in. Come in, uncle."[112]

The guard allows him to enter. His uncle asks Joseph if he thinks he will again escape the hands of his enemies. Joseph says, "My brother Hyrum thinks I shall." They preach to the guards and gain their confidence, so much so that the guards admit that they have been brought there to be killed.[113]

Cyrus H. Wheelock smuggles a six-shooter into Joseph. Joseph hands a single barrel pistol, which had previously been given him, to Hyrum, and says, "You may have use for this." Hyrum says, "I hate to

---

[110] HC 6:592

[111] Jones 100

[112] HC 6:598

[113] Jones 89

use such things or to see them used." Joseph says, "So do I, but we may have to, to defend ourselves."[114]

7:45 p.m. The prisoners eat supper.

8:00 p.m. Joseph is informed that Ford and the troops will march to Nauvoo tomorrow to gratify the troops. The prisoners are moved back to the upstairs bedroom at the request of Ford. Fifty men are left to guard the jail. The trial is postponed until the 29th.

9:15 p.m. John Taylor prays. Hyrum reads and comments upon passages from The Book of Mormon, *especially those that recount the imprisonment and deliverance of God's chosen. Joseph testifies to the guards of the authenticity of* The Book of Mormon *and the restoration of the gospel, that this was the reason for his incarceration. The prisoners retire to bed. Willard Richards stays up late writing. Richards and Hyrum sleep on the bed, and Joseph lies down on the floor between Dan Jones and John S. Fullmer. The men hear the sound of a gun firing outside the jail. Joseph tells Fullmer, "I would like to see my family again. I would to God that I could preach to the Saints in Nauvoo once more." Fullmer tries to comfort Joseph. When all are asleep, Joseph whispers to Jones, "Are you afraid to die?" Jones replies, "Has that time come think you? Engaged in such a cause I do not think that death would have many terrors." Joseph prophesies, "You will see Wales, and fulfill the mission appointed you ere you die."*

Midnight: Steps are heard on the stairway. Jones sees an army gathered outside the window, and hears, "How many shall go in?" They hear a rush of feet up the stairway, and they can hear the men breathing on the other side of the door. Joseph calls out loudly, "Come on ye assassins, we are ready for you, and would as willingly die now as at daylight." No one replies and they leave. They hear the mob outside the window all night long.[115]

---

[114] HC 6:608

[115] Jones 89

The next day in Carthage ain't real clear in my memory, Major. There warn't nothin' to do but stand in the dark all night with the other horses, and then stand all day out in the stable yard watchin' folks come and go from the hotel. All I know is that I never see'd Brother Joe that day, nor Hyrum.

But I see'd plenty of other comin's and goin's, that's for sure. There was more and more soldiers walkin' around the streets of Carthage all the time, and the militia officers was bringin' in their horses to the stable or takin' 'em out to ride. There was still a bunch of horses from Nauvoo with me, standin' around all day, waitin'. The militia horses come and went, but me and Sam stayed together in the yard with Lady Gray and Saucepan and Tramp and Pickwick, wonderin' when we would ride back to Nauvoo.

First thing in the mornin', after the three Hamilton brothers, Marv and Will and Dallas, had let all the horses out into the yard and gave us our feed, I stood watchin' the street in my new reg'lar spot. Will Hamilton was wearin' his gray militia uniform again that day. He had set his gun and cap to the side and was workin' on the water pump, fillin' up the water trough, when this militia feller dressed out in a red jacket wandered over and leaned agin' the fence. He jest stood there with one foot up on the rail, a-watchin' for a while. Then the soldier in red spoke up to Will Hamilton—

"Hey boy," he said "You part of the Carthage Greys?"

"Yes sir," said Will. "What company you with?"

"Warsaw," said Red Soldier. "These the horses of the damned Mormons?" he asked.

"Sure enough," Will said. "At least some of 'em. Most of 'em have already ridden back up to Nauvoo."

"Which horse belongs to old Joe Smith?" the Red Soldier asked.

Will pointed at me. "Big black stallion, yonder."

"Fine looking horse," said Red Soldier.

"He's a regular military horse," said Will. "I saw him a year back when Joe Smith rode him in a parade with the Nauvoo Legion. One black horse leading out in front of five thousand men or more."

"The Legion," said Red Soldier. "I just hope they never march on us."

Suddenly I spotted Blue Dan and Markham in the street. They was walkin' up to the hotel. I walked over to the fence rail and nickered right loud, but they didn't pay me no nevermind and went inside Hamilton's. They was inside for a spell, then come back outside and walked back down the street to the west.

A short while after Blue Dan and Markham left the hotel, I see'd the Gov'nor come outside with several of his militia fellers, and he walked down the street. After a spell he come back to the hotel and went inside.

Meantime, the streets was still filled with soldiers, though they warn't shoutin' and carryin' on like they done the day before. They was right sober, and I could tell a few of 'em was skeered, jest by the way they looked this way and that when they was out walkin'. I 'spect it was 'cause they was skeered of the Legion, jest like Red Soldier.

Later in the mornin', two of the Brethren rode up to the stable and left their horses. They was Cyrus Wheelock and John Fullmer, two stout and strong fellers who is great friends with Brother Joe. With 'em was Constable Green, the head of the Nauvoo policemen. When they unsaddled their horses, I noticed that Brother Cyrus pulled a six-shooter out of his saddlebags and put it into the side of his long ridin' boot. Then the three of 'em walked off down the street. Later on, Constable Green come back to the stable and saddled up his horse and rode away.

Not much else happened that day, Major. Jest lots of standin' in the stable yard and watchin'. 'Cept later in the day, when the sun was startin' to slant towards the west, I heared a big to-do goin' on down the street. There was once more lots of shoutin' and yellin', and I heared the militia drum bangin' away, so I knowed that there was some kinda musterin' goin' on close by, though I never see'd nothin'. Later on, Robert Foster come by and fetched his little mare, Charity, and rode off. By nightfall, it was gettin' right cloudy outside, and time or two I heared the sound of thunder off in the distance.

Brother Joe never come back to the hotel that day or evenin'. Long 'bout dark, Will Hamilton and his brothers come by and herded us all into the stable and locked the door all safe and sound for the night.

I stood awake for a long time, listenin' to the rain startin' to fall on the roof

THURSDAY MORNING AND AFTERNOON, JUNE 27, 1844

OLD CHARLIE SEES GOVERNOR FORD UP CLOSE –
BROTHER JOE'S FRIENDS ARE FORCED TO RIDE OUT OF
CARTHAGE ONE BY ONE – OLD CHARLIE SEES WILL
HAMILTON CLIMB THE COURTHOUSE TOWER

CARTHAGE, ILLINOIS – THURSDAY MORNING AND AFTERNOON, JUNE 27, 1844

There is a slight rain in the early morning.

5:30 a.m. The prisoners arise. There are about eight of the Carthage Greys who remain on guard. Dan Jones descends to ask the guard about the disturbance in the night. The guard responds with curses, swearing that "Joe Smith" and the others would "never come out alive" from that jail and that those who supported him were no better than he.[116]

Jones tells the guard that they, as guards, were under oath to protect the prisoners, and that he would soon tell the Governor about his threats. The guard is furious, "You'll see that I can prophesy better than old Joe that neither he nor his brother nor anyone who will remain with them will see the sun set today." Joseph sends Dan Jones to apprise Governor Ford of the threat. Jones goes to the Hamilton Hotel and reports these things to Ford, who dismisses them as idle threats.

7:00 a.m. Governor Ford orders the troops to disband except for the Carthage Greys and the Augusta Dragoons. The troops break camp and leave the city. Joseph and Hyrum are left in the jail with a detail of six

---

[116] Jones 89-90

men and an officer from the Carthage Greys guarding them. The rest of the Carthage Greys remain in camp in the public square.[117]

8:20 a.m. Joseph writes a letter to Emma: After allaying her fears as to an attack on the city, he says, "There is one principle which is eternal; it is the duty of all men to protect their lives and the lives of the household, whenever necessity requires, and no power has a right to forbid it, should the last extreme arrive, but I anticipate no such extreme, but caution is the parent of safety. . . P.S. Dear Emma, I am very much resigned to my lot, knowing I am justified, and have done the best that could be done. Give my love to the children and all my friends, Mr. Brewer, and all who inquire after me; and as for treason, I know that I have not committed any, and they cannot prove anything of the kind, so you need not have any fears that anything can happen to us on that account. May God bless you all. Amen."[118]

9:40 a.m. The prisoners are informed that another meeting, at which delegates from every state of the Union except three were present, has taken place to determine how best to stop Joseph Smith's career, "as his views on government [are] widely circulated and [take] like wildfire"; there is fear that if he does not gain the Presidency of the United States this time, that he will the next. Dan Jones, on his way back to the jail, sees a mob gathered, threatening to kill Joseph before the day is out, while Ford is away in Nauvoo. Jones returns to Ford to report the words and threats of this mob. Ford ignores him.[119]

Jones races back to the jail to inform the prisoners, but the guard refuses admittance. Jones returns to Ford to inform him of the guard's refusal, and to request a pass to enter the jail. Ford refuses, but consents to give a pass to Willard Richards to act as secretary. Ford proposes to march the entire army into Nauvoo, but decides in council that it would

---

[117] 1902 Hamilton Letter
[118] HC 6:695
[119] Jones 90

be "unjust" as well as "impolitic, in the present critical season of the year, the harvest and the crops."[120]

The prisoners also learn that Captain Dunn and his company are to accompany Ford to Nauvoo, while the Carthage Greys and members of the mob are to guard Carthage jail.

11:00 a.m. Ford departs for Nauvoo. Most militia companies are disbanded in Carthage, allowing the men to linger in Carthage.[121]

Willard Richards tells Joseph that he is willing to suffer and die for him. John Taylor also tells Joseph to give him the word and "I will have you out of this prison in five hours, if the jail has to come down to do it." Joseph refuses.[122]

Joseph tells Wheelock to warn the Saints in Nauvoo to avoid any military show, to remain perfectly calm and quiet. "Our lives have already become jeopardized by revealing the wicked and bloodthirsty purposes of our enemies; and for the future we must cease to do so. All we have said about them is truth, but it is not always wise to relate all the truth. . . . We have the revelation of Jesus, and the knowledge within us is sufficient to organize a righteous government upon the earth, and to give universal peace to all mankind, if they would receive it, but we lack the physical strength, as did our Savior when a child, to defend our principles, and we have of necessity to be afflicted, persecuted and smitten, and to bear it patiently until Jacob is of age, then he will take care of himself." So many oral messages are given to Wheelock that Willard Richards proposes writing them down. Hyrum says, "Brother Wheelock will remember all that we tell him, and he will never forget the occurrences of this day." The Prophet relates that night's dream: He was back on his Kirtland farm, which had fallen into disarray. A man began to quarrel with him for possession of the farm, to which violence Joseph said that the man could have his property. The man did not cease to

---

[120] Governor Ford's address, "To the People of the State of Illinois," *Times and Seasons* (July 1, 1844)

[121] "To the People of the State of Illinois," *Times and Seasons* (July 1, 1844)

[122] HC 7:100; HC 6:608

threaten him. Joseph removed himself away from the barn into some mud. The barn then immediately filled up with men, and they began to fight violently with knives amongst themselves.

11:00 a.m. Private William Hamilton and another private from the Carthage Greys are ordered to go on top of the Courthouse to keep a lookout. They watch in every direction with a large field telescope throughout the day. They see nothing suspicious until about 4:00 p.m.[123]

12:20 p.m. Dan Jones, sent to Nauvoo with messages for Joseph's lawyers, is detained by the mob, who believe he is trying to raise the Nauvoo Legion against them. Men wait in ambush, but he escapes by the mistake of his horse, which takes the road to Warsaw instead of Nauvoo.[124]

Dan Jones later makes for the road to Nauvoo, and tells the crowd awaiting the arrival of Governor Ford to hasten at once to Carthage to save the Prophet's life. The crowd decides to stay.[125]

1:15 p.m. The prisoners dine.

1:30 p.m. Willard Richards is taken ill; Brother Markham is sent for medicine. Upon returning to jail he is forced by bayonet onto his horse and out of town.

Stephen Markham wrote: "Hamilton, the Innkeeper, came out and said, 'You can do the prisoners no good and I will bring you your horse. . . .' He cried, and brought my horse up."[126]

3:15 p.m. The jail guard becomes more severe with prisoners. John Taylor sings "A Poor Wayfaring Man of Grief." Joseph requests him to sing it again, which he does. Hyrum reads extracts from Josephus.

4:00 p.m. The guard is changed, only eight men being left at the jail.

---

[123] 1902 Hamilton Letter

[124] Jones 91

[125] Jones 104

[126] Stephen Markham, letter to Wilford Woodruff, June 20, 1856, Fort Supply, 3-4, Original in Church Archives, copy in the possession of the author

The next mornin' was a strange one, Major. First, things was right crazy, with lots of folks comin' and goin', but then it got mighty quiet all of a sudden.

Right after Will Hamilton brung us outside at early light, I see'd Blue Dan runnin' down the street and up the steps into the hotel. Now what in blazes is he doin', I thought.

I didn't see Blue Dan again 'til after we horses had finished our mornin' eatin', but then I knowed somethin' was 'bout to happen when I see'd all the militia companies musterin' in the streets and marchin' down toward the west. Then I see'd the Gov'nor walk out of Hamilton's hotel and head down the street. The Gov'nor had all of his fellers crowded around him and a militia officer or two. I also see'd Blue Dan foller him out of the hotel and walk with him into the street. Blue Dan was talkin' to the Gov'nor, but it 'peared that the Gov'nor warn't payin' Dan no nevermind.

Well, they walked off in the direction all the other troops had gone, down the street to the west. From a distance I could hear the Gov'nor speakin' right out loud for a short piece, and then like a horsetail whiskin' away the flies, the streets started clearin' of all the soldiers. A whole bunch of militia officers come right over to the stable and got their horses. Pretty soon, the only horses left in Hamilton's stable was them what belonged to our Nauvoo fellers left in the city and the Gov'nor's big trotter, Napoleon.

But pretty soon, here come Blue Dan runnin' into the stable. He was breathin' right hard and 'peared to be mighty agitated. Lickety-split, he fetched his little bay gelding, Tramp, and rode out, jest like that.

By this time, the streets was mostly empty, and I see'd fewer and fewer soldiers about. Time or two, I see'd a company of soldiers marchin' down the street and could hear their feet hittin' the road all together and heared 'em as they marched further and further away.

Things started to get real quiet in Carthage. I kept wonderin' what was keepin' Brother Joe, and why he and Hyrum and the other fellers—John Taylor and the Big Doctor and Brother Cyrus and Markham and the rest—didn't come and fetch their horses and ride back home to Nauvoo.

Short time later, Will Hamilton and another young feller, all dressed up in their gray militia uniforms, come over to the stable. Will 'peared to be in a hurry. He fetched the Gov'nor's horse, Napoleon, and saddled him all up. Then the Gov'nor hisself strolled across the street and mounted up on Napoleon and rode off.

After the Gov'nor left town, there were fewer and fewer of our Nauvoo fellers left in Carthage. By the time the sun got high, Brother Cyrus and Brother Fullmer come to the stable and fetched their horses and rode away. I heared 'em talkin' while they got their horses saddled up.

"Do you remember what we are to say?" Brother Fullmer was sayin'.

"Yeah," said Brother Cyrus. "I got all the messages."

"Why didn't Brother Joe just write them down?" Fullmer asked.

"In case we get stopped," said Cyrus. "He doesn't want anybody reading what he had to say."

Well, I didn't rightly understand that, but I did know that Brother Joe was still in Carthage, so I 'spected him at any moment to come fetch me so we could head out with the others.

After that I see'd Will Hamilton fix his militia cap on his head and grab his gun, and then he and this other feller run off down the street. I didn't think nothin' of it, as I had see'd Will in his militia uniform the day before, but after a spell I happened to look over to the west toward the big stone buildin' with the tower on top, and sure enough, I see'd Will and his soldier friend standin' out on the tower, way above the streets of Carthage. Well, I thought to myself, what in the heck is he a-doin' way up there? Horses is able to see a long ways off, and I looked real intent like and could see how Will Hamilton was jest standin' behind a little railin' up in that tower. Then I see'd how he had a long bottle, and he was jest a-lookin' into that bottle with one eye, while he turned his head this way and that on top of that tower, jest like General Dunham done back on the Carthage Road with his bottles. 'Cept Will Hamilton had only one big bottle, not two little ones like General Dunham. It was mighty strange.

In fact, Major, the rest of the day was uncommon strange in Carthage.

There warn't much comin' and goin' in the street by the hotel, but still I could sense that somethin' was happenin' and felt right uneasy. There warn't hardly nobody in the streets, 'cept a few soldiers dressed in uniforms exactly like the one young Will Hamilton was wearin'. These fellers, all dressed in gray, was marchin' up and down the street slowly with their muskets ready on their shoulders. I felt a kinda tension every time one of these gray fellers marched by.

Short time later, I heared a commotion in the street and looked out to see a bunch of these soldiers in gray comin' down the street in my direction. I was s'prised to see Markham walkin' in the middle of these fellers, and they had their muskets and bayonets pointed right at Markham. He was talkin' to 'em with each step, but it didn't 'pear they was listenin'.

Jest then, Old Hamilton come runnin' out of the hotel and went right up to Markham. "Mr. Markham," he called as he run up, wipin' his hands on a cloth. "You can do the prisoners no good. I will bring you your horse." Markham stayed standin' in the street with the gray soldiers around him, pointin' their bayonets at him, while Old Hamilton run over and fetched Markham's palomino, Pickwick. He saddled him all up and led him out into the street. I watched while Markham mounted up on Pickwick. He looked around at the fellers with muskets pointin' at him, then shouted at Pickwick, and they rode off.

THURSDAY LATE AFTERNOON, JUNE 27, 1844

OLD CHARLIE WAITS IN THE HAMILTON HOUSE STABLE
WITH SAM, LADY GRAY, AND SAUCEPAN – CHARLIE
HEARS THE DISTANT CRACKLING OF MUSKET FIRE

CARTHAGE, ILLINOIS – THURSDAY LATE AFTERNOON, JUNE 27, 1844

Joseph and Hyrum's brother, Samuel, who lived two or three miles from Carthage, heads for the city with a fourteen-year-old boy driving the wagon. On the way they meet a mob, which attacks Samuel when they learn his relationship to the prisoners in Carthage. Samuel leaps from the wagon and escapes into the woods, while the boy continues into Carthage. Samuel makes his way home and "acquired a horse noted for its speed."[127] Samuel's daughter remembered that her father came in the house in much excitement and said, "I think I can break through the mob and get to Carthage." Samuel then "immediately mounted the horse and was gone."[128] Samuel rides to Carthage at great speed. Men hidden in a thicket shoot at Samuel and then pursue him. Samuel outruns them on his fast horse.

4:00 p.m. The Carthage Grey watchmen atop the Courthouse see "a body of armed men in wagons and on horses approaching the low timber, a little north of west from the jail, and about two miles distant. This was

---

[127] Kyle R. Walker, ed., *United By Faith: The Joseph Sr. and Lucy Mack Smith Family* (Salt Lake City: Covenant Communications, 2005) 230

[128] Ruby K. Smith, *Mary Bailey* (1954) 90

at once reported to the captain, when we were ordered to keep a strict watch and at once report if they come through the timber."[129]

4:15 p.m. Joseph converses with the guard on the subject of his persecutors. Hyrum and Willard Richards converse.

4:30 p.m. In the courthouse tower, Carthage Grey Private William Hamilton and another private watch through a field telescope as "a body of armed men—about 125—came out of the woods on foot and started in a single file, behind an old rail fence, in the direction of the jail. They were then about three-fourths of a mile distant. This we at once attempted to report, but could not find the captain; and . . . told another officer, who after considerable delay found the captain who ordered the company to fall into line."[130] *Hamilton wrote that the men were "grotesquely disguised by blackened faces."*[131] *Hamilton and his fellow private are ordered to return to the tower and watch to see if the armed men approach the jail.*

5:00 p.m. The jailer suggests that Joseph and Hyrum and the others go into the cell, which is safer. Joseph says, "After supper we will go in." Ford arrives at Nauvoo.

5:15 p.m. The guard turns to go out. A voice from below calls for him, and he goes down. Rustling is heard at the bottom, a cry of surrender, and the sound of three or four firearms. A mob encircles the building. Richards, peeking out the curtain of the window, sees a hundred men surrounding the main entrance of the jail.

Carthage Grey Private William Hamilton sees the mob reach the jail and commence shooting. He descends from the courthouse tower and runs "double quick for the jail."[132]

In the jail, John Taylor sees some men firing through the windows and others rushing up the stairs past the guard. Joseph springs for his

---

129 1902 Hamilton Letter

130 1902 Hamilton Letter

131 Letter from William R. Hamilton to Samuel H.B. Smith dated March 18, 1898, copy in author's possession (hereafter "1898 Hamilton Letter")

132 1902 Hamilton Letter

firearm, Hyrum for his, Taylor for Markham's large hickory cane, and Richards for Taylor's cane. The prisoners force the door shut. Hyrum shoots at the door, when a ball piercing it strikes him in the left side of the nose. He falls back, saying, "I am a dead man!" Three other balls enter his body as he falls. Joseph exclaims, "O, my dear brother Hyrum!" Joseph discharges his six-shooter into the hallway by opening the door a few inches. Taylor attempts to fight off the guns with his cane. Joseph's last words to Taylor are, "That's right, Brother Taylor, parry them off as well as you can."[133]

Taylor attempts to jump out of the window, is struck in the left thigh, falls on the windowsill, and cries, "I am shot." Another ball hits his watch; he rolls under the bed, struck by three more balls. Joseph drops his gun, springs onto the windowsill, and is struck by two balls from within, and one enters his right breast from without. As he falls out the window, he exclaims, "O Lord, my God!"

Carthage Grey Private William Hamilton joins his company, which "finally reached the jail, but not until the mob had completed their work and left in the direction from which they came. When about fifty yards away I saw Joseph Smith come to the window and fall out. One of the men went to him and partially straightened his body out beside the well curb. Just at this time I got up amongst the men and heard him say, 'He's dead,' when all the mob immediately left."[134]

Willard Richards escapes unscathed but for a slight wound to one ear, fulfilling a prophecy made by Joseph a year earlier that "the balls would fly around him like hail, and he should see his friends fall on the right and on the left, but that there should not be a hole in his garment."[135]

---

[133] John Taylor, "An Account of the Martyrdom of Joseph Smith" (June 27, 1854), copy in possession of Author. See also Mark L. Staker, ed., "John Taylor's June 27, 1854 Account of the Martyrdom" in *BYU Studies* 50:3

[134] 1902 Hamilton Letter

[135] HC 6:617-19

Willard Richards drags John Taylor to the inner prison and covers him up. A cry is heard, "The Mormons are coming!" which causes the mob to flee.

Private Hamilton wrote, "I went to where Smith was lying and found that he was dead without doubt. I then went up to the room where they had been quartered, where I found Hyrum Smith lying upon the floor on his back, dead. No person was in the room, or came while I was there. He was stretched out on the floor, just as he had fallen after being shot."[136]

That was one confusin' day, Major. After Jack and Pickwick rode off with Blue Dan and Markham, there was only four of us horses from Nauvoo left in Hamilton's stable—me, Sam, Lady Gray, and Saucepan. Besides us, there was jest a sturdy brown mare restin' in the stable. I figured she belonged to Old Hamilton. Besides the five of us, there warn't no horses at all left in Hamilton's stable.

With all the ruckus the day before and that mornin', things had been mighty stressful for the horses, 'specially for Lady Gray. She was mostly standin' near Sam and me all day, with her head down low and kinda shiverin'. In the mornin' there had been all the shoutin' and marchin' back and forth in the street out front of the hotel, and there warn't nearly any time when we didn't have one officer or the other comin' in the stable to bring his horse or fetch it up and ride off. There was also plenty of reg'lar soldiers what wandered up to the railin' to smoke some and talk real loud. But after the Gov'nor rode off, and then Blue Dan and Markham, I

---

[136] 1902 Hamilton Letter

scarcely heared a sound, and didn't see no soldiers anymore walkin' in the streets.

All of a sudden, it seemed right still in the stable yard, and I could even hear the birds flittin' around in the little trees what stood around the edge of the yard. But I didn't hardly see no one. Fact is, after the sun started slantin' down towards evenin', the only men I even see'd was that Will Hamilton and the other feller all dressed in their gray militia uniforms and standin' yonder up in that big tower. They was walkin' around inside the railin' right slow, and time to time holdin' that big bottle up to their faces for a look-see inside.

'Bout feedin' time I was startin' to wonder if young Will would climb down from his tower and come set out some food for us. I was sorta watchin' Will up on that tower yonder, when suddenly he and this other feller with him started to point with their arms out in a northerly direction. Then they passed that bottle back and forth and took turns lookin' into it. Then they climbed down out of the tower on a ladder, and I couldn't see 'em no more.

'Bout that time little Dallas Hamilton come across the street from the hotel and started to fix up our afternoon feed and pump out some fresh water into the trough. I watched him pumpin' away and heared the water splashin' into the trough. Across the street I see'd Old Hamilton come out of the hotel and stand on the porch with his hands on his hips, jest a lookin' down the street in the direction of the big tower. He jest stood there lookin' for a spell, then went back inside the hotel. By that time, Dallas had set out the feed, and Sam was startin' in on it with Saucepan and Lady Gray.

The brown mare left the shade of the stable roof and wandered over for a drink, and I looked her over. She was a fine young thing with a shiny brown coat and a pleasant demeanor. It looked like she was a goer, and right smart, too.

Before I went over for some feed, I looked back up towards the tower, and see'd that Will Hamilton was back up with his other feller, and they was lookin' into their big bottle.

I walked over to have a drink next to the brown mare, when suddenly there come the cracklin' noise of muskets—a whole passel of it way out yonder. All four of us horses pricked up our ears to listen. Sounded like a whole militia firin' off their guns at the same time, then for a long while a bang here and there, and then another bunch of 'em.

Will Hamilton climbed right down out of that tower with the other feller and disappeared.

After a short while the bangs stopped, and we finished our feed. Then I smelt the gunpowder, kinda driftin' out over the city.

THURSDAY EVENING, JUNE 27, 1844

OLD CHARLIE SEES CARTHAGE BECOME A GHOST TOWN – BROTHER SAMUEL ARRIVES IN CARTHAGE – WAGONS COME AND GO AT THE HAMILTON HOUSE HOTEL

CARTHAGE, ILLINOIS – THURSDAY EVENING, JUNE 27, 1844

Private William Hamilton, after seeing the dead bodies of Joseph and Hyrum, returns to the Hamilton House to "tell the news" to his family.[137]

Immediately after the killings, there is a scene of panic in Carthage. The cry goes from house to house, "The Mormons are coming!" Word spreads that the Nauvoo Legion is approaching the city. Virtually all of the inhabitants leave their homes and flee from the city on horseback, in wagons, or on foot. Doors are left open, businesses abandoned, food left on the table. The roads south and southeast of Carthage are jammed with fleeing people. Within an hour or so after the assassinations, Carthage has become a ghost town, empty except for a few sick or elderly who cannot flee and the family of Artois Hamilton, the innkeeper.

Samuel Smith arrives in Carthage immediately after the killing of his brothers. He is the first Latter-day Saint to arrive at the jail.[138]

Early evening: Willard Richards and Joseph's attorney James Woods attend the short coroner's inquest over Joseph and Hyrum Smith, held in the jail.[139]

---

[137] 1902 Hamilton Letter

[138] HC 7:110-11

[139] See Susan Easton Black, "Artois Hamilton: A Good Man in Carthage?" *Journal of Mormon History* vol. 31 no. 3 pg. 159

The bodies of Joseph and Hyrum are taken by Samuel Smith and Willard Richards to the Hamilton House, where they are washed, laid out, and placed in rough pine coffins.[140]

"Soon after," William Hamilton recalls, "Samuel H. Smith and three others came in a wagon and had the bodies brought to our house. . . . [R]ough pine coffins were made in which they were placed."[141]

Just before sundown William Hamilton "took all the county records in a wagon and took them some eight miles into the country east of Carthage for safe keeping. . . . I got home just at sunrise the next morning."[142]

8:05 p.m. Willard Richards sends a message to Nauvoo: "Joseph and Hyrum are dead. . . . The people of the county are greatly excited and fear the Mormons will come out and take vengeance. I have pledged my word the Mormons will stay at home . . . and say to my brethren in Nauvoo, in the name of the Lord—be still—be patient." Three messengers are sent, each of whom finds Governor Ford on his way back. Ford does not allow the messengers to continue on to Nauvoo, but turns each of them back, fearing an attack by Nauvoo citizens, and delaying the news of the Prophet's death.[143]

It was dead quiet in the stable yard after the cracklin' of the muskets stopped. Me and the other horses was standin' still, jest listenin' and a-sniffin' the smell of gunpowder in the air. It was mighty peaceful, Major. No sounds at all, 'cept the chirpin' of that little bird over in the scraggly tree by the road. We jest stood there, waitin', like always. We was jest waitin' for Brother Joe and Hyrum and the Big Doctor and

---

140 Thomas Bullock Journal, 17 April 18
141 1898 Hamilton Letter
142 1898 Hamilton Letter
143 "To Mrs. Emma Smith and Maj. Gen. Dunham, &c," *Times and Seasons*, July 1, 1844; HC 7:109-110

John Taylor to come and fetch us so we could ride back home.

Then everythin' started to happen at once. First we see'd Will Hamilton come runnin' down the street. I see'd how his militia cap blowed right off of his head as he ran. He run right inside the hotel. Then I see'd Old Hamilton and his boys Marv and Dallas and two or three ladies come out of the hotel onto the porch and look real intent like down the street, then Old Hamilton spoke to his boys. Little Dallas and the women folk went back into the hotel, but Old Hamilton went runnin' down the street hisself, follered by his boys, Marv and Will. I see'd other men and some ladies in the street, talkin' to one another. Some of the men was runnin' in the direction of the big tower.

Then I heared a feller a-shoutin' loud in the street. He was sayin', "The Mormons are coming!" Then I heared other folks say the same thing, "The Mormons are coming!" And then I see'd folks comin' out of their houses up and down the street and jest lookin' up and down the streets, this way and that. 'Bout that time Old Hamilton and his two boys come back to the hotel and went inside.

A little while later Will Hamilton come over to the stable. He had done taken off his gray militia uniform and was wearin' his reg'lar duds. He worked real fast, pullin' an old cart out of the back of the stable and settin' it all up in the yard. Then he brung out the lively brown mare and set her between the shafts on the cart, and they rode off down the street toward the tower.

'Bout the time Will rode off in his cart, I heared the sound of hooves gallopin' right hard, and who should race up like dad-burned lightnin', but Lather with Brother

Samuel, the brother of Hyrum and Brother Joe, ridin' in the saddle. I nickered at Lather as he galloped in, and he answered back. Brother Samuel reined him in real sudden like out front of the hotel, with dust a-swirlin' around Lather's legs and sparks comin' off his hooves where they struck the gravel. Brother Samuel didn't dismount, but Old Hamilton come back out on the porch in a hurry, and I could hear 'em shoutin' back and forth between 'em, real urgent like, though I didn't understand what they said. But Old Hamilton was pointin' down the road, and what do you know, but Brother Samuel whipped up Lather and rode full speed down the road.

By this time I see'd a bunch of wagons out on the street and lots of folks—men and women and lots of little children. They was carryin' stuff out of their houses and loadin' up the wagons, then headin' out like the blue blazes. They was in wagons, on horses, on mules, some even carryin' stuff in their arms and walkin'. I also see'd Will Hamilton ride by with the brown mare pullin' the cart, and it looked to be pert' near filled up with papers and stuff. He didn't stop at the hotel, but jest drove on, follerin' all the other folks who seemed to be headin' out of town.

It got awful quiet, Major. Pretty soon there didn't seem to be no one left in all of Carthage, jest Sam and me and the other horses, Saucepan and Lady Gray.

Then I see'd Old Hamilton come out of the hotel with his boy, Marv. The two of 'em come right over to the stable and opened wide the doors. Old Hamilton fetched Lady Gray and Saucepan while Marv drug a big wagon out of the stable. Then Old Hamilton and his boy put the two horses into the shafts of the wagon. I wondered where they was headed, as John Taylor and the Big Doctor might be showin' up any time and want to ride Lady Gray and Saucepan, what belonged to 'em. But Old Hamilton didn't seem to give that no nevermind, as he climbed up into the wagon box with Marv, waggled the reins and clucked, and the wagon headed off down the street.

By this time we was 'spectin' somethin' to eat at any time. But nobody come over to fix us up. The little warblin' bird in the scraggly tree flew off somewhere, and the crickets started to chirpin' in the dusk. Then it started gettin' dark, and I see'd some lights come on in the windows of the hotel yonder across the street. There warn't nobody out and about in the street, and it was real quiet. Sam and I stood alone in the stable yard, jest watchin' and listenin'.

Then I heared the sound of hooves on the road and the turn and crunch of wagon wheels, and Old Hamilton's wagon rolled up in front of the hotel across the street yonder in the dusk. The wagon was movin' with Marv drivin'. 'Cept Old Hamilton warn't ridin' with him on the wagon box. Do you know who it was, Major? It was the Big Doctor. Well, I was mighty s'prised to see him, as I hadn't knowed where he was off to since the night we rode into Carthage with Brother Joe and the rest. I figured since the Big Doctor was still in town, that Brother Joe must be somewhere close.

There was somethin' movin' in the back of the wagon bed. It was gettin' dark, but I could see a hand raisin' up, and then I heared John Taylor's voice. It sounded mighty different, like he was half asleep or somethin', but he called out the name "Willard!" That's the Big Doctor's proper name. Then I see'd how the Big Doctor and Marv carried John Taylor real slow and careful like out of the wagon box and up to the steps. The door to the hotel opened, and little Dallas Hamilton run down to help, while the lady folks stood 'round about the doorway.

They took John Taylor into the hotel and closed the door. Lady Gray and Saucepan jest stood there hitched to the wagon, 'til I wondered who was goin' to get 'em unhitched. But pretty soon the door to the hotel opened up again, and young Marv come out and got in and then jest drove off.

By this time it was right dark, so all I could see was the outline of Sam standin' stone still in the stable yard. The stars come out, and it was right peaceful and calm.

Then we heared the sound of the wagon again, and it pulled up once more by the hotel steps yonder. Marv Hamilton was carryin' a lantern up on the box and I see'd that Old Hamilton was a-drivin', and I also see'd that Lather was follerin' right along behind the wagon with Brother Samuel. He dismounted and stood by the wagon while Old Hamilton and Marv climbed down. A lady opened up the door of the hotel, and a yellow light kinda shone down the steps and out into the street.

It was plenty dark, but I see'd that there was two big bundles a-lyin' in the back of the wagon. I couldn't make out what they was, but I see'd how Brother Samuel and Old Hamilton and Marv carried 'em one by one into the hotel while the lady stood by watchin' in the doorway. Then they closed the door to the hotel.

Pretty soon Marv come back outside and unhitched Lady Gray and Saucepan from the wagon and brung 'em over and jest left 'em with Sam and me in the yard. Then he brung over Brother Samuel's ridin' horse, Lather, and unsaddled him and left him with us. He quickly set out some feed and water, then run back across to the hotel and went in.

We ate in the dark, then the others started to drift off into sleep. I stood awake for a piece, jest thinkin' on things. Since I see'd John Taylor and the Big Doctor, I figured that Brother Joe and Hyrum would be back soon, and then maybe we could all ride home. That gave me a right peaceful feelin', as I had been wonderin' where Brother Joe had gotten off to and when he was comin' back.

For a long spell, I jest stood listenin' to the crickets in the dark, and lookin' at the stars and watchin' the yellow windows of the Hamilton hotel yonder. The windows was burnin' bright all night long.

FRIDAY, JUNE 28, 1844

OLD CHARLIE AND SAM PULL WAGONS FROM CARTHAGE TO NAUVOO CONTAINING TWO LONG WOODEN BOXES – CHARLIE SEES TWENTY THOUSAND PEOPLE LINING MULHOLLAND STREET

CARTHAGE TO NAUVOO – FRIDAY, JUNE 28, 1844

1:00 a.m. Governor Ford flees Nauvoo and does not stop until he reaches Augusta, eighteen miles away from Carthage. Porter Rockwell cannot sleep, saddles his horse, and gallops towards Carthage. Rockwell meets Lorenzo Wasson and George D. Grant carrying news of the deaths of Hyrum and Joseph. Rockwell returns to Nauvoo and races through the town calling out, "Joseph is killed—they have killed him! G—d— them! They have killed him!"[144]

Early morning: Katherine Smith Salisbury, the sister of Joseph and Hyrum, arrives in Carthage early in the morning, sees her dead brothers, and later accompanies the bodies back to Nauvoo.[145]

Sunrise: William Hamilton reported: "I got home just at sunrise next morning. Soon after, Samuel Smith and three others came in a wagon—and in a short time the body of Joseph was put in their wagon and the body of Hiram [sic] in Father's and he and my brother John Dallas went to Nauvoo with them—returning late at night."[146]

A cloudy morning gives way to burning sun.

---

[144] Anson Call, "Life and Record" p. 27, copy in possession of author
[145] Reminiscences of Katherine Smith Salisbury, copy in possession of author
[146] 1898 Hamilton Letter

8:00 a.m. The two wagons bearing the bodies of the martyrs set out for Nauvoo, accompanied by Willard Richards, Samuel Smith, attorney James Woods, innkeeper Artois Hamilton and his two teenage sons, and a guard of eight mounted soldiers detailed by General Miner R. Deming, commander of the Hancock County Militia. John Taylor stays behind, gravely wounded, under the care of Atta Hamilton, the innkeeper's wife.

The journey takes almost seven hours. Prairie grass, brush, and Indian blankets are spread over the pine boxes to protect them from the hot summer sun.

10:00 a.m. The Nauvoo Legion is called out in Nauvoo and addressed by several, whose purpose is to calm the men down and prevent any act of vengeance for the killing of Joseph and Hyrum.

2:00 p.m. The Saints begin to gather by the thousands along Mulholland Street, which is connected to the road from Carthage. Virtually the entire city stands along the road—church leaders, businessmen, farmers, housewives, and children. It is reported that among the mourning crowds were hundreds of recent converts from Ireland and Wales, who begin a low moaning, which increases in sorrow and intensity theretofore unheard on this side of the Atlantic.[147] The crowds grow as Saints from outlying communities and farms arrive in the City. As the cortege slowly approaches, the vast throngs of mourners walk out as a group to meet the wagons, then follow behind.

2:30 to 3:00 p.m. The cortege arrives in Nauvoo.

Attorney James Woods wrote, "There was a great crowd to meet us formed in lines said to have been two miles long."[148]

---

[147] See, Donna Hill, *Joseph Smith: The First Mormon* (New York: Doubleday, 1977) p. 4

[148] Edward Holcomb Stiles, "James W. Woods," in *Recollections and Sketches of Notable Lawyers and Public Men of Early Iowa Belonging to the First and Second Generations: With Anecdotes and Incidents Illustrative of the Times* (1889)

The wagons carrying the bodies are slowed by the muddy roads. George Cannon, a recent convert from the Isle of Man, hastily makes a large sled out of logs to pull the wagons from the mire.[149]

The procession passes west along Mulholland Street. The Nauvoo Legion, in full uniform, stands at attention, along with the City Council and as many as ten thousand mourners.[150]

"Oh," wrote Dan Jones, "the mournful scene to be seen in Nauvoo that day! There has never been nor will there ever be anything like it; everyone sad along the streets, all the shops closed and every business forgotten."[151]

The procession passes the unfinished Nauvoo Temple, then south down Main Street to the Mansion House, where the bodies are carried into the dining room and the doors locked.

3:30 p.m. Though exhausted, Apostle Willard Richards speaks to the crowd gathered in front of the Mansion House. He asks the people to keep the peace and reminds them that any act of vengeance will jeopardize the life of John Taylor, who still lays gravely wounded in Carthage. The citizens of Nauvoo are then asked to leave and return to their homes until the morning.

Late evening: Three men wash the bodies of Joseph and Hyrum and plug their wounds with cotton soaked in camphor. The bodies are made as presentable as possible and lovingly dressed in drawers, fine plain shirts, white neckerchiefs, white cotton stockings and shrouds. At last, Joseph's wife, Emma, and Hyrum's wife, Mary, and their children are allowed to enter the room to see them.[152]

George Cannon makes death masks of Joseph and Hyrum.[153]

---

[149] David Henry Cannon, "History of David Henry Cannon," unpublished typescript, copy in possession of author

[150] "Mr. Orson Spencer," in *Times and Seasons*, July 1, 1844

[151] Dan Jones, "I Shall Ever Remember My Feelings," translated from the Welsh by Ronald D. Dennis, in *Church News*, June 24, 1984, p. 11

[152] HC 6:626-28; 7:134

[153] David Henry Cannon, "History"

Are you still a-listenin', Major? I was tellin' you about that last day in Carthage when we heared the cracklin' of muskets and then how all the folks jest cleared out of town.

Well, that night it was quiet—the quietest I seen in a long, long time.

Jest before daylight, folks started comin' in to the hotel. First, I see'd Will Hamilton drive up with the brown mare pullin' Old Hamilton's cart. Will unhitched the mare and left her with us in the yard and then went into the hotel.

Then 'bout sunrise I heared the clatter of hooves, and eight cavalry soldiers rode up in front of the hotel and tied up their horses yonder. At first I thought they was our Legion cavalry fellers, but then I see'd that they had on different uniforms, and I didn't recognize none of 'em. Ridin' right behind 'em was a lady on a clay-colored mare. It was Lady Katherine! She is Brother Joe's sister what spends most of her time with their old mother, Lady Lucy up to Nauvoo. I kinda 'spected Brother Joe and Hyrum to show up now, seein' how Brother Samuel and Lady Katherine was already there in Carthage. Brother Joe's family was always a bunch what stuck together. I see'd 'em all gatherin' in Kirtland plenty of times. Then, after we all rode off to Zion, they was back together again. Same thing in Nauvoo. That family was never far from one another as long as I knowed 'em, so I figured they was gatherin' all together again here in Carthage.

From the time Lady Katherine rode up and tied up her clay mare with the cavalry horses, I was rarin' to go and get on the road. Sam was the same. We had been cooped up in that stable yard long enough.

I figured I'd be saddled up and maybe have Brother Joe ridin' me, so when the three boys of Old Hamilton come across the street to the stable yard, I was stampin' my feet and nickerin' right out loud. But I was mistakin'. 'Stead of puttin' the saddle on me, they stuck me between the shafts of a long wagon next to Brother Samuel's big sorrel stallion, Lather. There was a second wagon, and Sam was all hitched up in the shafts together with Old Hamilton's brown mare. Then they drove the two wagons over in front of the hotel, mine in front and Sam's behind, and left us standin' in the street. Then I see'd how the Hamilton boys went back across to the yard and saddled up Saucepan and brung him over and tied him up by all the cavalry horses.

That left Lady Gray all alone in the yard, and she didn't like it one bit. She was tossin' her head and runnin' up and down the fence rail, lookin' over at us and neighin' somethin' fearsome. I guessed she warn't ridin' out with us that day. Maybe she would foller along later with John Taylor.

We stood in the street for a spell while the sun come up and started to climb up in the blue. It was fixin' to be a hot day. The flies was buzzin' around us, and I was already swishin' my tail a bit. Then the door to Hamilton's opened wide and all the folks come out into the street at once. There was Old Hamilton, all dressed up in a ridin' jacket, and his three boys and several women folk and Lady Katherine and the Big Doctor and Brother Samuel. They all kinda lined up down the steps while the cavalry soldiers brung out two long boxes, four of 'em carryin' each box. The soldiers walked with 'em down to the two wagons and set 'em real gentle like in the bottom of the wagon boxes. There was one big box in Sam's wagon and one in mine. Then I see'd how Will and Marv drug over some branches, and they laid 'em out over the boxes. Then they spread out a couple of colored blankets over the branches. Why they done that, I don't rightly know.

Then Brother Samuel helped Lady Katherine climb up front into my wagon. I turned around and see'd how Old Hamilton tied up Lady Katherine's mare to the back of my wagon. Then he and his boy Dallas got in the second wagon. The Big Doctor swung up into the saddle on Saucepan. Then all the cavalry mounted up, and it looked like we was ready to move. I kept lookin' around, waitin' for Brother Joe to come, but we lit out before he showed up. It looked like we was leavin' him behind in Carthage, or maybe he would catch us up on the road.

We headed up the Carthage Road toward Nauvoo at a slow pace, jest walkin' along easy. The Big Doctor on Saucepan walked along on the right side of my wagon. I looked over to him and see'd how he had done hurt hisself along the side of his face. There was a big red mark, but it didn't seem to bother him none.

Sam and the brown mare follered right behind me, and the eight cavalrymen rode along to the side and behind. The funny thing is there warn't no talkin' at all amongst the riders. Even the cavalrymen was more or less quiet, which is right unusual, as soldiers is always talkin' and yappin' back and forth as they march. For some reason everyone was as quiet as can be all day long. The only time they spoke was to talk amongst theirselves about how far they had come on the road.

We stopped for some water at Fellows' place, then went on up the Carthage Road. I knowed that road like I know the pasture by Brother Joe's place. It was jest different walkin' it with a wagon behind me 'stead of gallopin' up it with Brother Joe in the saddle.

The sun was gettin' high in the sky, and it was right warm. I was hankerin' to jest gallop off to cool myself down, but bein' hitched to the wagon I knowed that warn't happenin', so I jest kinda hunkered down and kept on movin'.

Right along 'bout the heat of the day, we was gettin' closer to Nauvoo. We come slowly up the Carthage Road close to Brother Joe's farm when I looked up ahead and see'd a whole passel of folks standin' on either side of the road. When they see'd us, the men folk jest took off their hats. I see'd Old Man Lott standin' there with his folks, with water jest a-runnin' down his face. Then I see'd most of the folks had wet faces. Well, after we passed by, I looked around and see'd that the whole bunch was jest walkin' in the road behind Sam's wagon. And there was more and more folks by the side of the road as we went. By the time we passed the Cemetery, there was hundreds of 'em. Then we got up to the crossroads, and I see'd that there was hundreds and hundreds more standin' along the Mulholland Street, lookin' at us right intent like, and takin' off their hats, and then bowin' their heads low as we passed by.

Then I heared a strange sound comin' from the crowds of people, which was gettin' bigger by the minute. It started out as a kinda low hummin' sound, but then I see'd how womenfolk and menfolk here and there started jest cryin' out, and then more of 'em cried out altogether, 'til there was a general buzzin' and cryin' sound. It was mighty puzzlin' to me, as I had never heared such a sound in my life, and I see'd how it was disturbin' to Lather, what was strapped into the shafts beside me, as he laid his ears flat and started to neigh right out loud and toss his head this way and that.

We rode on down Mullholland Street, and past the white stone walls on top of the hill. When we started down the hill I see'd that there was more people standin' down on the road ahead than I ever seen in my life. Must have been every person on earth down waitin' for us to ride by. We passed by the clump of trees where Brother Joe liked to do his preachin' and then turned down Main Street. I see'd that there warn't nobody goin' in and out of the shops, but they was all standin' by the road.

When we drove up in front of Brother Joe's Mansion House, I see'd that Lady Emma was standin' outside with her little ones, Julia and Little Joseph and Fred and Alex, and right beside her was Lady Lucy. I see'd that Lady Emma and Lady Lucy was wearin' black cloths over their faces. After we stopped, a bunch of Brethren stepped up and uncovered the branches from the boxes in the wagons and lifted 'em up real solemn and quiet like and carried 'em into the Mansion. Lady Emma, Lady Lucy, and the little ones follered 'em inside, and they shut the door.

After that, the streets 'round about the Mansion was fillin' up with more and more folks. There was hundreds and hundreds of 'em. More than I can count. Well, me and Lather jest stood hitched up to the wagon, and Sam and the brown mare the same, as folks walked all around us. Then I see'd how the Big Doctor dismounted from Saucepan and climbed slowly up on top of the wooden platform and started preachin'. Everyone crowded in to listen. I heared him say somethin' about Brother Joe and Hyrum, but what he said I didn't rightly understand. He then said somethin' about John Taylor and how he was stayin' down to Carthage for a spell, and how the folks needed to be peaceful and calm. He then told all the folks to jest go home and rest until tomorrow. Then he climbed down from the platform, and the folks started to move off slowly. It was mighty quiet, jest like on the ride up from Carthage. Folks was not sayin' much to each other, which was uncommon strange.

Then Lorin come over with some of the Legion fellers and unhitched Lather and me and brung us around to the stable.

And so we rested up some. I was mighty happy to be home and 'specially to be out in the pasture where there was green grass and lots of open space and good feed and fresh water and Lorin Walker to give me a nice rubdown.

So I slept like a plumb-tired colt that night in the stable. I 'spect you was sleepin' over to the Mansion House on the side porch, watchin' out over the folks there, and waitin' for Brother Joe to come back home.

SATURDAY, JUNE 29, 1844

OLD CHARLIE WAITS FOR BROTHER JOE – HE SEES
THOUSANDS OF PEOPLE GO IN AND OUT OF THE
MANSION HOUSE – HE IS SADDLED UP FOR A PARADE
BUT CARRIES NO RIDER

NAUVOO, ILLINOIS – SATURDAY, JUNE 29, 1844

Early morning: The bodies of Joseph and Hyrum are placed into coffins lined with white cambric and covered with black velvet, studded with brass. A glass lid with brass hinges is put over each face, and the bodies are laid out for viewing in the dining hall.[154]

8:00 a.m. to 5:00 p.m. The doors to the Mansion House are opened and as many as ten thousand people file into the dining room and past the coffins containing the bodies of the martyrs. The people move in slow procession through the house, pausing momentarily in reverence over the two coffins.

Dan Jones wrote: "On the streets around it was almost the stillness of the grave which reigned."[155]

5:00 p.m. At five o'clock a public funeral service begins in the grove beneath the unfinished Nauvoo Temple. The doors to the Mansion House are closed and the people are asked to leave the departed brothers to their families before the burial. The mourners walk up Main Street to the grove.

Behind the locked doors of the Mansion House, a secret plan is hastily carried out. It is said that before he left for Carthage, Joseph gave directions to members of the Quorum of the Twelve as to how he was to

---

[154] HC 7:134

[155] Jones, 94

be buried, should he not survive. The bodies of the martyrs are hidden in a tiny bedroom in the northeast corner of the Mansion House. Sandbags and rocks are placed in the coffins to simulate the weight of Joseph and Hyrum and are sealed shut. Then the coffins are placed in the hearse, and the formal cortege proceeds up Main Street to the Grove, where the leaders of the Church are conducting the public ceremony.[156]

As the hearse bearing the "bodies" of Joseph and Hyrum (actually the coffins filled with sandbags and rocks) passes the Nauvoo Grove, Church leader W.W. Phelps is preaching the funeral sermon.[157]

The coffins are transported in the hearse to the Nauvoo Burial Ground, where they are interred.

At midnight, under a small guard of armed men, the bodies of the martyrs, in simple wooden boxes, are quietly carried through the garden of the Mansion House to the construction site of the Nauvoo House. The boxes are then buried in the freshly dug basement. The surface of the hastily filled graves is swept, smoothed, and disguised by scattering wood chips and debris on the ground. The purpose is to hide the dead prophets from their enemies, who, it was rumored, were after Joseph's head for a bounty still offered in the State of Missouri.[158]

Come in, Major. I'm mighty glad of the company tonight. I can't sleep none, for all the thinkin' of what's transpired these past days. Fact is, I been mighty confused. I wonder where Brother Joe has gone off to. I'm one puzzled horse—as puzzled as I ever been in my life. It's bein' without Brother Joe that's got me puzzled. He warn't

---

[156] Letter of Ursula B. Hascall to Colonel Wilson Andres, May 2, 1846, in "Letters of a Proselyte," *Utah Historical Quarterly* (April, 1957) vol. 25, pg. 146

[157] See Richard Van Wagoner and Steven C. Walker, "The Joseph/Hyrum Smith Funeral Sermon in *BYU Studies* (1983) 23:1

[158] Job Smith, *Diary of Job Smith, a Pioneer of Nauvoo, Illinois and Utah* (Arcadia, California: Louise Smith Willard, 1956) p. 8

in today for a ride, though I 'spected he would be, since Sam and me got back safe from Carthage yesterday. I figured he had jest follered along somehow and would be showin' up at the Mansion, jest like he showed up un'spected that day in Quincy, after he got hisself away from the soldiers in Zion.

You still listenin', Major, old friend? Well, this mornin', after we had rested up from bringin' the wagons and them boxes back from Carthage, I woke up bright and early 'spectin Brother Joe to come any moment. But I didn't see him, nor any of the family all through the day. Lorin come in and gave me and the other horses our feed, but he was uncommon quiet and left in a hurry. It was good to be back with Tom and Joe Duncan and the rest.

I'm sure you see'd what went on inside the Mansion House all day. I see'd it from over here. First thing this mornin' I was out in my watchin' spot in the pasture, when I see'd how all the folks come back down to gather 'round Brother Joe's house. Pretty soon, somebody opened the door and then the people started to go right inside Brother Joe's house. Hundreds and hundreds of 'em, jest walkin' around to the front of the house and on inside. Pretty soon more and more folks walked up, until there was a long line of folks backed up all the way along Water Street. They didn't talk much, but jest stood there, walkin' forward real slow like until they got up to the front of the Mansion, then they went inside.

So most of the day I jest rested out in my watchin' spot in the pasture, watchin' the lines of folks come and go. I never heared no loud voices at all, but jest low sounds, like whispers, a kinda hummin', like the buzz of a hive of bees.

Lorin was in a time or two to feed me, and he was awful solemn and sad like. He didn't say much, but he sure did treat me well, pattin' me and talkin' to me, and givin' me lumps of sugar like Brother Joe likes to do. There warn't no hotel horses stayin' over at all. Jest Joe Duncan and Tom and me.

I kept waitin' for Brother Joe to come see me and maybe go for a ride in the mornin', like we usually do, but I didn't see a glimpse of Brother Joe, nor even of Lady Emma, nor Little Joseph, who usually helps Lorin with his chores of a mornin'.

Then, jest as the afternoon shadows was gettin' long, things started happenin' again. I was inside the stable in my box, jest restin', hopin' that Brother Joe would come for one of our long rides through the countryside or out to inspect the Legion. Well, Lorin come in with Old Man Lott and one other feller. They was all dressed up in their blue Legion uniforms. Then I recognized the smell of the other one. It was Brother Philo, who sometimes helps Brother Joe with his sword and pistols and such when we is on parade with the Legion.

Philo says to Lorin and Old Man Lott, "Gosh, Charlie's as strong as he ever was in Ohio or Missouri!" Old Man Lott jest stood there starin' at me for a while, and then the three of 'em, Lorin and the two other fellers, jest started strokin' me and talkin' to me. There was somethin' kinda low or downhearted about the way they talked to me. I remember 'specially that the feller Philo was one with the jokes, and always laughin' with Brother Joe, but there was none of that. Lorin and the others acted real solemn like.

Lorin got out the Legion gear, and they put on my bridle and saddled me up with all the Legion stuff, and then they polished every button and strap until it shone. Then Lorin fetched up a pair of ridin' boots. I knowed they was Brother Joe's Legion boots, as they had his smell on 'em. Lorin and Philo started a-fussin' with one of the stirrups on my saddle, and I turned my head to see what they was doin', and you know what, Major? They was puttin' Brother Joe's empty boot right in the stirrup, 'cept they had it facin' backways! Can you b'lieve that? Then they fussed on the other side, and they put the other boot in the other stirrup backways. I'll be durned if I can tell you what was the use of that.

Then they led me outside. I 'spected that Brother Joe would be there to ride me, but he warn't there, and there warn't any ridin' that day. In fact, although I had my saddle on, no one tried to climb up, which I thought was mighty strange. Outside the stable there was another Legion soldier standin' and holdin' Hyrum's horse, Sam. Sam's white coat was shinin', like he jest had a brush down, and he was also all dressed up for Legion work. I see'd that he also had a saddle on and a pair of Hyrum's boots in the stirrups facin' backways. Then the fellers led us both out onto Water Street and up to Main Street in front of Brother Joe's place.

Out front of the Mansion there was a whole crowd of folks, but they warn't sayin' nothin'. They was mighty quiet. General Dunham of the Legion seemed to be in charge. He was sittin' on his claybank stallion, Rambler, with a bunch of other cavalry. It looked like he'd gathered up a whole line of Legion soldiers all dressed in their finery, and they was lined up like they was ready to go into a drill on the parade ground.

In back of the soldiers was a sorta long wagon but covered with glass, with two black boxes inside. I see'd that they warn't 'bout to put Sam and me into the shafts, 'cause they already had horses hitched up. Then Lorin led me and Sam directly behind the wagon and held us steady. In back of us was Brother Joe's buggy, pulled by Joe Duncan and Tom Carlin, with Sister Emma and the children inside, all wearin' black, and behind 'em was a long line of people, hundreds of 'em. I felt mighty confused, and to begin with I was stampin' my hooves and jerkin' my head around, but Lorin calmed me down, strokin' my neck and talkin' quiet, and pretty soon I steadied down.

Then, after a while we set out and turned up Main Street. There was people linin' both sides of the street as far as I could see, and as we passed, they all walked right behind us and the crowd of people follerin' us.

We passed by the little clump of trees where Brother Joe likes to talk for hours, but I didn't see Brother Joe, jest Brother Phelps talkin' away to a whole crowd of people. They all turned their heads to watch us as we passed, and some of the faces of the ladies was wet, and they was wavin' their handkerchiefs at us. After we passed by, Brother Phelps even stopped talkin', which was unusual for him. I knowed him to go on for hours in the clump of trees. And then the whole passel of folks listenin' to Brother Phelps stood up and follered right along behind us.

We passed the white walls, which Brother Joe loves to visit, and then headed up Mulholland Street to where the Carthage Road bears off to the right, until we come to the Cemetery. Then, Legion soldiers walked 'longside of the glass cart in front of Sam and me, spaced out reg'lar like they was in a Legion parade, and then they stood together and lifted them two boxes out and carried 'em into the grove of trees, follered by Sister Emma and the children, to where they had dug two big holes in the ground.

Most of the people went on in underneath the trees after the men carryin' them two boxes. Sam and I jest stood around in a field of June grass with all the other horses. Time or two I looked over through the trees to see what Lady Emma and the kids was doin'. She had her two arms around Little Joseph and Julia and she was holdin' the hands of the two little fellas. I see'd 'em standin' right in front of one of them boxes. Lady Mary and her children was standin' in front of the other box. There was the boys John and Joseph Fielding and Hyrum's little girls, whose names I don't know. Lovina was there, too, and Lorin Walker was standin' with her, with his arm around her. Funny thing, though, I didn't see Brother Joe, nor Hyrum.

Then so many folks was crowdin' in, that for a spell I couldn't see anything at all, jest the backs of hundreds and hundreds of Brethren and ladies and Soldiers, all standin' together, bunched around them two big holes in the ground and the two long boxes. There was the sound of some preachin' and then singin' and then the crowd kind of opened up some, so I could see how the Legion fellers was lowerin' them two boxes with ropes right down into the two big holes in the ground.

It was right solemn and still like under them trees. There warn't no talkin', jest the sound of birds up in the trees, and the little muffled nickerin' and jinglin' sounds of all the horses waitin' in the field for their riders.

Well, that's about it, Major. After all that, Lorin brung me back down to the stable, and here I stand. Thanks for listenin', Major. 'Course you and I can't always understand what men are up to, can we? But I guess all this walkin' around with no riders in our saddles and follerin' them boxes up to the Cemetery made some kinda sense to 'em all. I'll be a whole lot happier when Brother Joe comes back. He'll set things right.

I'm expectin' that Brother Joe will be back any day now. I'm hopin' that tomorrow mornin' Lorin will come out while the birds is chirpin' and the sun is peekin' over the edge of the hill and get me all fixed up and ready to go for a ride. He'll saddle me all up and put on my bridle and cinch things up proper and then lead me outside the Mansion House. Then Brother Joe will walk out of the Mansion House door with a smile on his face and scratch my ears and pull a lump of sugar out of his pocket and reach it out for me. I'll lick it right off his hand, and then he'll stroke my neck and say, "Good boy, Charlie! Good boy!"

NOTES AND ACKNOWLEDGEMENTS

In this novel, *Last Ride to Carthage*, I have attempted to give a voice to one of the lowliest figures in Mormon history: Joseph Smith's favorite riding horse, Old Charlie.

Historical anecdotes about Old Charlie are numerous. He was a large and powerful black stallion with a regal appearance and a fiery disposition. He was with the Prophet and Emma from the early 1830's in Kirtland until his death in Nauvoo in the late 1840's. He witnessed from the ground level, so to speak, these pivotal events of Church history:

- The tarring and feathering of the Prophet at the Johnson farm in Hiram, Ohio, on March 24, 1832
- The laying of the cornerstones of the Kirtland Temple on July 23, 1833, followed by years of work in the stone quarry, and the events surrounding its dedication in March of 1836
- The Prophet's journey with Zion's Camp to Jackson County, Missouri, and back to Kirtland from May to August of 1834
- The Prophet's journey to Far West, Missouri, from September to December of 1837
- The Prophet's midnight ride out of Kirtland on January 12, 1838, to escape his enemies
- Joseph and Emma's eight-hundred-mile journey with their children from Ohio to Missouri from January to March of 1838, including crossing over the ice on the frozen Mississippi River
- The quarrying and laying of the cornerstones of the Far West Temple in July of 1838

- The Prophet's surveying tours of Northern Missouri in the summer and fall of 1838 to lay out "Cities of Zion," including Adam-Ondi-Ahman
- The "Mormon War" in Missouri in October and November of 1838, culminating in the great military siege of Far West and the arrest and imprisonment of the Prophet
- The journeys of Emma Smith and her son Joseph Smith, III to visit the Prophet in the Liberty Jail
- The grueling winter journey of Emma Smith and her little children from Missouri to Quincy, Illinois, in the Winter of 1839, including a second crossing of the frozen Mississippi River
- The arrival of Joseph Smith in Quincy, Illinois, on April 22, 1839, after escaping from jail
- The move to Commerce (later Nauvoo), Illinois, in May of 1839
- The building of Nauvoo during the years 1839 to 1844 from a small settlement on the Mississippi to a city of 20,000 inhabitants
- The creation and training of the Nauvoo Legion into the largest militia in the nation, with over 5,000 enlisted men
- The Prophet's months of hiding from his enemies, from August to November of 1842
- The kidnapping of the Prophet on June 23, 1843, during a family vacation, his dramatic release, and his triumphal return into Nauvoo on June 30 at the head of hundreds of horsemen
- The destruction of the *Nauvoo Expositor* on June 10, 1844, and the dangerous days to follow

- The Prophet's surrender at Carthage, Illinois, on June 25, 1844
- The death of the Prophet and Hyrum Smith on June 27, the return of their bodies to Nauvoo on June 28, and their funeral on June 29, 1844
- The completion of the Nauvoo Temple from 1844 to 1846
- The departure of the body of the Church from Nauvoo in the first months of 1846
- The "Battle of Nauvoo" in the fall of 1846, when the enemies of the Church descended upon and sacked Nauvoo
- The harrowing escape of Emma and her children from Nauvoo in 1846 and their return in 1847
- The destruction of the Nauvoo Temple by fire on October 9, 1848

Old Charlie was a silent witness to all of this and more. *Last Ride to Carthage* and the books that follow will tell his story.

I acknowledge sculptors Stan Watts and Kim Corpany for the spark of inspiration that led to the writing of *Last Ride to Carthage*. Ten years ago, in the autumn of 2004, I visited Nauvoo for several days with my wife, Julie, and my parents, Francis M. Gibbons and Helen Bay Gibbons. Over the years we had visited Nauvoo many times, but on this trip we wanted to see the newly reconstructed Nauvoo Temple. After leaving the temple the morning after our arrival, we walked outside in the sunshine to the overlook at the brow of the hill. From there you can see all of Nauvoo spread out below, like a map, and the wide sweep of the Mississippi River in the distance. There we also saw the beautiful eleven-foot-tall bronze statue sculpted by Stan Watts and Kim Corpany. The work depicts Joseph and Hyrum Smith mounted on their horses, Charlie and Sam, as they rode out of Nauvoo on June 24, 1844, on what would be their final ride.

Not far from the temple, Joseph turned in the saddle to gaze back one last time upon Nauvoo and said, "This is the loveliest place and the best people under the heavens; little do they know the trials that await them."

As I stood looking at this monumental statue and thought of those two faithful horses, which carried the martyrs to their deaths, the thought came to me, "Here is a great untold story."

Later that same day I bought and began reading a copy of Joseph Smith, III's memoirs, which paint loving and detailed portraits of Charlie and the many other horses owned by the Prophet.

That day I conceived a novel, or rather a series of novels, which would view Church history from the perspective of the Prophet's faithful horse. Little did I know that this spark of an idea would consume my life for the next decade. I spent 2004 to 2007 in broad historical research of Joseph Smith's home life, his animals, and his life during the 1830's and 1840's. I began the actual writing of a first draft of this book in November of 2007, while on a teaching assignment in Kyiv, Ukraine. Over the next three years members of my writing group, "The Inklings," including G.G. Vandagriff, David P. Vandagriff, Annika Paxman, Deedee Freestone, Scott Lockwood, Maure Albert, and Lydia Lindsay, read and commented on early drafts of this book. I interrupted my research and writing in the fall of 2010, when Julie and I were called by the First Presidency to serve as a full-time mission president and companion. During the years 2011 to 2014 I completely laid aside the book as we served a mission together in Russia and Central Asia. In July of 2014, I picked up the strands of this project once more. *Last Ride to Carthage* is the first fruit of this long and beloved endeavor.

Several people have been instrumental in giving me great encouragement and help along the way, including the following: my father, Francis M. Gibbons, the most prolific and best-selling Mormon biographer in history, who has offered counsel, advice, and generous financial support; my mother, Helen Bay Gibbons, a professional writer from the age of eighteen, who gave me much encouragement and advice; my lifelong friend and sounding board, Dr. Kelly DeVries, who has read virtually everything I have ever written, from my first historical novel written at age fourteen to my present scribblings; my writing mentors, novelist G.G. Vandagriff and "Passive Guy," the writer and attorney David P. Vandagriff, who have offered great encouragement and vision, and who have modeled for me what a successful writer in this presently shifting world must do to thrive; my son-in-law, Ryan Shawcroft, a fourth-generation rancher and horseman from Alamosa, Colorado, who read the manuscript and offered valuable practical suggestions; my late mother-in-law, Gwendolyn Wahlen Glenn, whose modest legacy has allowed us to make a "leap of faith" into the life of a full-time writer; my children, Annie, Jenny, Liz, Abby and Josh, who have endured my talk about "Old Charlie" for a decade; and above all, to my gifted and perceptive wife, Julie Glenn Gibbons, who has been a constant support and who has also edited and designed this novel with great skill. When I married Julie, my Dad told me, "Dan—you really lucked out!" He is right!

To Julie, I dedicate this work.

Daniel Bay Gibbons
May 18, 2015
Holladay, Utah

ABOUT THE AUTHOR

Daniel Bay Gibbons has aspired to be a novelist his entire life. Born in Salt Lake City, he began his first historical novel at the age of fourteen and has been writing ever since. A Salt Lake City trial attorney, he was educated at the University of Utah and Willamette University. During his professional life, he was also a  refugee sponsor with the Tolstoy Foundation, a long-time radio talk-show host, an elementary school chess coach, a founding member of the Holladay City Council, and a frequent guest lecturer in Ukrainian law schools. In 2001 he became a trial judge in suburban Salt Lake County, serving on the bench for ten years.

Dan walked away from his judgeship and his legal career in 2011 when he accepted a calling to serve with his wife, Julie, as an LDS mission president in Russia and Kazakhstan. He had previously served a two-year Church mission as a young man in Germany, as an ordinance worker in the Salt Lake Temple and twice as bishop. From

2011 to 2014 Dan and Julie lived in Novosibirsk, Russia, and traveled more than 750,000 miles throughout Russian Siberia and Central Asia, as well as in Eastern Europe, the Baltic nations, Ukraine, and Turkey.

Dan returned to the United States in 2014 with a determination to make his way as a full-time writer of historical fiction, novels of suspense, and Mormon history and biography. He is the author of several books, including the *Old Charlie and the Prophet* series of historical novels, the biographical series *Remembering Seven Prophets*, and the historical mystery series *Sherlock Holmes in the Country of the Saints*. He is the coauthor, with his father, Francis M. Gibbons, of two previous titles: *A Gathering of Eagles* and *Nethermost: Missionary Miracles in Lowly Places*.

Aside from his passion for writing, Dan loves reading books (he has a home library of more than 5,000 titles), learning languages (he is fluent in German and Russian, reads ancient Greek and has studied Biblical Hebrew) and running (he runs four to six miles a day and has completed seven marathons). He is married to Julie Glenn Gibbons, and they live in Holladay, Utah. They have five children—Annie, Jenny, Liz, Abby, and Josh—and five grandchildren.

DISCUSSION GUIDE

1. In *Last Ride to Carthage*, Old Charlie describes the events surrounding the June 27, 1844, martyrdom of Joseph and Hyrum Smith as a horse might have seen them. He witnesses well-known events from an entirely new perspective, "from the ground level," so to speak. How does Charlie's unique perspective affect your understanding of the martyrdom? What new insights about Church history did you gain from reading this novel?

. . .

2. Old Charlie is the narrator of *Last Ride to Carthage*, and he "speaks" in very simple language, modeled on a pre-Civil War Trans-Appalachian idiom. Can you think of other novels that are successfully narrated by inarticulate characters? Can complicated events of history be adequately described by such lowly characters and in such simple language? How might this relate to the seemingly limited abilities of inexperienced missionaries or even young children to talk about faith or religion? Is it possible that the heartfelt, inarticulate speaker actually has greater impact on the listener than the voice of culture and eloquence?

. . .

3. Old Charlie tells his story late each night in the stable to the Prophet's old, white watchdog, Major. What friend have you had in your life that you can confide in completely? How does Old Charlie change by being able to express the inexpressible to Major? Are we somehow changed when we write or tell our own stories?

. . .

4. Each chapter of *Last Ride to Carthage* begins with a brief historical chronology, followed by a narrative from Old Charlie's perspective. How important to you is the historical context in an historical novel? Why is it important for historical fiction to be faithful to the facts of history?

. . .

5. In what way is *Last Ride to Carthage* a testament to unconditional love and devotion? How does Charlie's unfailing devotion to Joseph Smith affect the story?

. . .

6. There were many instances of violent persecution in the history of the Latter-day Saints during the lifetime of Joseph Smith. In *Last Ride to Carthage*, the Nauvoo Legion plays a pivotal role in defending the city of Nauvoo against violence. Martial law was declared in Nauvoo on June 18, 1844, and overnight the city became an armed camp. How is Charlie's life changed by this event? How does his experience as a military horse affect him?

. . .

7. In many ways, Old Charlie was Joseph Smith's closest companion during his last decade of life. Although Charlie did not possess any deep understanding of politics, doctrine, or complex human relationships, he was with the Prophet more on a day-to-day basis than almost any person, other than perhaps Emma. Have you ever had a close friend or companion who did not fully understand you? Does such a friend offer help through difficult times? Can an animal play the role of confidant and friend in a person's life? In what ways did Charlie help Joseph Smith despite his lack of understanding of everything?

. . .

8. Horses have a great sense of and memory for places and will often reserve particular spots in a pasture, often on a hill, for loafing or observing. Horses like the sense of security in being able to see all around them. In *Last Ride to Carthage,* Old Charlie has a favorite spot in the pasture where he can be alone and observe what is going on at the Mansion House, the streets of lower Nauvoo, and the Mississippi River. Have you ever had a favorite spot where you go to rest and gain perspective? How did Charlie's time waiting in the pasture prepare him for the furious events that unfolded?

. . .

9. History records that Joseph Smith loved animals and he preached about the "salvation of beasts." Have you had a horse, a dog, or some other animal that you loved? How has that animal shaped your perspective on life? What can we learn about the Prophet Joseph Smith from his love for Charlie and his other animals?

. . .

10. *Last Ride to Carthage* depicts Old Charlie's deep puzzlement at various human activities, such as reading words on papers or books, or the traditions of funerals and burials. How does the novel help you see our lives in a new light and perspective?

. . .

11. *Last Ride to Carthage* gives vivid descriptions of Nauvoo. Author Daniel Bay Gibbons said that he received the inspiration to write the novel while standing outside the Nauvoo Temple overlooking the Mississippi River in 2004.

While gazing at the huge bronze statue depicting Joseph and Hyrum Smith mounted on their horses, Charlie and Sam, as they rode out of Nauvoo, the thought came to him, "Here is a great untold story." Have you ever been inspired by an historic place? How does the setting of a book enrich the narrative? Is it possible that a setting, especially in an historical novel, can almost become a "character" in the story?

. . .

12. In *Last Ride to Carthage*, Old Charlie does not witness the death of Joseph Smith and Hyrum. At the end of the novel the horse is left wondering where the Prophet has gone and longing for his return. How does Charlie's incomplete understanding of what has occurred heighten the emotional feel of the story? How does the experience of death or the painful absence of loved ones change us as human beings? How does death change *our* life stories?